Stevens, Marcus

The curve of the
world

DUE DATE		E266 24.95	

THE CURVE OF THE WORLD

THE CURVE OF THE WORLD

A NOVEL BY

MARCUS STEVENS

ALGONQUIN BOOKS
OF CHAPEL HILL
2002

Published by
Algonquin Books of Chapel Hill
Post Office Box 2225
Chapel Hill, North Carolina 27515-2225

a division of
Workman Publishing
708 Broadway
New York, New York 10003

Library of Congress Cataloging-in-Publication Data
Stevens, Marcus, 1959–
    The curve of the world : a novel / by Marcus Stevens.
    p. cm.
    ISBN 1-56512-336-0
    1. Americans—Congo River Valley—Fiction.   2. Congo
(Democratic Republic)—Fiction.   3. Wilderness survival—Fiction.
4. Congo River Valley—Fiction.   5. Missing persons—Fiction.
6. Married people—Fiction.   7. Rain forests—Fiction.   I. Title.
PS3619.T49 C87 2002
813'.6—dc21   2001056530

10 9 8 7 6 5 4 3 2 1
First Edition

For Diana

ACKNOWLEDGMENTS

THE DEMOCRATIC REPUBLIC OF THE CONGO, already on its knees from thirty years of the Mobutu dictatorship, has suffered a devastating cycle of wars over the last decade. The loss of life, especially in the eastern part of the country, staggers the conscience. Even in other parts of Africa that have been spared the fighting, poverty is endemic and daily life is a struggle. It can be hard to imagine sometimes, for a Westerner, how society continues to function under such duress. And yet it does, with dignity and joy. I set this novel in Africa's heart, in part because it cries out for our attention, but also because despite the hardships of their struggle, the courage and indomitable spirit of the people I met in my travels across that continent humbled and inspired me.

This novel was written with a great deal of help. Lokoko Kitenza translated and corrected the Lingala used in this story and offered suggestions in portraying the DRC where he grew up. My friend and United Airlines pilot, Scott Mulder, meticulously advised me on emergency landing procedures. Lori and Michael Siewecke in Accra, Ghana, provided insight into the lives of foreign diplomats in Africa, and Lori dug up obscure but important books on African witchcraft. David Kissledu, Hayford Nyinaku, and Kobina Nyarico translated local stories and shared their wisdom about the rainforest. Rebecca McNatt encouraged me with her optimistic spirit and enthusiasm and assisted with research. Doug Hylton e-mailed French translations, and Corinne Madden provided thoughtful criticism on an early draft. Readers' comments were invaluable throughout the writing—my thanks to Elizabeth Rose, Michelle Orton Stevens, Camille Burkard, Megan Ault, and Lucy Leadbeater, also Marisa Tranquilli, who shared her personal insights into monkey bites and the color of rabies serum.

I am deeply grateful to my agents, David Hale Smith and Sylvie Rabineau, for their unwavering support, my dear friend Kelly Romick for believing in my writing and passing it on, and to my editor, Antonia Fusco, who edited this story with her heart. She stayed late and worked many weekends rereading the manuscript, asking the thoughtful questions that challenged me to account for every word.

I would like to thank my children Haley, Madison, and Wyatt for their understanding and patience when I was unavailable because I had to write and for their boundless energy and enthusiasm traipsing across Africa. Lastly, I could not have written this novel without the love and support of my wife, Diana, my first reader, whose passion for Africa introduced me to that beautiful and inspiring part of our world.

The world is what it is; men who are nothing, who allow themselves to become nothing, have no place in it.

—**V. S. NAIPAUL,** *A Bend in the River*

THE CURVE OF THE WORLD

KOBUNGA NZELA—DISPARANT—VANISH

THROUGH THE THICK GLASS of this porthole, the night sea is dim and indistinct, barely defining a line between sky and water. Thirty thousand feet beneath a pillow of air, the ocean's blackness swallows even the indurate light of a full moon, and it is only the clouds lingering ten thousand feet below him that offer some faint sense of promise or hope. Beyond that there is a void that extends under the silver clouds to some unfathomable infinity, like something missing, or everything missing—the way Lewis has always imagined blindness.

Most of the other passengers are sleeping, mouths agape like escape hatches flung open. The businessman across the aisle from him looks like a child this way, a desperate boy who hopes no one will see through the disguise and perceive his pillowy kindness. Lewis's eyes meet those of the only other passenger who is awake, an African man, a Muslim. He wears a white djellaba, which in the dim cabin is so brightly lit by his reading light that it gives him an ethereal look. Beyond him a flight attendant sits calmly in the jump seat, flipping through a French edition of *Vogue,* her stiffly made-up face lit by the warm light bouncing off the magazine.

Lewis turns back to his window. That must be Africa, slipping by beneath the clouds. He presses his face against the cool glass, which is delicately traced with frost on the outside, trying to see some detail, even to confirm that what he sees is land, but there is only an unappeasable darkness and merely his imagination to illuminate it. It seems to approach silently and steadily like sleep. He watches until the faint glimmer of the ocean is consumed by it completely and they have crossed over. His gut stirs with unease. There is an unrealness to his relationship with this place, so thoroughly insulated is he by the dull roar of the turbines, the soft bumps of turbulence in the jet stream. There is also something vaguely threatening.

Who goes to Africa? he thinks. A few camera-laden vacationers on "safari," transported by four-wheel-drive buses, still a bit aloft, or some dusty, sweaty businessmen, miners or arms salesman, the kind of men you never see in the suburbs of America, mercenaries in suits and ties, and doctors, missionaries and Peace Corp volunteers. Lewis never expected to go anywhere near Africa. Not that he avoided it, either; he just never thought of it. Not once. He changed planes in Paris for the ten-hour flight to Johannesburg without a thought of where he was going. It could have been anywhere. Selling Coca-Cola to foreign markets takes him all over the world. One of the local distributors will meet him at the gate, help him with his bags and take him to an office not that different from what he has seen in Australia or New Zealand. At first he won't even be able to distinguish the accent. They will treat him, as he is accustomed, like a client. There will be a basket of biscuits and South African wine and a hat and sunblock waiting in his hotel room.

Somehow he must have fallen asleep with his head against the window. He looks up for a flight attendant—perhaps some water. At first he cannot find her. She is no longer reading. Then he notices the African man staring with an odd intensity at the galley, where she's talking on the interphone. Something in her stance, the way she looks at the floor, the tenseness of her body, seems a bit off. Lewis presses his face into his hands. There is in this unfirm place, this moment between consciousness and unconsciousness as his mind struggles to reassert command, such fertile ground for doubt. In his stomach he can feel the plane descending. He looks for his watch; it seems early, but it could be the time zone difference. His watch isn't set right.

Then two of the other flight attendants join the first. Lewis frowns. He can't shake the impression that something is not right with this scene. The first flight attendant takes the phone away from her mouth and says something to the other two. They nod, listening intently. She gestures with some urgency, and they move off in a hurry. The African man leans out into the aisle, and with a calm hand touches the hem of the flight attendant's uniform.

"*Qu'est-ce qui se passe?*"

She leans down to explain, but her voice is too soft to make out. From across the cabin she catches Lewis's eyes on her as she finishes, and it's easy to see that whatever she just said was a lie. As if to prove it, the left wing of the jet dips sharply as the plane makes an abrupt course change, and the lights come on suddenly as the cabin blinks awake.

"*Mesdames et messieurs, votre attention s'il vous plaît.*"

The tone of the captain's message is disturbing, and it's

maddening to have to listen to it first in French. Lewis makes out the words *la fumée,* "smoke."

"What the hell is going on?"

"English, please!"

Two flight attendants race by Lewis with a service cart rattling with loose items. They aren't taking time to gather anything from the passengers, and they are yelling as they go. "Seat belts. Tray tables and seat backs up."

"Ladies and gentlemen. May we have your attention . . ." That much he got already, but it is oddly reassuring. He senses that in the worst kind of emergency, the kind you don't survive, there would be no time for formalities, and even though the plane is descending, it still feels normal, still under control. He can feel the subtle pressure building in his ears. The passengers are all looking up at the speakers above their heads as if to hear better.

"We are experiencing smoke in the cockpit. To ensure your safety, we must land immediately at the nearest possible airport. Flight attendants are preparing for a possible emergency landing and evacuation. Please pay close attention to all flight attendant instructions and demonstrations."

"Please take your safety cards out. Look at the brace position." The flight attendant closest to Lewis holds up her card. The passengers take them out like hymnals at church. "Lean forward and hold your ankles," she says, and then she nearly falls as the nose of the plane suddenly drops and the engines rapidly power down to an idle. There are screams throughout the cabin. The plane is falling like a rollercoaster dropping at a carnival. All around him he sees passengers grabbing their armrests. Lewis quickly tightens his belt and reaches for his safety card. The flight attendant has regained her balance, and she is leaning forward with her feet wide apart to compensate for the steep angle of the descent. She's doing her best to remain calm and demonstrate how the passengers are expected to brace for landing, but she is close enough to Lewis that he can see the fear in her eyes.

"Lean forward and hold your ankles. If that is not possible, cross your hands and place them on the seat back in front of you. Lean forward and place your head on the back of your hands. Flight attendants, check brace position." It comes rapidly, first in French and then in English, but it is hard to hear over the terrific noise of the air rushing outside the plane. They are descending at six thousand feet per minute.

"Christ." Lewis drops his card, leans forward and grabs his ankles for the rehearsal. He looks across the aisle—hands on ankles everywhere. He still has that sick feeling in his stomach. If they hit the ground going this fast, this drill will amount to nothing.

"Please sit up. Check the security of your area. Any loose or sharp objects should be removed and placed in a safe place such as a seat pocket. Flight attendants brief helpers at exits. *Appel aux hôtesses. Préparez la cabine pour l'atterrissage.*"

The last part of the announcement is clipped by a sudden noise and vibration over the wing. The air brakes have been deployed and now the whole frame is shaking. Lewis catches a brief glimpse of the cockpit as the lead flight attendant opens the door. There is no obvious fire, but the gray-white smoke in the cockpit is dense. The pilots are wearing heavy oxygen masks and smoke goggles. They are working frantically with checklists, scanning gauges and switches. He can see them shouting to try to communicate.

"Where?" someone yells. "Where are we landing?"

"Africa. Somewhere."

Lewis looks outside, where dawn has begun to unravel the

night's grip on the continent below. What was an indistinct mass is now a deeply textured green. Land? Of course, it looks soft, a verdant carpet of luxurious tropical plant life. It is easy to imagine lying down there in a soft whisper of ferns and yellow birds, but clearly this is a forest below them, a canopy of trees, great trunks of hardwood. At ten thousand feet they are already in the forest's embrace. The patches of white cloud that race by almost have a sound to them, like showers of hailstones. A road appears, like a bright reddish-brown rip in the green fabric, and then passes behind them. At four thousand feet the plane passes over the great curve of a brown river that flashes faintly in the dawn, and then another red gash.

The engines spool up and down now as the pilots struggle with the difficult approach, making rapid corrections. A hint of the sharp smoke invades the cabin. It smells toxic—burning rubber or plastic.

"Please do not be alarmed." Alarmed. It's a strange word in the Frenchman's mouth. It sounds as if it is being eaten whole. "We will be landing soon. Flight attendants will signal when it's time to assume the brace position by shouting, 'Brace!' Remain in the brace position until the airplane has completely stopped."

The landing gear rumbles into position, and the plane slows further. Their attitude is less nose down, and the terrific noise of the air rushing outside has calmed down. At about three hundred feet a flight attendant comes over the intercom.

"Brace! *Courage! Baissez la tête!* Brace!"

Lewis watches as the cabin obeys, everyone bent over like puppets with their strings cut. The businessman bends over his knees. His face is slack with fear, and he is praying. The words fall from his mouth with the faint smell of alcohol. His toiletries are gripped tightly in his hands, as if for some final ablutions. The African man's hands look powerful and strong on the seat in front of him. The flight attendant closest to Lewis notices him still sitting up.

"Brace!" she shouts. He leans forward, but he cannot take his eyes away from the window. The trees seem smaller than he thought, but he realizes that his sense of scale is off, that they must rise a hundred feet or more. They pass a road and a fence at about the time they come level with the treetops.

"Brace! *Baissez la tête!* Heads down!"

"Not until I see pavement," Lewis thinks aloud, as the blur of trees reaches up under the belly of the airplane as if trying to grab them, pull them down. Then the pavement is there, cracked and overgrown with weeds. Lewis puts his head down.

He closes his eyes, anticipating the impact like a child who left his body in a dream or nightmare and is now falling back at the realization that he cannot fly. He breathes in deeply and holds it. The plane hits the ground hard and twists sickeningly to the left, popping open several overhead bins as the engines thunder deafeningly in reverse, trying to slow the tin rocket. As the pilot brakes, the pull of inertia threatens to rip Lewis from his seat, and all of the baggage that fell from the overheads on impact now flies forward, violently striking the terrified flight attendant who has belted herself to the forward jump seat.

The runway is rougher than it looked, and the pilot has trouble keeping the plane straight. The plane shakes and vibrates desperately as the pilot tries to slow its reckless speed. Lewis lifts his head to see what he can. Alongside the black asphalt runway the dirt is blood red. Suddenly there is a terrific noise, and then, as a reward for his temerous curiosity, Lewis is slammed into the seat in front of him like a rag doll. There are a few shouts, barely audible above the incredible sound of the front landing gear failing. The plane lurches violently forward, eliciting more screams from the passengers, then comes to rest, and it is awesomely quiet except for the sound of bottles rolling through broken glass in the aisles.

The turbines wind down, as they would upon a normal arrival. The cabin is in chaos, debris scattered everywhere. As if caught between heartbeats, no one moves, expecting another blow. Then a child crying somewhere in the back restarts the order of things. Suddenly in many languages the passengers shout and yell and thank god. The flight attendant at the bulkhead struggles stiffly to get out of her seat. Around her battered legs is the scattered garbage of the carry-ons, an odd collection of bottles of wine and liquor from Duty Free, cameras, cards, hairbrushes, lipstick and broken vials of perfume.

"Someone's hurt here! For god's sake, someone is hurt," comes a shout from the back.

Lewis watches the hurt flight attendant approach the exit. Her eyes are red from crying, and already her cheek is swelling where she was hit. She looks out the window, with an arm stretched out to keep people away, something she has learned in a drill, then she rapidly clears the door. Warm air pours into the cabin, condensing and creating a lush steam. There is the fantastically loud hiss of the emergency evacuation slide inflating.

"Release your seat belts and get out!"

All around Lewis, passengers are already unbuckling. "*Sortez par la sortie en avant. Vite!*" The flight attendants yell at passengers to leave their things and get out. "*Sortez maintenant! Vite vite vite!*"

Lewis jumps onto the slide behind the businessman. The drop down the slick yellow slide is quick and he's glad to have someone to catch his hand as he lands. A young man with wide eyes waves them to a gathering place just past the wing tip. His urgency has everyone running, but Lewis lets the others hurry by.

Now that his feet are on the ground, the emergency seems over to him. The tropical air feels good.

He turns when he reaches the group and looks back at the fallen jet. A faint blue haze of smoke hovers over the main wheels. The nose is dipped from the partially collapsed front landing gear. Otherwise the airplane doesn't appear significantly damaged; at least, there is no obvious fuel spill. There are no buildings along the runway, no airport. Some of the grass growing out of the cracks in the tarmac is quite tall. The runway obviously hasn't been used for a long time. There might be a road entering at the far end; otherwise on all sides the forest looms, cut back to a perfect sharp border, yielding just enough room for the pavement and a fifty-yard swath on each side, which has grown back almost chest deep in some places.

One of the flight attendants is kneeling by a big red-haired Dutch man who has injured his head. She drops strips of bloodied gauze on the pavement. His eyes are red, and his black suit is wrinkled, his face wet with tears. A bright green and blue bird sails over the passengers' heads and then settles on the tip of the airplane's wing and flaps its own as if gloating.

The flight crew walk slowly away from their wrecked airship; they seem both elated to have made the landing and shaken up by it. The captain checks to see that the flight attendant has what she needs to help the injured man, and then he approaches the group of more than two hundred passengers. He looks over the faces of those closest to him. They are waiting to hear when they can get back on the plane and how soon they will be taking off again. He has to shout to deliver his message, first in French, then in English.

"The situation in the cockpit, an uncontained fire, was very serious, and it was critical that we get the aircraft on the ground immediately, wherever possible. We have landed in central

Africa, the Democratic Republic of the Congo. Unfortunately, this runway is not intended for an aircraft of this size. To attempt a takeoff is impossible. Air traffic control was advised of our position and circumstances. It is important that everyone stay in the immediate vicinity of the aircraft. I'll give an update in about a half hour when we have more information."

The Congo. Lewis almost says the word aloud. For him it's not a name that conjures images of an actual country, a real place, more of an ominous river coiled in a hostile jungle—dark tales of misadventure whispered by a seaman who counts himself lucky to have survived. Lewis looks up at the sky, but the clouds have closed it off. They are so low now that they seem to be dragging in the tops of the highest trees. That's something to be thankful for, he thinks, that the clouds held off, long enough for them to find the field and make this landing. Around him many of the passengers have sat down on the pavement, and they are looking up, too, as if trying to decide whether this could be called unfair.

He wanders a few yards along the edge of the cracked tarmac, away from the group. His white dress shirt clings in the damp current of air that drifts up the runway like the soft breath of the rainforest. The green lushness contrasts vividly with the withering autumn he left behind, and it feels good to rest his eyes on this exuberant wilderness. He thinks of Helen, who has always delighted in a lavish tropical breeze, and vacations on the beach that left him biting his lip. He tries to remember what country she went to with WorldAid, long before he met her, some remote place, a jungle like this, wild and humid —Burma.

He looks out at the wall of vegetation before him. A breeze animates the tops of the towering hardwood trees and trembles in the thick green bush below. It occurs to him that when Helen talked about Burma, she never mentioned what it looked like or felt like, how beautiful it must have been. She talked about the people, her enthusiasm to help, the feeling that their efforts felt largely irrelevant to the crushing weight of poverty they were fighting. What will she think when she finds out about this accident? There's no excuse for how he left things with her. He shakes his head and looks down at the warm, crumbling asphalt. Under better circumstances she could laugh about it, find a little irony in his being stranded like this; maybe she'd make a joke that he has earned this banishment.

About a hundred yards down the field, the captain and the second officer find an old set of air stairs that must have been abandoned with the runway. It's half buried in the grass and covered with rust. A couple of passengers help them untangle it from the mass of creepers and twisted weeds that have already laid claim to it. Lewis is about to walk over to help, too, when they manage to pull it loose and wheel it over to the wreck. They pull off the evacuation slide and line the stairs up to the front boarding door. The captain and his crew walk into the plane to a round of applause, wave and go inside to check the status of their equipment and try to make radio contact.

For a while there is a buzz of conversation, as if the passengers anticipate some new development, expect the captain to come out and announce that they've found some surprise solution, the flight engineer has ingeniously rewired the airplane, they're going to be able to take off after all. But he doesn't come out, and time passes slowly like the sullen clouds settling into the treetops.

The deluge comes suddenly, as if released by a clap of thunder. The rain bounces back from the pavement nearly two feet. Instantly, all two hundred passengers are up and running for the shelter of the wing. Water pours off the control edge in

waterfalls, and even though the wing is big enough to accommodate everyone, the tarmac is flooded with half an inch of water within minutes. The air is heavy with the scent of the rich
red mud at the edge of the runway. Everyone is left standing,
looking out at the gray torrent, getting wet despite the overhead
cover.

"Laissez nous réembarquer sur l'avion!"

"Let us back on the airplane!" someone repeats in English.
One of the flight attendants pokes his head out of the door.

"Laissez nous réembarquer sur l'avion!" another passenger
yells. A chorus of voices shout in agreement. The flight attendant says something to the captain, who has joined her. It is still
raining, but the initial downpour has settled into a faint mist.
Some of the children have already ventured into it and are playing on the slippery evacuation slide that extends down from the
wing.

After a few minutes, the flight crew decide to let the passengers back on. They stand at the front door and make people
take their original seats, and by the time everyone is on board
again, the cabin is so humid that the walls sweat and the windows fog up. Lewis clears his with his wet hands just enough to
see that the rain shower has now completely stopped.

It's uncomfortably hot in the cabin, even without the sun. He
looks up at the flight attendant, who again stands by the door
as if guarding it. Ahead of him, the African man sits calmly, his
hands in his lap, his eyes gently closed. Most of the passengers
seem so relieved to be back on the plane, they act as if they have
already been rescued. The loud mix of voices and laughter coming from the main cabin sounds more like a cocktail party than
the aftermath of a plane crash. The flight attendants have begun
passing out drinks in first and business class, as if these were at
least reasonably normal circumstances.

"What would you like to drink, sir?"

Lewis looks up at the young man incredulously. Then it occurs to him that there is nothing else to do, really. He's glad to be back on the airplane, especially glad to be in first class and seated by himself. "Just some ice," he says.

The attendant meticulously scoops the ice into a cup and neatly hands it to him with a napkin and snack and moves on. Lewis tilts the glass back and lets the ice tumble into his mouth. It melts slowly as he looks out again at the new world. The sun is already out, burning the rain off the runway in a thin vapor. Lewis watches it shift in and out of the clouds.

He closes his eyes and lays a hand against the damp glass of the window and imagines his seven-year-old son, Shane, at his mother-in-law's house in Spokane, sitting before the dining room window with his hands resting on the cool glass. Helen sits at the table, sifting through bills, the reassuring sound near him of shuffling paper. Shane leans his face against the window, which trembles faintly with evidence of the outside world. He is listening to the rain, feeling the patter of it with the tips of his fingers. He has been blind since birth.

The hall of the maternity ward was empty at four-thirty the morning after he was born. There was no one to see Lewis alone with him, to see this tall young man looking so helpless, his own brown eyes lost in the long shadows of the corridor. He held his baby, and he worried that he wasn't up to this—to be father to a blind child. He felt wholly unprepared. Love, the kind of love a son would need from a father, could not be taken for granted. It would require something more than just empathy or a facile sense of obligation to do what is right. The numbness he felt could merely be shock. It would fade. But sometimes when Shane played with his toys, especially when he was very young, he was unable to find a toy that was inches away from him, and watching him grope for it became unbearable. Even though he knew that Shane had to find it on his own, if he ever was to learn, Lewis would give up first and put it in his small hand and then quietly stand up. Perhaps he was guilty of the obvious mistake of putting too much faith in the seen world. He would walk away and believe, because Shane could not see him, that the boy could not hear his footsteps receding down the hall.

He tried to make up for it in other ways. When he lay Shane in his crib, he reassured himself that he could work hard and provide Shane with all the things his genes had deprived him of. He jumped at the new job with Coke, even though it meant a lot more travel. He knew from the moment when Helen first caressed Shane's face that she was braver than he. She left the seeing world out of it and loved Shane with touch and sound. He was always in her arms, and in the beginning this was a relief for Lewis. She could hold their son for his whole life, enough for both of them.

The businessman interrupts his thoughts.

"They should be telling us something. We have a right to know what's going on."

"I guess they're trying to figure that out."

"So what do we do? Spend eternity sitting on this damn airplane?"

"There's not much out there."

"I want a plan. I want to know what the plan is."

The businessman leans closer. Lewis can smell his breath, sharp with fear. "I wish this was an American flight. At least they'd speak goddamn English. It probably wouldn't have happened, either." He gives a conspiratorial nod that says, We're us, we are Americans, and thank God for that, at least.

Some passengers have gone back to sleep. The woman in

front of him looks like she is dreaming. Her hands are moving faintly as if she is fending something off. The orange juice on her tray shakes quietly over her lap. The African man is reading, calmly turning pages. Lewis can hear the soft jingle of the service trays in the back. The children have quieted down, too. It is just still enough in the front cabin to hear some of the forest sounds—a bird calling, and the delicate buzz of insects warming up with the sun.

"We'd have been there in two hours, if this hadn't happened," says the businessman, petulantly. He looks at his watch as if doubting that such an outcome was ever taken for granted.

Lewis tumbles the last bit of ice from the glass into his mouth, relishing its coolness. He leans his head back against the pillow. As long as the ice holds up, it'll be all right.

Then someone yells from the back, and the excitement spreads through the cabin. *"Ils arriveront!"*

"They're coming, they're coming."

Three or four military jeeps approach the plane from the opposite end of the runway, racing like the cavalry charging over the hill. The jeeps are old, the soldiers in them are dressed in a hodgepodge of military uniforms, some even appear to have feather headdresses more like women's hats than helmets, and most of them are very young. There is not an ambulance or fire truck among them, the kind of emergency vehicle that might be of some use. Lewis can't resist the traditional superior response, the thought that *they* still haven't learned how *we* do things.

"Please remain seated while the captain greets the rescue crew. When we disembark it will be by section. Until then, please, you must remain in your seats."

The jeeps screech to a halt, and the soldiers jump out and run to the exits. The captain has emerged from the cockpit, buttoning the cuffs of his uniform. He smiles as the commander of the rescuers approaches the open forward door.

"Je vous en prie; l'escalier n'est pas parfait." The captain chuckles uncomfortably at his own joke about the condition of the ramp, which is two feet too low for the door.

But there's no response, and he has to back up quickly to get out of the way as the commander enters with two young soldiers, each with a different make of automatic weapon and mismatched uniform. The commander steps past the captain to the first row of seats. He is much older than the others, in his forties maybe. He isn't tall, at least six inches shorter than the French pilot just behind him. His eyes are tired despite the anger set in his jaw, and he looks, if not for the handgun gripped tightly in his fist, like anyone who feels uncomfortable making speeches in front of a group.

The cabin gives a cheer of welcome, which quickly dies out as one of the guards knocks loudly on the closed cockpit door.

"Ouvrez la porte!" He swings his rifle to hit the door, but the copilot is already opening it, and it swings back at him with amazing speed, hitting him in the face as it bounces violently shut. He opens the door again, slowly, then sits down, holding his bleeding nose, and the third pilot quickly switches off the radio and removes his headset. The soldier chases them both out and shuts the door on the empty cockpit. They find seats near where the captain is standing. He starts to say something to the commander, who simply ignores him.

The commander compensates for whatever stage fright he might be experiencing by shouting. He doesn't bother to translate his heavily accented French. Through the whole speech, the woman in front of Lewis stares out the window. When the commander finishes, he leaves one of the soldiers by the door and walks slowly down the center aisle. He stops to question the African man, not in French, but in Lingala. Lewis cannot hear the response, but the commander snaps something back and then walks on. The flight attendant steps into the galley, staring at the floor, trying to be invisible.

Everyone is careful not to meet the commander's gaze. Lewis, too, avoids his eyes, but glances up at his face as he passes. There are scars on his cheeks, symmetrical, inch-long diagonal lines clearly put there purposefully. He has the strong, acrid, sweaty smell of a man who has been working in the tropical heat, and his boots make muddy red tracks on the carpet. He takes fifteen minutes to make the trip to the rear of the plane. He stations the second soldier by the aft exit. When he returns, he has three or four passports from different countries in his hand. He stops where he made his speech and looks over the cabin, which is silent.

Then he turns to the captain. *"Venez avec moi."*

The captain obeys, standing stiffly, trying not to make too much of his superior height. He stoops under the door frame as they leave.

The soldier left to guard the door leans casually against the bulkhead, and after the commander leaves in his jeep, he motions to the flight attendant. "Coca-cola."

Lewis looks up.

"Do you want ice? *Du glace?*" the flight attendant politely offers.

The soldier shakes his head, and opens the drink with a soft *pop,* obviously very pleased with his assignment.

KOSESA—SÉPARÉ—APART

THE HUSHED MURMUR OF voices mixes quietly with the occasional showers of rain that wash over the hull of the airplane. Water pours down the windows and then beads up. Outside the soldiers have pulled off the yellow evacuation slides and have laid them out under the wings like rafts. Some lie on the inflated sides; others sit in groups, leaning back as if they are at the beginning of a long voyage. They look like refugees this way, or like navy men whose ship was sunk by a U-boat in the Atlantic, who now wait to see what will come first—rescue or sharks.

The businessman fidgets in his seat. A steady drip of condensation has pooled over the seat and seems to follow him as he moves, so that he has become gradually more agitated. "Hell of a rescue."

"What?"

"What are the they up to?"

Lewis shakes his head.

The businessman leans over the seat in front of him and clears his throat. "Excuse me."

"Yes?" The woman slowly turns to look up to him. He looks straight down at her like a child playing over the seats.

"Do you speak French?"

"*Oui.*"

"What did he say?"

She doesn't immediately respond, but looks ahead, playing abstractedly with her shoe, letting the heel slip on and off. Then she looks at Lewis across the aisle, half-whispering in case the soldier with the Coke speaks English. "Do you think it matters what he said? Do you think any of it was the truth?"

Lewis shrugs.

"I'll tell you what he didn't say." She smirks. "He didn't say when he was coming back. He didn't say when, or if, we were to get off the airplane. He didn't ask if anyone was hurt."

The businessman sits back down, rolling his eyes conspiratorially to Lewis. He looks at his watch again. "I was supposed to hit the links in an hour. It's the best way to beat jet lag. I go straight from the airport."

Lewis isn't sure how to respond. He doesn't want to encourage him. He half smiles and tries to turn away, but the man is not easily deterred.

"You a golfer?"

Lewis knows better than to say yes and spend the next who-knows-how-long talking about how he marks his golf balls. "No. Not really."

He wishes this guy would sit back in his seat. He turns deliberately to the window this time, but in his peripheral vision he can see the businessman fiddling with the phone. Eventually the man realizes that it isn't going to work; instead of hanging it up, he lays the phone in his lap. Lewis looks at his empty cup, wondering if he could ask for more ice. Outside the sky is now so blue it almost hurts his eyes, and the wall of forest looks formidable, green at its soul.

He thinks of Orly International in Paris, just a few hours and worlds away. He rode one of the long, shiny tube escalators that in drawings must have seemed like a daring, modern vision of the future, but having gathered dust and grime from years of use seemed hopelessly anachronistic. The woman at the executive lounge checked his ticket and took his coat with such a pretty accent and hushed tone that he didn't want to leave her. He stood there smiling at her a beat longer than seemed normal before going to sit in one of the long sofas with an anticipation of luxury and a desire to let himself relax. But within a minute he had to stand up, and desperate for a goal, he headed for the bar, where he got a scotch he did not really want, and returned to the stillness of his seat. After a sip and a bite of ice, he was on his feet again.

He found a phone in a plush, librarylike booth, but when he slipped the door shut the sudden silence reminded him that he did not know what he was going to say. He felt relieved to get the answering machine and then stammered through an awkward message that he was in Paris and leaving for Johannesburg in an hour, and love and hugs to Shane. As soon as he hung up, he knew that the message would just make her mad. She would be expecting more. He could do better. He looked at his watch, trying to calculate the time in Spokane. Still the middle of the night. She was sleeping, no doubt, on her stomach, an arm tossed over her head. He knew the position exactly. Perhaps she would be talking in her sleep, or just breathing softly, her quiet face appearing to have forgiven him.

Then he remembered the fight. He remembered starting it.

"Why *can't* she come out to New York, get her out of that ratty old house in Spokane?"

"It's her house."

"And she won't leave it? You know that?"

"She can't. She isn't well enough."

He could load her into a Lear jet with a nurse and fly her out.

She caught him rolling his eyes. "She broke her hip. She's eighty. Don't you get it?"

"If she's that hurt, she should go to some kind of nursing facility, assisted living or whatever it's called. You could commute out there to check on her."

"She lived for forty years in that house with my grandfather. Who are you to make that decision for her?"

He didn't say what he thought, that he was the man footing the bill, the man who was going to end up living alone for god knows how long. He looked at her, but she wasn't looking at him, luckily. She'd surely have read his mind.

"What's the difference, I guess."

"What?"

"Whether you're here . . . technically."

Helen sat down, looking at him as though he just hit her.

He felt lavishly willing to betray himself. There was something here that he had always avoided saying. This wasn't it, really, it wasn't what he meant, though on some childish level he felt it, and this resentment wouldn't let him address the real problem. He wished he could simply say that he was still in love and he wanted her back. Couldn't they just unslip themselves somehow?

Instead he said the thing that would cause the most harm. He was drawn to it like revenge.

"You left a long time ago."

Helen turned her face from him. She was so angry she almost laughed. "*I* did?"

Lewis knew he could still back out, turn it around. But he didn't. "We've had this conversation. A thousand times."

"Oh, that one." Helen shook her head and walked away from him.

"He takes all of you, Helen. There's nothing left."

"He's blind, Lewis."

"Thanks for the information," he seethed, "you know what I mean."

"This is all about you, huh?"

"I do my part." They were yelling now.

She looked at him as if she didn't recognize him. She might have wanted him to talk her out of going. Not now.

"So you need credit? Is that it?" She shook her head and started up the stairs. Halfway up she stopped. "I work my ass off," she shouted. "You don't know what it takes. You can't."

"I work, too, Helen. Every day. I *pay* for all of this." He knew it was lame the minute he said it. What a stupid point to bring to this argument. This didn't have to be a fight.

"Good. You pay." She waved her hand at him wearily. "I give up."

"And now you're actually leaving," he said, feeling the blow.

Helen looked down at him with reddened eyes.

"Yep."

Without another word she walked to the bedroom, and Lewis took his keys from the table and stopped just once at the car, intensely aware of the cool air drifting down through the branches that loomed over him. What was this unexpected feeling? This sense of relief. Like some burden being lifted? No, that was ridiculous, it wasn't what he wanted. Was it pride or just stupid anger? Something kept him from going back inside. He couldn't argue himself out of it.

Since then he has been haunted by the memory of something he never actually saw, but refined in his imagination. Helen sitting at the top of the stairs, her hair shorter than it had ever been, the hem of her dress brushed carefully down over her knees. The house is still and there are boxes and suitcases by the door. Shane is at school and their plane doesn't leave until late afternoon, but she's already packed. It isn't supposed to be a separation, but it will look that way to anyone from the outside.

Lewis looks up now at the soldier who has just finished another Coke. He watches him as he struggles to lower the jump seat. The flight attendant helps him with it, and when he sits his body looks so relaxed that he seems absolutely satisfied. His weapon leans carelessly against the toilet door. Lewis wonders what kind of conversation he might have had with his wife this morning. Maybe he's too young to have a wife, or maybe he has more than one. What is he thinking about? Is it something that happened to him as a child? A father's rebuke? His mother's voice singing softly at dawn? Or is it something else altogether, the unsettling curve of a young woman's body?

Outside the soldiers have moved the slides out from under the wings. Somehow they must know that the rain is over for a while. It's getting hot. Two of them are working carefully in the back of one of the vehicles, but other than a set of black jumper cables, he cannot see what they are so focused on.

It's barely dawn, gray with no promise of sun. Helen wakes up, aware of the empty bed like a cold hand on her back and the unfamiliar smells of her mother's house. There is the muffled quiet of new snow piled against the windows. Shane can hear it. He always knows first. Before anyone else has a chance to look, he'll be half dressed, anxious to get outside. Helen marvels at how quickly he is getting used to her mother's house and the small-town rhythms of Spokane.

While the coffee brews, she checks for messages on the answering machine she brought with her and plugged into her mother's phone, one of those with oversized numbers and buttons, like a child's toy. Lewis's is the only one. She shakes her head and erases it, quietly cradling the phone.

"Come on, Lewis," she whispers to the empty house, "what else did you expect me to do?" Even though he didn't say anything specific, more than the necessary information, the question is there in his tone. She can barely force herself to hear the actual content of the message. Still, she writes down his flight number out of habit.

She hears a loud bang and rushes to the family room, but it's just Shane outside. He's thrown a snowball against the window, and he's laughing. He picks up another and hits the window again.

Still laughing, he runs out into the yard. The soft blanket of white has recreated the world for him. It sounds exactly the way it looks—the trees and bushes, everything is covered, tempered, made mute by the fallen snow. He runs to the middle of the yard and stops with his arms up in the air, catching snowflakes with his fingertips. He turns slowly, as if measuring the space around him, and then he stops. To Helen he looks lost, particularily small in the snow, wandering on a blank page without a guide. For the ten thousandth time she resists the instinct to pick him up, to shelter him.

In the kitchen, she makes his breakfast and cleans up, carefully clearing some of the obstacles for Shane but leaving the house mostly as it is. Even though her mother may not make it out of the bedroom, Helen doesn't want her house to be too greatly altered. She eats a bowl of cereal by herself, standing at the counter. When she finds where she set down her coffee, it's lukewarm. She's struck by how familiar this role is becoming— caretaker, nurse, and single mother.

"The toilet is overflowing," the businessman says to the soldier, who has not moved from his seat for the last three hours. The young man looks at him with a passive expression that can be interpreted as either compassion or contempt. Obviously, there is nothing he can do about it, and even if the businessman could manage a bit of French to communicate his complaint, the soldier might just wonder why it's supposed to be his problem, surprised by that peculiarly Western idea that makes authority also responsible.

"And it stinks."

The businessman sits down in a huff. Lewis turns his book over and reads the back cover again. It's not a book he chose. Someone at the office gave it to him because he was going to Africa—*Through the Dark Continent,* by Henry Morton Stanley. There is something in the portrait on the back that makes Stanley seem more tired and world-weary than the bold adventurer the book touts him to be, charting the blank spaces on the map of Africa. Just a few hours in this humidity and already the paperback has nearly doubled in thickness.

Outside his window two soldiers are asleep on the wing, bare feet on the warm, slick metal. They've pulled the ramp away from the door to get up there. The rest are in the rafts, playing some sort of gambling card game, drinking from a pile of soft drinks commandeered from the jet. Lewis opens the book and turns a damp page.

"It's fucking hot," says the businessman.

Lewis tries to ignore him and reads from Stanley's journal, *"Where are the brave fellows to be my companions?"* There are no volunteers, so Stanley chooses some from among his men and, in chains if he must, drives them into the wilderness by the sheer, brutal force of his will. *"We glide down narrow streams between palmy and spicy islands, whose sweet fragrance and vernal colour cause us to forget for a moment our dangerous life."*

"Our 'rescuers' have taken all the ice and all the drinks."

Lewis turns another page. *"Our blood is up now. It is a murderous world and we feel for the first time that we hate the filthy, vulturous ghouls who inhabit it."*

"Have you figured out what this place is? How it is that there's this paved runway in the middle of nowhere?"

Lewis sets his book down to answer. "It was probably built for a state visit, or something. The president of Mexico did it, built a big runway in Baja because the local runway wouldn't accommodate his jet. It's never been used since."

"They could have made it a bit longer."

The waiting has worn everyone down, except for the children, who can't sit still, as if they would like to see how it feels to run down the runway, arms stretched out like the wings of birds. The adults have already accepted the captivity of their waiting, anticipating with undue optimism that what comes next will be an improvement. Time, slow and hot and damp, ebbs like a weak tide.

The soldiers outside jump up and start madly lacing their boots. The gamblers ditch their cards. At the end of the field, the commander is returning. The soldier by the door stands and collects his weapon as they push the ramp back over. Lewis can see the captain, sitting in the back of his jeep. He looks resigned, wilted in the heat.

Again the commander wastes no time on pleasantries. His French is brittle, only the words that are needed, or perhaps it is only the tone that is needed. Then there is rustling in the back of the airplane. Even the woman reacts. She gathers her purse and pulls her carry-on from underneath the seat in front of her.

"Are we getting off?" the businessman asks, looking around. Most of the passengers in the business class cabin have not moved. Neither has the African man. He is looking straight ahead, not wishing to draw attention.

"*Les dames et les enfants.*"

"What the hell? Why? I don't get it."

The woman has already turned away from him and is waiting for the order to go. A soldier in the back starts shouting to separate the families from their husbands and fathers. Some dare to shout back, and a couple of the soldiers rush back with their guns, shoving their way through the aisle to enforce the order. For a few tense minutes of shoving and threats, the situation begins to escalate into something worse, but then the soldiers get the women and children moving. One father in the back is still yelling as the flight attendants help crying children out the front exit, lifting them down onto the air stairs. The commander follows the last of them out, and he offers no help to a woman who is carrying two children and desperately trying to persuade the third to move along.

They gather in a group on the pavement, as if expecting a bus. Then there is more shouting, and reluctantly they begin walking down the runway. Even though it is too short for the heavy jet, it is almost a mile long. The commander gets into his jeep and drives slowly behind. Strangers pick up children who are too small to walk.

Lewis watches them until, like a small band of refugees, they disappear into the bush at the end of the runway. His gaze returns to the soldier by the door. Both of the soldier's hands are on his weapon, and now his expression seems unequivocal. The ramp is pulled away from the door.

"That's it? That's it? We stay?" The businessman sits down and lays his face on his hand, wiping the perspiration away, and he looks up. "Jesus."

KOKIMA—S'ENFUIANT—RUN

HELEN'S CELL PHONE RINGS in her purse. She stops in the middle of the busy mall, sets her bags down and searches frantically until she finds it.

"Hello," she answers, a little out a breath.

"Helen Burke?"

"Yes."

"Your husband is Lewis Burke?"

"Yes. What's wrong?"

The statement the airline representative delivers about the "incident" sounds overly rehearsed. Helen nearly sits down on the floor, right where she is, but she manages to get over to a bench. She can barely listen to him. His tone is appropriately sympathetic, but he offers little in the way of factual information, except perhaps the claim that the passengers are presumed to be okay. Helen cuts him off.

"Where are they?"

"They have not released that information as yet."

"They? I thought you were they."

"Yes, I am a *representative* . . ."

"Who do I talk to who can answer real questions?"

"Well, I—"

"*You* don't even know where the plane is." She considers throwing the phone into the fake plants in the planter behind her.

"Please remember, this plane disappeared in *Africa*. Not Idaho or North Carolina. We are getting the answers out as efficiently as we can."

Helen gets a number and flips the phone shut. She stands and looks around the mall, searching for some confirmation that this news could be real. The shoppers move by her as if animated by an outside force, pressed unwillingly through their day. She leaves her shopping bags where they are in the middle of the floor. Instead of the escalator she takes a side exit with bare concrete walls and stairs, with simple floor numbers. Her footsteps echo dryly as she descends, and her thoughts gather into a storm. She pauses at the heavy metal fire door at the bottom of the staircase, wondering if she has taken the wrong way down.

My God, Lewis, where are you?

She pushes hard, and the door grudgingly opens. The wind outside is bitterly cold and blows snow up from the pavement. She takes a minute to orient herself in the unfamiliar parking lot and remember where she left the car. Her fashionable shoes are inadequate for the weather, and her hands are numb before she can work the lock open and climb into the refuge, the cold stiff seats of her mother's Ford Taurus. She shuts the door and turns the key in the ignition, the car beeps at her, the fan springs dutifully alive though it blows cold air. She sits there without moving.

The night of the fight, she turned back from the bedroom to see him, and he looked, suddenly, like a stranger who had trespassed in their house. She suppressed the desire to throw something at his retreating back. He must have thought she was crying. But he had no idea. She sat at the top of the stairs and marveled at the feeling of calm. She would make the decision that would shake him up or leave him behind, one or the other. Not speaking felt violent and satisfying. But he had never left that way before. They had crossed another line.

Sitting at a stubbornly red traffic light, she is shaken by how easily they created this mess, that she did nothing to try to fix it. She packed up and left. It was exactly the opposite of what she meant to do, exactly what she was mad at him for, but it felt powerful because it was so certain to wound him. At least they're saying he's alive. She rests her hands on the steering wheel to keep them from shaking.

———

Lewis unfolds his arms and sits up. It is raining again, and it's getting dark. The night is a great relief from the stunning sauna of day. He wonders if they are going to turn on any lights. They were given water, but it was warm and tasted of mud. Some of the passengers wouldn't drink it, but he was too thirsty to be so picky. It seemed more important to keep hydrated than to worry about African parasites. They haven't officially been designated hostages yet, no one has said it, and Lewis has to doubt if anyone ever will. When it is done, these men will claim that they simply came to the rescue, a purely humanitarian gesture, that once again the Western powers have misrepresented their intentions.

The soldiers seem not to notice the fading light or the rain. They stand or sit, immobile and implacable. They aren't much of a guard, really, and Lewis half imagines slipping past them in the dark. The only real obstacle is the long jump from the open door without the ramp. It must be at least ten feet. There is also the soldier drinking Cokes by the door. But after that the bush is only a few dozen yards away. It tempts him like the irrational urge to jump from a bridge or swerve into oncoming traffic, to test the realness of the world—disappear into that unknown, perhaps, but still it would be an escape, a choice made.

Finally one of the men turns the headlights of the jeep on, and they cast an eerie light that reflects off the puddles and dances on the ceiling. The passengers settle in for sleep, but Lewis cannot bring himself to close his eyes. Sleep has never been that easy for him, anyway. It has always been a luxury that his mind begrudges him. He thinks of Shane, who sleeps without completely closing his eyes. When he rocked him as an infant, he had to wait for the signs of sleep in his limbs. He would feel Shane's thoughts slowly wander and calmly leave his body. Closing his eyes did not help Lewis drift off. It merely blinded him, and for a long time just that thought itself would keep him awake.

The businessman across the aisle is fast asleep, his head back and to the side. Lewis pulls his wallet out of his pocket—it's been putting his leg to sleep—then he looks up at the soldier to make sure he hasn't noticed. He tries to slip it quietly into his shirt pocket, but he ends up dropping it, and it flips open on the floor. A few of the photographs fall out, images of Shane as a baby, his blond hair in curls. He picks them up carefully, as though they have some special fragility. It's hard not to want someone to blame for his son's blindness.

He pulls out a more worn picture. One he hasn't looked at in a while. It's of Helen, dimly visible in his hands like the memory of when he took it. He used to fancy himself a photographer; at least, he had all the gear. He had brought his new camera back into the shop, and to demonstrate what he considered to be its malfunction, he turned to take a photograph before he fully realized that Helen was to be its subject. She just happened to be standing there, waiting for a salesperson. This picture, now faded, represents precisely the first moment he ever saw her. First sight. But it wasn't love, at least not in the real moment of it.

"I want that negative," she demanded.

"Huh?"

"You can't take my picture without my permission."

"I was just testing the camera."

"I want the negative anyway."

He remembers looking at her and the profound sense of delay he experienced between what she was saying, what the issue was, and his ability to comprehend her.

"There are other photos on it already," he offered. "Most of a roll."

"You can't take my picture without my permission," she said again.

He began to focus on her. Her eyes first, green and bright, and her soft face, but also strong and intimidating, her straight brown hair tumbling loosely onto her bare shoulders.

"Give me the roll. I'll develop it and give you your pictures back. I'll leave them with this man."

He didn't really care about the photos; they were just some still lifes that seemed worth taking at the time, but now, they seemed pathetic, enough to make him regret the lenses, the Haliburton case, the malfunctioning camera—all of it.

"Look, I'll throw the picture away. I'll destroy the negative. I've got no use for it."

Something in his tone finally calmed her. She shrugged. "I'm sorry. I just don't like having my picture taken by a total stranger."

He raised his hands to apologize again, but she had already started to walk away. He turned back to the repairman. "Look, obviously it worked fine just now. I don't know." He glanced over to her, but she was out the door.

When the photographs came back, the still lifes were just as bad as he had thought. But the picture of her had an unexpected quality to it, and though he didn't know her, it seemed then, as it always seemed afterward, to capture something of her essence. He broke his promise. He kept the picture and the negative. The print lay on his desk among the others, and he became familiar with it, with her image. He could not get her out of his mind. He found himself looking at her photograph on his desk before he did anything else. Then he began to feel guilty for breaking his word, and one Saturday on an impulse he took the picture and the negative in an envelope to the photo shop. He toyed with the idea of making a copy, and he had decided to do it, but when he got to the shop the guy recognized him, and so he gave him the envelope with a note apologizing for taking so long to return it. As an afterthought he added his phone number. Then he tried to put her out of his mind.

IN THE MORNING the commander returns and goes through the cabin, checking passports. He takes a long time with the African man, asking him questions or making demands in a clipped, angry voice. The African man seems shaken. His strong hands cannot find a calm place to rest as he tries to keep his answers short and confident, as though the commander is just wasting his time. The soldiers watch him coldly. The commander shouts one last thing at him, and he moves his head away, tightening his jaw as if he expects to be hit. But the commander turns his back instead and grabs Lewis's and the businessman's passports from their hands, barely glancing at them before giving them back and moving on.

They have brought some *fufu*, cassava cooked and then pounded into a putty. The young soldier at the door eats his with obvious satisfaction. The businessman looks at his as though someone might be trying to poison him. But hunger makes a convincing argument and Lewis eats his ration, though to his American palette, more used to accepting a Big Mac, it tastes like unleavened horse-hoof paste.

His mind wanders over their predicament. How long can these soldiers hide the fact that they are holding a planeload of foreigners? Does anyone out there know what's really going on? What will Helen have heard about it? That they survived? It's hard to imagine her sitting quietly by for very long as they feed her vague information that doesn't make sense; that wouldn't be like her. Even the soldiers seem unsure of what they will do. Amid the sheer boredom of waiting, it is hard to concentrate on what is happening enough to be able to register it, except in little shocks. The thought of just how suddenly this could find an unacceptable ending gives him a sick feeling in his gut. There are brief moments of panic, when he must close his eyes and try to control his breathing while his imagination searches for glimpses of Helen's face or simply the sound of Shane's voice reaching out for him across this enormous distance.

Perhaps three times before noon the soldier guarding them gets up and urinates directly out the door on the cargo side. Then he takes another can from his private stash of Cokes, which in the heat have reached a dangerous level of instability. He loses half of each one he opens. The ice is gone, having been allowed to melt unused. The toilet now truly stinks. In this tropical heat its stench manages to keep well ahead of the senses' ability to accommodate and ignore it.

The Dutchman has taken to singing folk songs, crooning in his native language. He sounds like a combination of Chaucer and Dylan. He starts softly, and soon he is getting along mournfully. The man who sat next to him has moved even though it put him nearer the toilet. The soldiers don't seem to like the singing much better. They go back and yell at him until he stops. Then, except for the raspy cough of an old man at the bulkhead, who probably should have been sent off with the women and children, it is quiet.

There aren't many answers to Shane's questions. Helen holds his hands on the globe they have found at the library. She moves his fingers across the mountains of northern Idaho to the edge of the desert basin of eastern Washington.

"This is Spokane."

She takes his other hand and moves it slowly down from the pole to give him a sense of where it is in the northern hemisphere. Then she moves it over to New York. His fingers cross the Hudson.

"This is our house in New York. This is how far we came."

"Where's Dad?"

The globe is big, nearly two and a half feet in diameter. She has to stretch his arms for him to reach. His hand crosses the glassy smoothness of the Atlantic, then encounters the bumps of Braille that identify it.

"What does this say?"

"Try to read it. Sound it out."

"At-lan-tic O-cean." He caresses it lightly with his hands. "It's big. Tell me the color."

"On this map it's blue, honey."

"Blue," he says slowly, trying to hear the quality of color in its sound. "Like a bird?"

"Yes."

"This is Europe. And Paris."

Then she moves along the route of Lewis's plane, across the Mediterranean and the mountains of Libya.

"More ocean?"

"Desert. The Sahara. Then the plane had to land because it had a problem—in the Congo."

His hand stops on the spot, and he holds it there as if trying to divine from the map something about what has happened to his father. His whole body seems more alert. His reaction when she first told him surprised her. She expected it to scare him more; she knew he would hear the concern in her voice. But he focused more on the exotic adventure of it. He wanted to know more about Africa. She would like to think of a way to communicate the danger of what has happened without upsetting him.

"Which way is out?" He moves his hand around.

She looks at him. He seems serious: he wants to feel the path.

"I think he would have to fly. Or take a boat," he says.

"I think you're right."

"Can we go get him, Mom?"

Helen takes a deep breath. "I don't know, Shane. It may be best to wait. He should be back soon."

"Will he come to New York or to Spokane?"

"I think . . ." she starts. "He'll come wherever we are."

"What if he's hurt?"

"They said he was okay," she answers, as confidently as she can manage. "I think we should trust them." She doesn't say that she hasn't heard anything more today, that she doesn't know how long it will take.

Another night. In shifts they have been allowed to get up and walk the aisle of the plane. Lewis stands by his seat. If he had any idea where they were, what lay beyond the thick bush and canopy of rainforest that line the runway, he might use the night to slip away, follow a road to a town. He still has his money. He could pay someone to hide him. U.S. dollars have to be worth something.

Lewis leans down to peer out the window, as if something might have changed—the forest yielded to a real airport, a gate, a way out. They have not seen the captain since the last time he left with the commander. The other pilots have come out to sleep in some of the empty seats in the back, though otherwise they spend as much time in the cockpit as they can. They haven't been allowed to use the radio since the "rescuers" arrived, but things have become more casual over two days. They all talk with the guards, trying to get information, but the soldiers don't know much more than they do. The French-speaking passengers play card games among themselves, drink their warm, muddy water as though it were whisky, laugh and wait.

The African man hardly gets up. Most of the time he seems to be meditating or quietly praying. When he does move, it is just to stand for a while. The guard always reacts, becoming suddenly more alert, and the African faces away from him. At first Lewis presumes this is because the African would have the best chance of escaping. But there is something else—they treat him as though he has a chosen side in this conflict, as an enemy.

Lewis sits down, his back against the wall and window. There is no moon yet, but the bright, starry sky confirms that there is no significant source of light, no city streets nearby. Eventually he sleeps.

He dreams of the airport in Paris. Now the glass tubes and escalators appear endless, and all the space between them is filled with billboards and large Diamond Vision video screens with Coca-Cola advertising, logos and slogans. When he comes to the end of one escalator, he is in a vast mall and then in one of the megastores that sell videos, books and CDs, anything that speaks and is for sale. The woman behind the counter, or the girl (she can't be more than nineteen), leans bored and cool, disdainfully watching one of the many monitors playing competing music videos. He waits to get her attention to ask a question. She lifts her heavy eyes and approaches him. In her navel there is a gold ring with a small diamond, her arms are bare and long; she lays her hands on the counter, subtly rocking her hips, shifting her weight from one foot to the other.

"What do you want, Lewis?"

He opens his eyes to the ceiling, to the round circle of light from the window, and when he returns to sleep, she is gone.

THE NEXT DAY, the third day, the monotony of their waiting is disrupted. Before the light has really come up, when darkness can still pretend to be infinite, Lewis wakes to several lights bouncing down the runway. The commander storms onto the plane, accompanied this time by several more soldiers. He waits impatiently while they search for the two copilots. Fear shakes the sleep out of their eyes as they are paraded up the aisle. The commander yells at them and they are pressed into the cockpit. A dim light comes on, and Lewis can see one of them sit down at the radio, pulling his headset on. The commander shouts again, and the copilot takes it off; he raises his hands as if to protest, and one of the soldiers strikes him without warning. There is discussion about something to do with the radio. The other pilot reaches overhead and flips a couple of switches.

The auxiliary power unit spins to life in the tail of the plane, building up from a low whine. Then a cool vapor begins to pour out of the air-conditioning vents, and the passengers groan. The soldier by the door grins at their reaction and leans out to see where the sound is coming from. Lewis quickly slips his wallet and passport into the seat, burying them between the life jacket and the seat cushion. He slips a hand into his pocket to get his money, but the soldier is watching him now, so he has to leave it. He slides his book into the seat pocket in front of him, and then sits back and closes his eyes. The pilot speaks quickly in English, but Lewis can only make out a few words of it. He has contacted the control center, identified the aircraft, and he is just about to tell them that the plane has been taken hostage, when the commander threatens him again, and the copilot switches to French. He says a few brief words, and then they wait. Someone is being summoned on the other end.

As soon as it is light enough, the soldiers begin going through the cabin; they start a few seats in front of Lewis. They open each overhead bin and pull out the contents. They are taking money, jewelry, anything they can find. They rifle through Lewis's bag and then yell something at him. He raises his hands to indicate that he doesn't understand. They make him stand. They search his pockets, take the money and his watch and then move on. There is plenty of loot to be had, and they're in a hurry because another group has started from the back, doing the same thing. Lewis sits down, and outside he can see that the soldiers have pried the baggage compartment open. Soon the runway is littered with clothes and toiletries, papers and pajamas, as they argue over the spoils.

The copilot is back on the radio. After a minute he hands the microphone to the commander. He seems impatient with what he's hearing and starts to get angry but stops himself and orders the pilot to turn off the radio. The APU shuts down again, and the air-conditioning cuts off. The commander walks back into the cabin and shouts for the looting to stop. He studies the passengers as if he is looking for something among them. Then his eyes fall on the African man. He gives an order to the couple of soldiers near him. For a second it looks as if they might shoot this man on the spot. Both soldiers cock their rifles and aim them at him. He raises his hands to fend off any blows and stands up. The commander yells at him. The man looks shaken, but he is not pleading. He stops. He seems afraid to leave the planeful of witnesses. A soldier butts him in the shoulder with his rifle, shoving him hard to get him moving, and they parade him off the plane. Lewis watches as they push him into the back of one of the vehicles and speed off down the runway. The commander takes the two copilots with him, leaving an additional guard to sit in the cockpit, where he fiddles with switches, turning the emergency floor lights on and off in the cabin until another soldier yells at him to stop.

Helen walks into the backyard without a sweater and shuts the door behind her. When she finally lets her breath go, it floats away in a cloud. She tightens her hands into fists and lets the cold wash over her. She finds herself staring at the snowman Shane has made, or half-made. It's about his size and looks like a wonderfully misshapen elf.

The day after Shane was born it was blowing snow. To get him from the hospital to the car they had to cover his face with blankets because the wind was whipping down the streets of

Manhattan with such ferocity. Lewis carried him in the car seat and she hurried ahead, trying not to slip on the icy sidewalk. The wind was so strong that it pulled the door from her grip the first time she opened it. Lewis held his body over Shane to shelter him until she got it open again. Though the trip from hospital door to car took only a few minutes, it had the dramatic feeling of a rescue. They sat in the car for a moment, catching their breath. Helen lifted the blanket from his face, and he was already sleeping, helpless, consigned to them.

"Are you ready?" The question came out meaning more than Lewis intended.

"I don't know."

Lewis reached across the seat and kissed her, and held her hands until they were warm again. "I'm sorry."

She didn't react then, but she always remembered that apology. What was it for? Was he taking responsibility for Shane's blindness? Or for not being ready himself? At the time she took the strength in his face, the way he held her hands, as a promise to take his share in this bit of fate.

Helen steps back into the house and slides the door closed as if to put that thought away. She runs over in her head what the woman from the state department just said, looking for any other way to interpret the information—looking for any way at all to take it at face value, not hear the improbability behind it. Why deny that they are hostages? Why make such a point of it, if that isn't exactly what they are? If they are not hostages, why aren't they out of there already?

The media have bought the story, as if anyone is supposed to believe that in the twenty-first century there is still some kind of "heart of darkness" in Africa, some place so remote in the jungle that military helicopters couldn't be there in a few hours. How gullible is she expected to be? Her impulse is to get to

Africa tomorrow and knock their door down, show them this isn't just another "situation" that they can leave on their desks at five to make it home for dinner.

Helen pours water over a tea bag, watching the steam rise from the cup. She is counting, trying to keep breathing. She stirs a spoonful of honey into her tea and goes to the phone. She listens to the dial tone for a moment before committing herself; then she dials the number. She gets a recorded announcement that she has reached WorldAid. The official tone does not conjure the small scrapped-together office that she remembers. She finds the extension she needs and waits while the call is forwarded.

"Danny? It's Helen Burke."

"Helen? Wow, it's been a long time."

"Do they still have you chained to the office?"

"They don't even let me out to sleep anymore. I haven't been to Asia since you were there. What's that? Ten years?"

"More, I think."

"He's how old now, your son?"

"Shane is seven."

"How's motherhood?"

"Great. Challenging."

"I'm sure."

"Look, you probably wonder why I'm calling. It's not about my job."

"If you want it back, we're offering the same shitty no-pay scale for volunteer work stateside."

"No, really. Shane still takes up all my time. That's my life." She takes a breath. "I need some help, Danny. Have you heard about this Air France thing?"

"Mmm, not sure."

"Africa. The Congo."

"Oh, yeah."

"Lewis was on that plane."

"Oh, shit."

"Have you heard anything?"

"Just that it landed in some remote place in the bush and they're having trouble getting the passengers out."

"It's been three days. Not a word, no plan of when they're being evacuated, nothing. It doesn't make any sense. Do you buy it?"

"I don't know, I've worked with governments that can be pretty incompetent when they want to be."

"Are you guys still over there? With all the fighting going on?"

"We're always *over there*—especially when the fighting is going on. It's easier to get money for emergency aid."

"What's it like?"

"I haven't been there, but I know some people who were pretty recently. The eastern part of the country is in trouble. The basic infrastructure has been so badly disrupted by the influx of Rwandan refugees and the war that what help we manage to get in there comes too late, or ends up going to the wrong people, the *génocidiers* or the militias, who are no better than armed thugs. The U.N.'s trying to keep a cease-fire in place with about two thousand troops for the whole country. Uganda and Rwanda are trying to look like they're cooperating, so the fighting has calmed down some, for now."

"I'm thinking of going."

"Where?"

"Just the capital, Kinshasa. The state department is stalling. I think they need to feel some pressure. I can't just sit here."

"You'd be on your own. I'm sorry, I just can't afford to piss off . . ."

"I understand."

"What can I do?"

"Get some press on it. One or two of your friends. Have them make some noise."

"What am I going to tell them?"

"Tell them it's a good story."

Helen takes a long sip of her tea, waiting for him to think about it. Then she changes the subject to give him a chance to decide if he's going to commit.

"I'm taking Shane." There's a brief pause. She suspects that he can hear that this is the first time she has seriously considered it. "You're not answering."

"I'm thinking about it. It depends on what you need to do. Kinshasa is pretty much the same as it's ever been, which isn't great. It's going to be different from when you were in Asia way back when, but not *that* different. You're smart enough. Just stay away from the soldiers and keep clear of the disputed areas."

"This all has to happen pretty fast."

"I know. I'll get to work on the press. I have a couple of ideas, but it isn't going to be anybody from *Newsweek* or the *Washington Post,* so don't be too disappointed."

"I didn't think . . ."

He can hear the shift in her voice, a little emotion slipping in. "I'm sorry. It's got to be rough."

"I don't know what else to do. Wouldn't you go?"

"Probably," he says. "I'm not surprised to hear you considering it."

Helen exhales, trying to compose herself.

"Helen, it's going to be all right."

"Thanks."

"I'll get back to you as soon as I can."

Helen quietly sets the phone on the counter. She walks back to the window, and over the gray afternoon outside she sees her reflection in the glass. Her eyes are red and damp. She stares hard at the image, looking for the strength she will need to cope. She can't simply wait this out, sit by the phone and hope. Her heart tightens suddenly in her chest—if she let herself, she could panic. Lewis needs her.

She hears her mother coughing in the other room. When she gets to the door, her mother is already sitting on the side of her bed, preparing to lift herself onto the walker.

"Mom, let me help."

"No, dear, I can manage." She struggles with it, but she does manage. "Where's Shane?"

"Playing in the den."

They slowly make their way into the living room. Helen's mother looks relieved to be sitting again.

"This chair feels good."

Helen smiles.

"So, you're off to Africa?"

"It's just an idea. I haven't decided. I can wait."

Her mother puts her walker out of her way and leans forward.

"No. You can't wait." Her bright eyes belie the crippled condition of her body. "There's no time. Your cousin Miriam can come help me for a few days."

"Mom."

"It's okay."

Helen looks at her silently.

"What about Shane?" her mother asks, avoiding direct contact with her eyes.

"It'd be too hard on him to leave him behind."

"But it's Africa."

"A real place, full of people."

"It's dangerous."

"What's the option?"

Her mother seems genuinely worried but still ready to trust her. She doesn't feel she has a choice to make here, no matter what anyone else might think about it.

"What am I supposed to do, Mom? He belongs with me. This is his father."

Sometime after noon they bring the dynamite on board in two bunches tied with hemp, along with a greasy old car battery and jumper cables presumably for detonation. Most of the sticks look very old, sweating in the humidity and encrusted at both ends with pale green and white corrosion. They look dangerously unstable, as though they could explode spontaneously. The soldiers dump both packages in the galley up front, as if they are unsure what they are supposed to do with them. Lewis winces at their cavalier handling of the explosives, but neither they nor the guard seem much concerned. He sits calmly with his feet next to them, tapping on the stock of his rifle.

Lewis finds himself staring at the dynamite, watching over it as though his gaze could keep it harmless. What's the plan, then? To blow up the plane? With them in it? Is this some final desperate measure because negotiations over the radio have been unsuccessful? The palms of his hands are sweating. It's time to do something, whatever it is, take action. Lewis looks up at the friendly face happily sipping an American soft drink. The man returns his gaze without losing the smile.

Would you kill me?

Then one of the Frenchmen a couple of rows back stands up. He doesn't leave his seat, but he starts yelling at the soldiers.

"Que voulez-vous faire avec cette dynamite?"

At first they ignore him, but the Frenchman keeps shouting. Finally one soldier walks over to him, cocks his weapon and points it directly at the man's chest.

"Assieds-toi, espèce de salaud." He yells, and then he laughs. *"Nous allons éclater ce putin d'avion, sale conard—avec vous tous dedans."*

It's not hard for Lewis to guess the man's meaning, the way he points at the dynamite and the laugh, the tone of the insult. They are serious about this. What would be the point of making a show of it? Who's watching that matters?

An hour later one of the soldiers returns. A couple of the other rebels help him wheel the ramp back into place. Apparently, he was supposed to put the dynamite over the wings, nearer the fuel tanks. He tries picking it up himself, but it is awkward and heavy with the two batteries and he ends up dropping the whole mess. The guard watches him, more amused than alarmed, and he drops it again; this time the battery falls on top of one of the bundles of dynamite. Lewis has to look away. Finally the soldier enlists the guard's help. At first they try to take both packages at once, and it looks like they will drop them again, but after some arguing they take just one along with its battery and cables and head back toward the wings. Lewis stares at the remaining package, the dynamite and the unguarded door beyond. The ramp is still in place. He tries to slow his breathing, pressing his hands into the seat to force some calm.

"What the hell are they going to do now?" the businessman asks of no one in particular. He means to sound bored, but his voice is shaky.

Lewis doesn't even try to answer. He looks back down the aisle. The soldiers and guard seem to be waiting for a passenger to leave his seat. Then the soldiers outside are shouting, and he hears the distant throb of helicopters. Lewis looks out the window. Several of the soldiers drop behind one of the jeeps and begin shooting. Most of the passengers duck and cover their heads. There is the flat smack of bullets hitting the fuselage— somebody has started shooting at them. The guard and soldier yell now for the passenger to clear his seat so they can put their load down. Lewis turns. The soldiers are working fast, frantically hooking the cables to the dynamite. They shout something to the soldiers outside, but it is impossible to hear because of the gunfire. He reaches under his seat and grabs the wallet and passport. For some reason he grabs his book too, and he runs for the door. He stops there just long enough to see what the soldiers are so excited about. Two military helicopters are approaching just over the trees about halfway up the runway, and the soldiers are all firing in that direction.

Lewis is out of the airplane and running before he has time to think about what he's doing. He grabs the railing with his free hand and takes the stairs three at a time. At the bottom he turns hard and runs for the nose of the plane to get out of view as quickly as possible. From there it's less than eighty yards to the edge of the forest. He sprints across the open asphalt without looking back. There is no way to know if he's been spotted or if the shooting he hears is directed at him. Any minute he expects the dynamite to ignite the fuel tanks and the heat of the explosion to engulf him. He makes it to the bush in eleven seconds, though it feels more like eleven minutes. The first several feet are denser than he thought and rife with thorns. He uses the book to protect his face and thrashes his way through, clawing at the vegetation. Twenty yards in, it lightens up, and he can move faster. There is even a vague trail to follow. He's making good progress when he catches a shoe on one of the many creepers that interlace the forest floor, and he goes down hard, knocking the wind out of him and injuring his shoulder.

As he struggles to get his breath back, he can hear the helicopters thunder overhead and for a few minutes some furious shooting in his direction. Then it calms down, and the helicopters fade into the distance. A few leaves drift down from the canopy. He sits up and listens hard for any human noise above the shrill buzzing of insects. Then he hears some muted shouting. They must have discovered that he has escaped. He gets up and runs again, watching the ground in front of him carefully, following the suggestion of a trail, arms ready in case of another fall.

He runs for an hour, maybe less. The sun breaks through the canopy only in shattered fragments. When it clouds over, it becomes impossible to judge time at all. At last he stops. He's a couple of miles into the forest. There is no noise, no sound of anyone following, no helicopters, no shooting. His captors seem to have resigned him to the forest and the din of insects and birds and the rotting humidity of the bush. It takes him a long time to catch his breath. The air is so muggy that it's almost impossible to breathe. He has been running hard. It's a lot of exertion after several days of inactivity, and he can feel it. He closes his eyes to keep from throwing up. His head is pounding. When he opens his eyes, the mass of vines and creepers, great trunks and small, flat, wide leaves and spongy earth looks otherworldly. It takes him a long panicked moment to remember which way he came from. And then, much sooner than he would have thought, night begins to fall, and it starts raining— a sudden, hard, tropical rain, as if someone just threw a switch. He finds shelter against the trunk of a tree that must be at least eight or ten feet thick. Its roots extend into the soft mulch of the ground in long ridges that are higher than his head. The light fades so imperceptibly that he cannot distinguish the exact moment when it becomes absolutely dark.

———

At five in the morning the house is cold, and sunrise is still a couple of hours away. Two more days have gone by, and the state department has had nothing new to say. Helen hasn't slept much, thinking about what she must take. She put Shane to bed in comfortable clothes he could wear on the airplane, and she is letting him sleep until the last minute. She takes a blanket to the car when she goes out to start it up. The wind is blowing, and a fine snow shifts and dances in the porch light.

Miriam is supposed to arrive by six. Helen and Shane have to leave at twenty after at the latest, though she's ready to go at a quarter of. She stands for a moment in the living room. It does not feel like a place where she belongs, and she feels guilty for the feeling of relief to be leaving already, shedding this responsibility, if only temporarily. When Helen peeks in to check on her mother, she is sleeping. She walks quietly into the room and stands by the bed. Suddenly she feels that she is doing absolutely the wrong thing. Not what's right for her mother. Not for Shane. And not for herself. It seems pointless. She has the panicked thought that maybe she should just cancel the whole plan.

Then she hears Miriam set her super-size Diet Coke on the kitchen counter with an icy *slush*. If she is going to cancel, go to the car and put Shane's blankets and bunny back in his bed, she will have to tell Miriam first. She'll have to apologize for getting her out of bed so early on a Sunday morning, and then explain why she has decided to do what all the sensible folks already know she should be doing. Stay put. Wait by the phone. It's easy to imagine Miriam's smirk when Helen tells her. Helen has always been a misfit here. As parochial as her family has always seemed from a distance, when she is here among them she feels at a tremendous disadvantage. All her supposed city savvy is discounted as pure foolishness. She cannot avoid their judgment that there is something frivolously wrong with her. She can see it in Miriam's face when she looks back from the refrigerator. There is no way to do it. Escape is all she can think of; better to be committed to precisely the inexplicable, irresponsible thing they expect of her than to awkwardly capitulate. Thinking of it this way refuels her resolve. She has taken care of Shane virtually by herself, and now her mother. She has the strength of will to do this.

"Thank you, Miriam. I don't know what I would do—"

"Oh, don't worry about it."

Miriam smiles, and Helen gives her a hug, which surprises both of them. She goes into her mother's room and kisses her softly on the cheek. Her mother stirs but does not wake. She feels as though the kiss has entered her mother's dreams as a brief respite from her pain. Then her mother opens her eyes and reaches for her hand.

"Be careful."

"I won't be gone long." She squeezes her mother's hand.

Helen gets Shane out to the car and wraps him warmly in a blanket. He sits up and yawns as they back down the driveway.

"Mom?"

"Yes?"

"Does Dad know we're coming?"

"I don't think so."

"Then it will be a surprise." Shane smiles and lies back in his seat.

ZAMBA—LA FORÊT—FOREST

THE SPIDER HAS SOMETHING in its grasp—a pale sac, something that will be removed, eggs perhaps—which it manipulates with its eight legs, exuding onto it some slick and sticky goo. It is just light enough for Lewis to see the white and blue speckled arachnid, which is the size of a mouse and so close to his face that he can barely bring it into focus. He is possessed with the idea that he must have been hearing it at its sticky labor for hours now. His skin crawls, clammy with the revelation. He nearly gags. The spider's front legs extend and pull back mechanically like the work of a coroner, his blunt scalpels and bone saws dissecting a cadaver, which would be the same pale blue color, the bared mechanics of life, viscid and gummy.

The cold roots of the tree hurt Lewis's back as he looks up at the canopy for a faint glimpse of the sky that has abandoned him to this green-choked abyss, but all he can see are fragments of unnaturally bright whiteness. Once he has scooted away from the spider, he feels safer. All night the rain came and went and the din of insects ebbed and flooded over him. In the darkness he could see nothing and everything. His imagination was like a light on black parchment, composing his fears in the language of generations of white men who have been haunted by Africa. For hours something screamed, somewhere close by, right over his head in the canopy. He would listen intently, trying to fix its position, and then it would stop, leaving only the sound of insects and rain filtering though the leaves and the doubt that he had really even heard it. Then suddenly, like a Harpy ready to spring onto his back, the screaming would start again. It was impossible to imagine the source as any kind of real animal. But if it were, because it must be, he thought that the screaming would drive even that simple beast insane.

He heard poison in the spaces of quiet, could almost imagine the beating of drums, the chanting of cannibals Stanley claimed to hear daily on the brown Congo as it drew him to the cataracts. He felt a leopard brushing his back, like a cat, purring, then slowly biting into his neck. At first, like a dream, it was even vaguely erotic: the rough, wet tongue and the hot breath and even the pressure of the teeth before they broke into his skin. Yet when he put his hands to his neck, it was wet but only from rain, and the night was made of liquid sounds, water from leaves dripping in pools, rain scattering across the broad canopy high above, gurgling among the roots, and that sticky sound which must have been the spider.

Lewis looks into the indecipherable bush. The plane should lie in the direction he is facing. He can't help thinking about his escape in terms of straight lines, but instinctively he knows that that cannot be right. He must have deviated many times, run in circles. No matter what, though, he cannot afford to just sit here. He stands and picks the direction that feels most like a return and begins walking. If he can get close to the runway he might be able to find a road. It's the only reference he has; otherwise it is just an unknown track of empty forest, and he could easily end up walking parallel to a road for days without knowing it. He has to breathe deeply to keep calm.

Something itches on his leg. He looks down, brushing at his ankle, and his hand comes back with blood. He pulls up the muddied cuff of his pants. His socks are tacky with it. He follows the blood up his leg, looking for the wound, but finds instead a fat, wet leech sucking midcalf. He jumps, brushing madly at it, but it clings on. Finally he forces himself to quiet down and slowly, precisely, grabs the slimy thing with his nails and pulls it off. It comes in pieces, and it only makes him bleed more.

"Goddamn it!"

His voice dies close to him, dampened by the near liquid greenness. Still, he wishes he had not made the noise. The great trees tower over him, turning like strangers suddenly aware of this foreign creature. The birds seem to have quieted, too. He waits, dreading some answer. But nothing comes, except perhaps a swell in the buzzing of insects.

He notices the book that lies by his feet and thinks to leave it, he even takes a couple of steps away, but it looks out of place there—a book. He can't leave it. It's like a mirror, the only civilized object he can see outside himself. He picks it up and starts walking, not knowing whether he is heading in the right or wrong direction, whether he is making his situation worse or better. But it's not an arbitrary choice, either, and not exactly his own. He finds the path that is easiest—the way the forest asks him to go.

After he has gone only a few hundred yards he feels something else climbing on him. He slaps at it, frantically turning in circles, trying to see what it could be. Then he realizes that it's only his wallet in his pants pocket. It has nearly fallen out in the struggle with the thicket. He starts to slip it back, but takes it out instead. He opens it and finds the picture of Helen. He feels a sudden tightness in his throat. He remembers when Helen called him, laughing. She'd just got the photograph and negatives.

"I just had to call to apologize. I'd forgotten all about this picture. I'm sorry you bothered. It doesn't look like me at all."

"No?"

"Oh, God. I hope not!"

There was an awkward silence. Lewis wondered if he should protest that the picture isn't really that bad, but he worried how that would sound.

"You didn't make copies, right?" she joked.

"No." He laughed, relieved to be able to say it. "No. No copies."

"That's a break. I've been plagued with blackmail lately. I can't keep up."

"I have to tell you, I thought about it."

"You did, huh?"

"Yep."

"And you decided not to?"

"I'm not much of a blackmailer. Anyway, I couldn't come up with any demands."

"No one can these days."

He laughed. There was a comfortable pause. Then he spoke without thinking. "Actually, I do have one condition—before I give you the duplicate negative."

"See, I knew it."

"Meet me for coffee sometime."

"Why?"

"Why not?"

Silence.

"Well?"

"And you got this idea to ask me on a date . . . from this photograph?"

"I suppose."

She was quiet again.

"Just a cup of coffee?"

"Okay," she said.

He slips the wallet back into his pocket, takes a deep breath and starts walking again. The trees that tower over his head are magnificent: mahogany four feet thick and silk-cotton trees whose webbed roots spread twelve feet across, spiked trees and stunted cola trees and parasitic vines choking the great rotting hulks of their dead hosts. Now and then, when he can see up far enough through the vines and broad-leafed bush, there is a flash of colored wings, like a message.

Without the sun there is no way to maintain his bearings, but there is a gentle rising slope to the forest. Following it up feels the most like progress, as if he might actually be able to climb out of it or reach some apex where he can get a view. His mind chatters as he walks, like a bird in a cage with nothing else to occupy its attention. Too much longer and he will be talking to himself out loud, just to fill the void of words. In the city there is always something in the form of language to occupy his mind, people and conversation, signs and advertising. It occurs to him that he virtually cannot think without words.

A spiderweb across his path nearly knocks him down. It's as wiry and thick as elephant hair. He backs up a couple of steps. The bush is closing in. The only open path is the way he has come. At first he thinks to go back, then remembers how overgrown the foliage was where he entered the forest. He can't see more than thirty yards into the gloom, but all this undergrowth might mark the edge of a clearing, or a road or village or God knows what. He lunges in.

The resistance is impressive. He claws with his free hand and after a mighty struggle he has succeeded in lodging himself a few yards into its leafy embrace. He kicks with his feet. His hand finds a vine with a twisted flat thorn that is as sharp as razor wire. It slices into his palm. He realizes that he needs two hands if he is going to get anywhere, but he is still reluctant to cast the book aside, so he tucks it into his shirt, and he pushes on, swimming in vegetation. After an hour, he has exhausted himself and the bush has not relented. He can feel the life in it like some malevolent intention, as if these plants might actually eat him, or merely strangle him, just to watch him die. He has to stage a real fight to keep down a growing sensation of drowning.

Breathe. Breathe. Oh, God.

Moving slowly is the only way to make progress. He tries to go back but he is disoriented. It shocks him, like a blow. He has become hopelessly lost in a distance shorter than a city block.

Slowly. Slowly. There is a way out of this.

He wades and tears and pulls and kicks until finally he staggers into a clearing created by one of the great trees. He slumps down among the wet roots and stares blankly at the jungle that nearly defeated him. Absentmindedly he bats at the swarm of flies that harass him. They are all over him, especially along his brow and his neck, and they look more like bees. He stands up and shakes them off, violently, but they immediately come back. He starts the dance again but quickly gives in. They are only after his salt.

He's thirsty. The heat is wringing the moisture out of his

body. High over his head it sounds like it might be raining, but it is not making it down to him, except in slow fat drops, like the one now splashing on his knee, every twenty or thirty seconds. He takes a broad, waxy leaf that lies in the mud near his feet and begins to catch the drops. It seems absurd, but it takes all of his concentration. When he isn't paying attention to the exact spot where the water is falling, he misses a drop, and the wait for the next is interminable. One drop at a time he gets enough for a sip. It isn't cold water, but his tongue tingles with delight.

What he needs is a quart, at least. As the water drops into the leaf, he tries to calculate how much he is getting. It takes at least ten minutes to get a tablespoon. Four tablespoons in a quarter cup, times four to get a cup, times four. If it keeps raining, if he doesn't miss too many drops, he might get a quart in about ten hours. He takes another sip, but then it stops. The dripping must have moved with the shifting leaves of the canopy. He looks for another spot where the water might be falling more steadily, walking around with his palms up, as if in prayer. He finally feels a drop. It's much slower than the first, and it takes a half-hour to get the tablespoon the leaf will hold, and by then his desperate hands are shaking and he nearly spills it.

It's not enough. There is little question that he will die of thirst in this rainforest if he doesn't get out soon. He starts walking again. He makes it a hundred yards—not too bad. There is no end to it yet, but the going has become easier. Then he nearly jumps.

A path! For the first hundred yards he runs. Then he stops. His odds are about even; he is headed either in or out. Now it feels like going downhill will lead out. He turns around and quickly covers the distance back to where he crossed the trail. He stops running but continues on for a long while, walking.

Whenever the trail starts to peter out, he begins to worry. When it picks up he walks faster, assuming and then praying that a clearing will appear.

How far can it be to get out? He couldn't have gone that far last night. He can't really remember now. His sense of time is slipping, choked in the perpetual dim light. If only he could climb one of these trees to get a view. But none of the bigger trees has a branch lower than fifty feet above the ground. The only thing to do is to keep moving. But what if this is the wrong way—away from the airstrip? No planes. He has not heard a single one, but who is going to fly in here now just to be shot at? He nearly shouts at himself to shut up. Then he trips hard on another creeper. He lies on the ground, aching, trying to get his lungs to trust him and breathe again. He looks down at his wingtips, which are muddy and so slippery that they are worse than useless, a bit of fashion conspiring against him.

A centipede a foot long ripples across the ground near his face. Something tells him that it must be poisonous. It pauses as though capable of some conscious thought, as if thinking, What is this animal, trampled and foul, lying on the forest floor? It raises its antennas, and they tremble. Or maybe it's more sinister than that. Perhaps this insect behaves this way because of a wicked spirit that rides in its belly. Now it's looking for some tenebrous root to hide under. It crawls a little closer before vanishing into the shadows.

He lies there feeling the strength abandoning his body. He closes his eyes and the world seems less frightening. He touches his face with a trembling hand, lays fingers to his eyelids so that he can feel the panic there. It amazes him to think that he could sleep.

In the airplane Shane touches his mother's face.

"Why are you frowning?"

"I don't know, honey," she replies softly, aware of his close-ness. "I guess I'm just anxious to get there."

"Flying feels funny."

"Yeah?"

"Like a cloud. Like thunder in a cloud."

"You need to sleep. It's a long flight."

She makes room for him to be comfortable and leans back in her own seat. She looks across the aisle at the sleeping faces of strangers. It's an intimacy that everyone will be happy to leave behind at customs. This shared journey is short, relatively, but the body still has some sense of what is transpiring, the unnat-ural disjunction of space and time. Through the window there is the unrelieved blankness of the Atlantic Ocean.

It would be easy to recreate the world without Lewis, with-out his heavy steps coming in from the cold, already dark evening or at dawn. He has become like an occasionally erotic dream, a sleepy shadow in polished black shoes disappearing down the hallway. But there was a time, years ago, when he would leave work early on days he knew she would be working at home on a newsletter she still edited for WorldAid. He camped out in her office, waiting for her to wrap up. And they lay in bed afterward at odd angles and whispered while the sun drifted across the room and faded, and finally it got too dark to see and they grudgingly untangled their limbs and turned the lights on.

Once, Lewis broke the silence. "We should eat."

"Mmmm."

"We have some frozen dinners. I don't know how they got there."

Lewis raised his leg and pulled his arm from under the pillow so she could roll onto her back. He sat up, looking away from her, squinting into the light.

"You look good naked," Helen said in a voice somewhere between a murmur and a whisper.

He turned and grinned.

"Stand up, please," she said.

"No."

"Yes."

He stood up, making a show of it. Under protest. "I'm hungry."

She ignored him. "I never get to look at you."

"That's for your own protection." He struck a pose, some imitation of David.

"Don't do that."

Lewis put his arms down. She saw first his stomach, and then the slight dimple of muscle at the bend in his arm. She skipped over his penis, which was quiet now and as usual too ridiculous to contemplate. But his thighs looked strong. And his neck. Still, there was something there that eluded this visual cross-examination, some ineffable quality, like the taste of their intimacy still lingering in her mouth that made all his imperfections absolutely desirable.

"What are you doing?" he asked.

"I'm just checking my order. You know. Is this what I asked for, or just what I got?"

"Maybe it's like those frozen dinners. Who knows how they got there?"

"You're like a frozen dinner?" She laughed.

"Yeah, pretty much."

She watched him walk to the bathroom. As he leaned over

the sink to wash his face, all she could see was his butt, just in view through the door frame.

"Hey, nice ass!"

He couldn't hear her over the running water, but he leaned forward anyway, sticking it out more clearly in view as if he had heard. She fell back on the bed, allowing her arms to fall away from her like a child, and she laughed.

Helen opens her eyes, and Shane stirs where he has laid his head on her lap. She quiets him with a hand and breathes in, trying to calm her own electrical storm of sleeplessness. The steady roar of the engines has been keeping her awake. She can't shake the awareness of those turbines or subdue it into something routine and acceptable, instead of what it is, an explosion of jet fuel just barely under control. And she cannot separate this anxiety from her own, which chatters in her mind, cataloguing the myriad possible outcomes for this journey. *As long as he's okay,* she thinks.

SHE'S RELIEVED WHEN THE flight attendants get busy, preparing to wake the cabin for landing with orange juice and instant coffee. She opens the shade on the window, just a crack. At the horizon there is the faintest hint of sunrise paling the sky, and the plane is descending. The gentle pop of her ears clearing accompanies the smooth arrival in Kinshasa. They walk down a long, bare hall; the paint is old, and the fluorescent light hurts. The hall ends in a line. Three men in uniform are checking passports. One of them waves her over. It's not surprising, really, that she has been singled out. There is not another white woman traveling alone with a child. She leads Shane with a hand on his shoulder. They must look American, because they're directed to an officer who speaks English.

"Where are you staying?"

Helen digs in her purse to find the answer. The Hotel Intercontinental.

"How is it?" she asks in as cheery a voice as she can manage this early in her morning.

The officer doesn't answer; he pretends to be studying her passport. She looks over at the station next to them, where a slightly disheveled European man is watching one of the officers dismantle his baggage and rummage through its intimate details. He seems bored, as if waiting for the right moment to offer a bribe so he can move on.

Helen looks back at the officer, who has her passports and a hand on her bag. He's looking at Shane, and he seems disturbed. Shane is holding onto her sleeve with his head tilted to one side as he concentrates on what he hears in the busy, echoing hall. In this attitude, his expression conveys the suggestion of divination. His blindness seems to have thrown the officer off balance.

"What's your business here?" the man challenges, trying to regain his nerve. Helen follows his eyes to Shane and instinctively she pulls her son closer, sheltering him with her arm. She should have anticipated this question, planned her answer.

"We're here to meet my husband."

"What's *his* business?" The man looks at her intently.

"Coca-Cola."

"What?"

"Pop, soft drinks, you know—Coke."

The officer pauses.

"Why must he come to Kinshasa, Congo?"

Helen shrugs. He's obviously playing dumb. "I guess people here must drink Coke, too. He's here to make arrangements to sell it."

"He can make money this way?"

Helen doesn't quite know how to answer.

He continues with his line of reasoning. "I think there must be more money in diamonds in the Congo. He must do something with diamonds."

The officer seems to be digging.

"No, just pop."

He frowns and makes them wait before he finally stamps the passports and hands them back to her as though they were gifts.

"You will take him to the zoo?" He nods to Shane.

"Is there a zoo?"

"Gorillas, Madame. Everyone must see the gorillas."

Not two steps past the barrier a man in a worn black suit approaches them. He reaches out his hand.

"You are English?"

"American."

"I am Mr. Dury," he says in a heavy accent that sounds not quite French. He acts official, but he probably isn't. "I must help you with your travel arrangements."

"That's okay, we're fine."

He ignores her and turns as if he expects to be followed. It seems to be the direction she has to go anyway. He pushes open the double doors that lead out of the customs area, and a wave of noise and a rush of people nearly overwhelm her. Now she is glad to be following Mr. Dury, who is carrying a stick and threatens the first several men who rush to help them with their bags, before choosing two. They have to push their way through the crowd of jostling bodies, warm and fragrant in the heat. She takes a deep breath and squeezes Shane's hand. This is just the airport, she reminds herself. It was like this in Burma. It'll be easier once they get to town.

He gets her a taxi, a small, once white car that has seen

better days, though it's hard to imagine it shiny and new. Helen realizes that she has only U.S. dollars, no local money.

She holds up a five, "Okay?"

Mr. Dury takes it as if he should be disappointed. She gives him another five.

"*Restez ici,*" he says, and he heads off into the crowd. The two men wait with her by the taxi.

Around her people shout, cars smoke and airplanes rumble, some distant ragged palms move lazily in the sticky wind. Her skirt clings to her legs in the heat. She looks down at Shane. What must it all sound like to him! But when she looks around she realizes that seeing only adds to the chaos of sounds and smells. He seems delighted.

Eventually Mr. Dury returns. He hands her a wad of dirty Congolese francs. She gives him half of the pile, then most of the rest and then tries to indicate that he is to share it. The men who have waited with her seem perturbed. They don't trust him. They want their money directly. But Mr. Dury enforces the arrangement.

"*Salut.*" He helps her into the cab. "Have a nice day," he adds stiffly, and smiles. He shouts at the cab driver, "*Allez!*"

They drive through a smoky, sprawling industrial area, passing billboards with smiling faces, their slogans in French. Perhaps because they're in another language the advertisements seems particularly blatant, not at all subtle. When they come to a stoplight boys and men walk among the cars, holding up a bizarre collection of goods for sale—things people might need, like batteries and toilet paper, and oddities like an ab exerciser with the picture of a fit blond woman on the purple and blue box. They have gum and plastic trinkets from Asia and sandwich bags knotted to hold water. Helen tries not to meet their eyes, to express any interest; still, they hold their wares up as if she might spontaneously be converted.

"What does it look like, Mom. What do you see?"

"A city, honey, very crowded. It looks like it sounds, like a room with too many people." She caresses the back of his neck, a little surprised at the confidence she feels there. He seems so brave.

"It's noisy."

The screaming is preceded by loud crashes, like trees falling or branches ripping from their trunks. Whatever is making the sound rushes directly at him, almost faster than Lewis can react. He scrambles for the nearest cover, to a tree that succumbed to some kind of parasitic vine. He climbs into the soft, rotten hull, praying that there are no snakes or poisonous insects or God knows what else already hiding there.

The screams turn his blood cold. He breathes slowly. It almost sounds human. A chimpanzee suddenly bursts into view, silent, out of breath, looking for a place to hide. The source of the noise is still a little way off but moving in his direction. The animal looks hurt. It crouches close to the ground. Lewis can see blood soaking the fur of its arm.

Then another chimpanzee crashes through the bush. It has a branch over its head and charges the wounded ape, which starts to back away but is surrounded as four more come from all sides. It cowers, and the five attack at once, furiously beating it with sticks and jumping on it. Now it, too, is screaming. Its voice is distinguishable from the others' by its anguished pleading, which has no effect on the murderers.

Lewis can feel bile catching in his throat as he witnesses the violence. Fear. Fear for himself. And terror for the victim. Two of the apes grab the nearly limp body and drag it a few yards closer to Lewis's hiding place. Now that it can no longer fight back, they begin biting and kicking.

After a while they leave the ruined ape and settle a few yards away. One of the younger chimpanzees grooms a silvery companion. They seem suddenly calm. Lewis's throat is raw from taking rapid, shallow breaths. He feels his whole being convulse in an effort not to jump when the biggest ape screams again and leaps on the body. Then they all join the attack again, hitting the dead chimp about the head, dragging it in circles. When they finally run off leaving the dead ape, its arms are flung over its head and it is laid out like a man stretching in his bed in the morning.

Lewis stares at the body. He never thought of animals as committing murder. The worst kind of violent killing for food, sure—but innocent even it if is savage; not wanton or premeditated killing like this. He struggles to get his fear to subside to a manageable level. He leaves his hiding place and crawls as close as he dares to the dead chimp. He reaches to touch the outstretched hand, which lies open, palm up in the detritus of the forest floor. The dark skin is soft, and still warm. He jerks his hand back and scrambles away a few feet, breathing hard. When the rain comes again, he finally leaves. His foot hurts from sitting on it for so long, and he has to limp to walk. It burns and tingles as the blood finds its way back.

He starts running though it makes no sense. He's going back the way he came. His heart pounds, and his breathing drowns out all thought except to look over his shoulder to see if he is being pursued. Every time he begins to slow because his exhausted legs are pulling him down, a rush of adrenaline sends him careening onward. When he gets to the place where he first found the path, it's dark again. In a delirium of thirst, he presses his back to the cold trunk of a tree and braces himself. The unimaginable is about to happen—a second night.

Mposa—La Soif—Thirst

IT BEGINS TO RAIN HARD. The soaking din silences the birds and insects. He holds his eyes unnaturally wide open to gather as much light as possible, and in the blackness, he has to keep reminding himself to relax them, let it be, give up on trying to see. At least the rain brings some water. He licks it off the leaves and where it comes in rivulets down the trunk of the tree, and after a while the tyranny of his thirst eases. The body is willing to accept this as a victory.

His defeats are more significant. His clothes are in tatters and his skin is covered with insect bites and cuts from the brush. Another day has passed, and he is only more lost. He runs his hands down his face to force it into calm, and exhales a trembling imitation of composure.

A day. A day is not much—not in this forest that once stretched for millions of years and thousands of uncontested miles. At the girth of the world, the African night passes exactly as long as day. Lewis closes his eyes. This blindness is good. He can see whatever he chooses.

Helen. He remembers her sitting across the bare, ring-stained table of the coffee shop. She was right, she didn't look like the photograph at all; but her eyes were full of an unexpectedly familiar light. She seemed to be teetering on the edge of a smile through the whole date, as though there were some joke ringing in the back of her mind. His eyes followed her hands, which were nervous, in the air, on the table, holding her cup of coffee, then setting it down. He remembers getting completely lost in her arms and neck and in the spell of her.

Once, after rocking Shane back to sleep in the middle of the night, after endless laps around the dining room table, through the kitchen and finally back to Shane's crib, he collapsed on the couch without turning on a light. He sat there holding his hands together to keep them quiet, unable to escape the tyranny of a wakeful kind of dreaming, an awareness of some uncertain truth that haunted him but would not rationally articulate itself. Helen got up and came into the kitchen, unaware that he was there, and leaned on the counter. Her unclothed body looked relaxed, still adrift in a breeze of sleep. Even in that vague light he could see the woman he'd had coffee with years ago. And he felt as if he had not seen her that way in a long time. He did not speak. He dared not breathe, afraid to disturb the moment, and leaned back into the shadows.

She ran the water in the sink, letting it pour over her hand, waiting for it to get cold before she filled a glass. He thought of how the day would go. The early-morning rush—her single-minded focus on Shane, who was turning their lives upside down just because he was learning to walk. It was so difficult for him in his blindness that he would end up screaming. He would hit Helen and then struggle to get out of her arms when she tried to comfort him. This was why he wasn't sleeping nights. Lewis would have to leave without much more than a wave from Helen, and Shane would only yell louder.

The buzzing of a mosquito, its soft whine, brings him back for a moment nearer the edge of consciousness. Lewis shoos it away, but another lands softly on his neck, drawing blood before the sting alerts him. It pays for the transgression with its life. Then another bites, and it is merely irritating until the significance dawns on him—malaria—and for a while he is more alert. Hunger grinds in his stomach. He stands up, and with his hands in front of him to avoid walking into unseen branches, he walks out a few paces. He unzips his pants and lets his penis out. The urine splashes back onto his shoes. It has a strong, chemical smell that is out of place. He backs against the tree again and sleeps until morning, until, on some impossible angle, the piercing light of a new sun finds his haggard face. It shines incarnadine on the warm inside of his eyelids. When after a moment the sun leaves his face, he reaches up and catches in his palm another shard of light where it splashes across the skinlike bark of the tree.

Helen is wakened by the thunderous noise of cab horns and diesel trucks slamming into potholes. Shane is already awake, sitting on her bed, fitting the brightly colored pieces of a puzzle together. The hotel room is something of a refuge. The switches are European. The lights work. And though it is plain and smells of insecticide and mildewed carpet, the room is clean. Shane hears her stir and leans over for a hug.

The TV has a few channels, though almost everything is in French. She finally finds CNN, but there is still nothing about the Air France flight.

Shane listens intently. "Are they going to say something about Dad's airplane?"

"I don't know, Shane, but that's why we're here. In case they forget."

"What are we doing today?"

"We're going to the American embassy. Are you hungry?"

Shane nods.

On the main floor of the hotel there is a mall and a restaurant. They eat chocolate crepes, drink fresh orange juice, and Helen relaxes into the idea of Africa. A soothing breeze eddies around them in the open courtyard, and nearby a tall man cleans leaves from the pool with a luxurious patience, sweeping his net through the water like a meditation. Shane is finishing his third crepe, this one with strawberries, when a Congolese man politely approaches them with the offer of a car. He speaks a fair amount of English, specializing particularly, he claims, in guiding Americans. He tells Helen he needs a thousand Congolese francs in advance to get gas.

"Madame, you must ask the doorman. You may trust Kalala." He points to the jacketed man by the front door as if he expects her to get up and check his references. She hands him the bills, worth less than ten dollars.

"When should we meet you?"

"Whenever Madame and son are ready."

After he leaves to get gas, Helen wipes the strawberry from Shane's face and they take a short walk through the hotel mall. They stop at a store that sells masks. One whole wall is covered with them, coming from all over Central and West Africa — some are animals, some human faces, contorted and disquieting. Shane finds one that is shaped like the great, round face of a spaceman. His fingers delicately trace the weathered paint and rough, carved surfaces, running over the circular mouth, strange, short spikes of yellow hair, and large, curved ears. His hands stop on the eyes, two very small holes.

"Are these the eyes, Mom?"

"Yes, I think so."

"Can he see?"

Helen looks at the face of the mask. "I think it would be hard through those tiny holes."

Shane feels them from the back side. Then he holds it up in front of him. He laughs, and the giggle from behind the mask is unnerving. The salesperson looks up from her desk. She looks a little frightened by the small white boy in the mask.

Helen lifts it away. "Let's go find our car, Shane."

BECAUSE OF SOME ROAD work, getting out of the hotel area involves a detour through the gas station, creating a traffic jam every time someone stops at a pump. They must wait for another driver to get his tank filled and then find someone to pay before they can get through and back into the general snarl of the streets. Kalala offers air-conditioning, but it is entirely inadequate against the heat and they end up with their windows down despite the noise.

They drive for several blocks through the downtown. The sixties architecture looks as though it might once have shined, but the buildings have not aged well, and now the modern dream has faded. The other colonial buildings are falling apart, too, ghosts of the departed Europeans who knew it would be like this after they left. Their sneer hangs in the fallen-down shutters and the vacant monuments to independence. Kalala eases the car amid a jam of wooden carts bearing heaps of colored plastic dishes and tin pots. There is little to remind Helen that this country is at war, that vast areas have been cut off. The busy city maintains an almost convincing air of normality. Then

a military truck rattles by, loaded with young men toting automatic weapons. Kalala pulls to the side to let them pass. Something about them seems out of place to Helen. Perhaps it is the
men themselves, who look cast from a single mold, taller than
the people crowding the street, and different.

"Those are government soldiers?" Helen asks.

Kalala laughs. *"Oui Madame,* today they are." She catches a
glimpse of his ironic grin in the rearview mirror. "It is almost
a year since they came to Kinshasa. They walked all the way
from Uganda. They still look tired, don't you think?"

"They're not Congolese?"

"Oh, yes, Madame, they're from the east, from Katanga.
Like Kabila. But you must already know, an assassin got him
just a few months ago."

"His son is president now, right?"

Kalala nods, but he doesn't say anything.

"Is that good?"

"Perhaps, Madame. At least the Rwandans and Ugandans do
not hate him so much."

Kalala turns in to the U.S. Embassy. Its plain walls extend to
the open gutters of the street. Inside the gate is a small courtyard, and a pole with an American flag.

Helen and Shane enter the unimposing lobby of the consular
section, which is mostly empty except for some green chairs
and a single desk occupied by a Congolese woman with elabo-
rately braided hair. Helen approaches with her passport in
hand. Each footstep echoes in the carpetless room.

She hands the woman her passport without being asked for
it and refers to a scrap of paper for the name of the consul she
hopes to see.

"Please wait," the woman says, coolly but politely.

Helen sits next to Shane, running her hands through his hair.

The woman leaves and returns without saying anything, and after a while Helen approaches her to ask how long the wait will be.

"Mr. Corbeil is in a meeting."

"How long?"

"I don't know."

She returns to her seat, thinking that bureaucracy could be considered one of the great exports of Western culture after T-shirts and Coca-cola.

An hour passes in fly-buzzing silence before the consul appears from a back room. He gives her a big Texas wave, and taking Shane's hand, she follows him down a narrow corridor to a small office. On his desk are pictures of his wife and two girls.

"Ms. Burke."

"Helen."

"Helen." He clears his throat. "You should have stayed home."

She doesn't respond.

"Perhaps you felt you would be closer to things here." His smile looks fake now. "But you'd have a much easier time getting information in the U.S."

There is a long silence punctuated by Shane slipping off his seat and then wiggling to get back up. Helen lifts him into her lap.

"I hate to disappoint you. I can give you my direct number, so you don't have to wait next time. You can also call me at home, though the phones are not always reliable. I'll call you as soon as I know anything. We simply are not a party to the negotiations."

"Negotiations?"

"Well, negotiations is not the right word. Uh . . . discussions, you know, the details of getting these people out. They're in a very remote area."

Helen studies him for a moment. What a bore it is to take for granted his chauvinism.

"Mr. Corbeil, I am already aware that this *is* a hostage situation. Can we skip the pretense? What I don't know is where they are. That you must know."

The consul's face falls flat. He seems to feel that she has broken some code that says he is to be excessively nice and polite and she is to leave the thinking to the professionals. She is being rude.

"I have no information whatsoever that I am at liberty to share with you."

"The wife of one of the hostages."

"There are no hostages. It's much more complicated than that."

"But there *are* negotiations, sir."

He seems to be wavering between anger and sympathy, so Helen softens her approach. "I only want to know where my husband is, and if he is in danger. You can understand that."

He looks at her long and hard; then he gets a scrap of paper and writes something on it. He hands it to her. "That's the closest town in the official government-controlled area. This is a very complex situation. It's not just rebels on one side and a corrupt official government on the other. This war has divided the country into several zones controlled by different ad hoc militias and rebel groups supported by foreign militaries. Some areas are relatively safe, others are not."

"Thank you."

"No, please. Don't thank me. Just don't make my life miserable by turning this into a media circus back home. Give us a chance."

KALALA IS WAITING, leaning against the door of his car, relaxed and nearly asleep. He jumps up when he sees them coming and opens the door. Helen sits back in the warm seat.

"*Où allez-vous*," he asks, forgetting his English for a moment, "to the hotel?"

"No." She looks out at the glare. "Is there a cool place . . . a market?"

"The market is not cool, Madame."

"But there is a market?"

"Of course."

"Then to the market."

The sun makes Lewis feel better. Even if only a little light filters through trees, he can look up and see a shrill blue sky singing in fragmented patches in the canopy. Vapors steam off the floor of the forest, slipping like ghosts or spirits into the boughs and leaves. There is a stunning perfection to this climax vegetation, an overwhelming beauty to the arches of lush green beyond anything he could have imagined from tales of this Eden. Thirst pounds in his head again. It's a debilitating requirement, and insistent. He feels that he should be smarter than this. He should be able to find water in a place that gets daily rainfall. The evidence is everywhere in the chaos of plant life, but when he digs down into the soil, where he can pry through the dense mat of roots, there is only sand: tropical forest disguising a desert. Every bit of water and nutrients is used by some other living thing the moment it becomes available.

He walks for two hours, though the trail eventually comes to nothing. The sun gives him the sense of maintaining a direction, though it is too fractured and indistinct to really count on.

Then clouds obscure the sun and the light dims. He begins trying to maintain points by visually marking trees; but the undergrowth is often impenetrable, and he must constantly detour.

Instinctively he stops. A chill spreads down his back. He has found a small clearing; it is trampled and torn up. There do not appear to be any animals in the immediate area, but he waits for a long while, hiding at the edge, just in case the apes return. His only guesses for what creatures may have been here come from books he has read to Shane, who could not see the pictures that made them look almost like pets but must have imagined them as Lewis does now—wild, unstable images that he cannot tame. Everything is still except the sweat bees that fly into his eyes and crawl down the neck of his filthy shirt. A breeze would be good, but he doubts that any wind could penetrate this fortress of vegetation. Eventually he leaves his hiding place and walks out among the trampled leaves.

The ground is littered with discarded rinds of some kind of bright red fruit. The limbs of the trees have even been torn off, in the apparent frenzy to get at all of it. He digs around, looking for something that may have been left uneaten. But the apes have done a thorough job, and it takes him a long time to find half a fruit, and even that is mostly rotten. He sits down with it, anyway, and carefully eats what remains. The fruit is pithy, but the sweetness of it fills his head and makes him almost dizzy; moisture tingles on his parched tongue. He finishes it and begins searching desperately for more, and after a while he has managed to eat four or five fruits, mostly seeds and rind.

He sits again, feeling the exhilaration from the food bring a glow of optimism. After a few minutes of rest he will rise up and stomp his way out of this mess. Instead he ends up falling asleep, and when he wakes his stomach is in a knot. He crawls a short distance, and then the coarse, barely chewed fruit and bitter seeds pass back through his mouth and teeth onto the crushed leaves. Whatever moisture he had accumulated goes with it. He sits back, holding his face with his hands, dizzy and weak. He lifts his wretched body, swears out loud at it, and threatens it not to betray him again. Then he walks on.

It doesn't take Helen long to get lost in the market, the press of bodies, the endless rows of hawkers selling fruits and bitter-skinned tomatoes. There are thousands of people here, but it seems like a family reunion. Groups of women dressed in bright shades of orange, yellow and green sit with their wares, sur-rounded by their children, talking and laughing, telling stories. Their hands dance in the air like smiles. The riot of smells over-whelms the noise—sweat, mud, onions, chicken, goat excre-ment, urine, sour coconut milk, rotting pineapples, greasy smoke, overripe meat, and the sweet, sour smell of garbage. Helen buys Shane a bunch of small red bananas, something that doesn't have to be washed, and even then she douses Shane's hands with a waterless disinfectant soap.

He is getting a lot of attention, a blond, blind child in the market. Every time she rounds a corner the women shout with delight and take Shane's hand and hold it, half singing to him in Lingala. The children walk with him to the end of the next row before running back, laughing. It's not that he is just a nov-elty. They seem to see him as some kind of charm, as if the power of this child might pass to them through his touch.

The men selling cloth are more aggressive, and they ignore Shane. They expect Helen to buy like a tourist and provide them with that one sale that could make a month or a year. She finds herself walking faster, weary of her French-accented "No, no." When they pass on to a new part of the market, she realizes how lost they have become. She keeps a firm grip on Shane's hand now, and avoiding the salesmen, she detours in the direction she believes they came from. It leads to a dead end. She turns back to try again, but the eddies of the market only take her farther in the wrong direction. Finally she leaves the press of the stalls altogether, hoping to circumnavigate the market to get back. The road they find themselves on borders an open dump of burned trash and the slum that engulfs the old city. A meager-looking cow grazes along its edge among the knots of plastic bags and Styrofoam. The smell is strong, and the smoke of burning garbage dims the sun. On top of the hill of trash, a young girl washes herself in a plastic bucket, her thin, dark, naked form drenched with white suds.

When Helen turns back to the dirt track, she nearly trips over a man sitting among some plastic bags. Then when she does see him, she gasps involuntarily and steps back. With his good hand the man holds up a plastic cup. This is the first beggar she has seen here. It hadn't occurred to her how unusual that is, given the intense poverty of this city. He must have no relatives, none of the family connections that provide security among the poor. He is missing an arm; a savage pink scar marks the point where it was taken. The stump moves as if the arm were still there. The man tries a toothless smile. Helen gives him some wadded bills, half doubting that that is what he is actually reaching for. She tightens her grip on Shane's hand and hurries him away, relieved that he cannot see.

Helen stops where the road climbs a gentle hill, trying to get her bearings. She desperately fights back a growing sense of panic. This feels dangerous. It's just the kind of stupid thing that everyone who would have had her stay home expects.

Then a car rolls quietly to a stop behind her, but it's not Kalala. She is startled and ready to run when the driver rolls his window down.

"*Êtes-vous perdue?*"

This much French she can guess at. She *is* lost. "*Oui.*"

His response is too fast and too complicated, and she realizes that she must appear confused.

"*Vous ne parlez pas français?*"

"*Un petit peu.* Only very little."

"English? Mine is not perfect. Do you need a ride?"

She looks into the face of the man addressing her. He could be older than he looks, maybe forty. He is wearing a white shirt, which makes the skin of his face seem very dark and his eyes bright. There is something in his broad smile and piercing eyes that seems optimistic. At home she would never consider such an offer from a stranger, but he seems genuine, and besides that, she has no real choice. They climb into the back, and it is not until she has scooted Shane across the seat and buckled him in that it occurs to her how unusual it is to find a car without passengers. He turns and gives his name, Malik. He owns, he says, one of the finer grocery stores in town.

They look for Kalala for a half an hour, but he seems to be gone. Finally, Malik offers to drive them to the hotel. He asks only a few questions, but there is something so charming in his smile that along the way she finds herself telling him her story. He lets her finish before offering an opinion.

"I don't trust this new government. Not these French. I'm sorry, not the Americans, either." Then he worries that he may have alarmed her. "The whole thing will probably just blow up."

Helen looks up, a little shocked.

"I'm sorry, my English. What do you say?"

"Blow over?"

They pull up at the hotel, and Malik jumps out quickly to get the door, as though he were now her chauffeur. He helps Shane out and notices his blindness for the first time.

"He is blind since birth?"

"Yes," Shane answers cheerfully, as if that were the good news.

Malik smiles at him and lays a hand on his shoulder. He kneels next to him so he can look up at Helen from Shane's perspective.

"Then he has never seen how beautiful his mother is."

Helen smiles; the comment feels good, something personal that for a moment makes her feel less isolated.

"Madame, if you need help, I am easy to find."

He writes a number on a piece of paper, and Helen slips it into her purse. As Malik drives away they return to the shelter of the grand hotel lobby, the air-conditioning and the almost familiar world.

———

The forest begins a gradual slope down and then flattens into a shallow swamp. Lewis walks into it up to midcalf. The water is tepid, choked with algae and tangles of green lily pads with brilliant pink flowers. He takes another step; the gummy silt pulls at his shoe, and a black cloud boils up into the water, smelling of sulfur and rot. He has to fish out one of his shoes and nearly falls when he tries to get it back onto his foot.

His body cries out for a drink, and he kneels, finds some clearer water not fouled by his steps, and he takes a calculated risk. He knows that if he does not drink this water, he will not make it out. He also knows that if he does drink it, he will almost certainly get sick, but perhaps not right away. He might make it out first. And then antibiotics might save his life. If not, then it comes to the same thing. He can only drink.

He drinks a lot. The water tastes of roots and the faint putrid taste of the silt but also sweet and scented with flowers. He can feel it flowing into his blood through his tongue and down his throat before settling in his stomach.

He is so excited about finding water that he does not immediately consider that he is once again faced with turning back or at the very least taking a wide detour. This swamp may go on for miles, and it seems unlikely that there would be a road here. He backs out of the water and accepts a course that is basically a return, back up the hill, edging around the swamp.

Soon the forest seems to change, dominated now by towering trees, which make the undergrowth less dense, and it is easier for him to walk. It may also mean that he is only going in deeper into regions of the forest where few people ever go, but he is so exhilarated by the feeling of progress that he does not consider what the change in vegetation might signify.

It is late in the day by the time he stops. Before him a huge chunk of granite, a kakba, rises out of the forest like a temple. His feet trample the plain leaves of wild yams that grow there, that could feed him if he knew what they were. He climbs up, thrilled to see above the trees, sure that he will have only a little way to go, that he will at last have a sense of where he is.

When he gets to the top, the sun is already seeping down into the haze. He sits, stunned by what he does see—a world of verdant forest that stretches to the far curve of the horizon. He lays his hands together and watches the evening gather on him again like a choking gas.

TEMBE—LE DOUTE—DOUBT

THE STARS—MILLIONS MORE than he ever knew were there—
are scattered across the sky in clouds that tease the limits of his
vision. It's hard to sleep on this rock. He drifts in and out of
consciousness, from dreams to half-delirious thoughts that
might not be dreams but are more like memories. And in this
nether state he feels Helen and Shane as an ache that pervades
both the dreams and the dervishes of his mind's ramblings.

He remembers watching Shane running in tight circles in the
living room, making sound effects like an airplane flying straf-
ing runs at him. He was just home from work and still in a suit.
He lay on the floor, ducking Shane's passes, and it took some effort to force the stress of the day from his face. At least Shane
could not see his fearful mask as he made a slightly wide turn,
his toes digging into the carpet for traction.

Lewis rolled over onto his back and closed his eyes, and the
inevitable happened—Shane fell. Lewis jumped up to lift him

off the floor and gently rocked him, which only encouraged Shane to cry harder. He buried his face in his father's neck and sobbed. His reaction seemed out of proportion to the fall. Lewis held him away so he could see his face to make sure there was nothing seriously wrong.

Helen came into the room. "What happened?"

"He fell."

"We still have to watch him so closely." She patted Shane's back, unaware of Lewis looking at her, wondering if there was another way to take that comment.

"Shhh," Lewis whispered to Shane, and lay him against his shoulder again. "I thought maybe he'd really hurt himself."

"He's just tired. Let me take him upstairs," Helen said, and took Shane from Lewis.

While he undressed, Lewis could hear Helen changing Shane, her warm voice and his giggles and cooing. He got into the shower and let the water pour over him. The sound of it drowned out the laughter coming from the other room. With his eyes closed what he could see was reduced to something that seemed infinitely small or infinitely large and empty, as if there could be a complete world between his cornea and eyelids. He shut off the water and opened his eyes wide. He was tired. Each morning when he had to leave, Shane would be just up, in bed with Helen. She'd slip in and out of sleep while Shane climbed on her as though she was a jungle gym. Lewis would get a sleepy kiss and leave for the day. By the time he was home after his commute, Shane was almost ready for bed.

He leaned over Shane's bed to say good night. He waved a hand over his face, and Shane grabbed at him as if it were a game; he could feel the movement of air.

"You shouldn't do that, honey."

"What?"

Helen leaned past him and kissed Shane on the forehead.

"Let him sleep."

Lewis stood a moment longer by the bed and then followed Helen out of the room.

"Good night, Shane."

Helen shut the door except for a crack and then turned to Lewis. She squeezed his hand and went downstairs ahead of him. He found her in the pantry, on the floor, sorting through old boxes of cake flour and dusty, half-used bags of Indian spices.

"Can we take a break?"

"This is the only time I have to do this. His naps are too short."

Lewis leaned against the door. He watched her filling a garbage bag with uneaten food.

"Such a waste," she says.

"What."

"This food we buy and don't eat. It would go a long way somewhere else in the world."

"I guess it's just an issue of distribution."

"It's more than that."

Lewis's shoulder began to hurt from leaning on the doorjamb. He started to leave.

"Don't go. Stay and talk to me."

He turned back.

"I'm not going back to work," she says. "I don't see how. And I'm dropping the volunteer work, too. I can't get it all done."

"What about when he starts school?"

"I don't think I can. I need to be here when he gets home. I need to pick him up. He needs me more than that. It isn't ever going to be normal."

Helen stopped what she was doing; she was looking down at her hands, her hair hiding her face.

"What's wrong?" Lewis asked quietly.

Helen put down a stack of cans and leaned back against the shelves with her legs crossed.

"I don't know."

Lewis felt he should move over to her, but the pantry was too small and cluttered.

"I just . . ." She stopped and sighed. "I'm tired and I'm afraid." When she looked up at him, he could see that she was trying not to cry. She reached up for him to take her hand to help her stand. She stepped over the cans and boxes she had organized on the floor and into his arms. As soon as he had her in his embrace, she let go.

Somewhere in the middle of the night, he rolled away from her onto his back. He didn't really mean to open his eyes. He knew it would wake him and he'd spend the next couple of hours trying to get back. Then the ceiling felt too close to his face, and in his chest he could feel the press of claustrophobia. He got up and pulled on the sweats and T-shirt from beside the bed as quietly as he could. Helen was asleep. He peeked through Shane's door. He also seemed asleep in another land.

Lewis walked out into the yard and sat in the glow of the porch light, watching the moths dive-bomb the screen door. How distant everything felt at this time of night. He could be anywhere but where he was. Even the cold stone of the patio could not ground him. He should have been in bed. He should have been sleeping with his wife. In the morning, he should have been rocking his son, throwing him laughing into the air.

A CRASHING DRAWS him back out of sleep—something around the base of the kakba. At first he thinks of hiding, that the apes have found him, climbing the rock with hairy black arms and stunted thumbs. They beat on him with their fists, bite him, and drag him to the edge of the rock and hurl him off. His body catches in the crook of a tree and rots there, to be eaten by civet cats or pecked at by bareheaded vultures until there is only his yellowed skeleton. And then even the hard bone is eaten by molds and lichens and tiny ants.

But whatever he hears sounds bigger than that. He climbs down carefully to try to see what it is. His hands tremble on the ancient rock. He stops on a shallow ledge, where he can make out a shape in the dark, a shadow the size of a small truck. He is too afraid to yell. The branches of a small tree near him shake violently, and then a whole tree goes down. He scrambles back up, tearing the soft pads of his fingers on the rough stone. For hours he can hear rocks being overturned and then trees shaking. His mind will not reason. Every explanation for what might be out there comes to him from the Middle Ages—winged ants the size of wolves, black, flesh-eating birds that reek of death, snakes with two heads spitting balls of blue fire.

Lewis does not think of elephants. Not until they are gone and it is quiet again. When light comes, the mists settle below the rock and he is on an island, and above him there is no sky, no line to distinguish a beginning or an end. It paralyzes him, watching the unchangeable jungle. If it is growing, it is also dying—a constant, immutable chaos.

The pushcarts, bikes and people mixed in with the jam of cars have traffic stopped dead. Kalala still seems upset about yesterday, even though Helen paid him double and apologized. Perhaps it was too much—too much money, too easily spent and therefore arrogant and insulting, or too much apology. He isn't talking or driving through the crowded streets with the same enthusiasm. Minutes pass without progress.

"Can we walk from here, Kalala?"

"No, Madame. You must not walk."

"Is it that far?"

"*Oui, Madame, à cause du gamin.* Too far for the boy."

She sits back and looks at the note that was delivered to the hotel this morning. "Good news! Passengers evacuated. Come to the embassy for details."

"Is there another way, Kalala, around the market?"

"No, Madame. Everyone must go by the market. The roads are made that way. *C'est fait comme ça par le gouvernement.*"

She tries to sit back and force herself to relax. It's hard to be this hot so soon after breakfast. Shane has his arm out the window as if trying to gather breathable air in handfuls. Helen watches the crowd. Women with infants on their back carry heavy loads on their heads; men in somewhat aged, tattered wool suits defy the heat; and younger men with lean, athletic bodies, in Western T-shirts, suck cool water from plastic sandwich bags. One particularly big man proudly wears a tight-fitting shirt that says "Don't mess with me, I'm a Mother."

Helen has to laugh, but there is something disturbing in it that she can't define, some challenge there, as if somehow she should take offense at this twisted imitation of a Western city. She pulls Shane's hand in.

AFTER THE NOISE of traffic, the quiet of the consul's office is welcome, even with the rattle of the ineffective air conditioner in the window. Mr. Corbeil shifts in his chair, looking for her file in the small pile on his desk.

"When do we find out if he's on that plane?" asks Helen.

"When they get to Paris."

"Paris?"

"They were taken out by helicopter to Gabon to be flown back. We weren't notified until the plane had already left."

"But he's not on their list?"

"No."

"What does that mean?"

"I don't know yet."

"I hope you are telling me everything."

"I'm telling you everything I know."

"Yes, but what are you thinking?"

The consul looks uncomfortable. "We should really wait until the flight gets to Paris before we begin to speculate."

"When is that supposed to be?"

"Two hours. An American embassy official will meet the flight and debrief the American citizens. We'll have a better picture then. You should go to the hotel."

"We'll wait here."

Helen leads Shane to the lobby.

"Don't worry, Mom, I think Dad's okay."

She closes her eyes. "Me, too, Shane."

She digs a small cassette player from her bag and slips the headphones over his ears. He holds her hand because otherwise, without his hearing, he is completely cut off. Helen looks around the undecorated office. She feels numbed. She did not expect this. She closes her eyes to keep from crying. *Where in hell is he? Safe. He's safe. He's on that flight. It's just a mix-up. But if he's not?* However this ends, it is unendurable to imagine the way things might be left to stand between them.

THE CONSUL IS SURPRISED to see Helen still waiting when he emerges for his lunch. It's been two hours.

"I see you are already developing a refined notion of African patience."

Helen looks up, but she doesn't smile. The consul clears his throat and tries again.

"I haven't heard anything yet," he says. "We can call together after lunch. Would you and your son like to join me? There's an expat place a short walk from here."

The busy cafe, bustling with people and French food, would pass for any place in Brussels. Shane relishes a milkshake, slurping loudly while they wait for their food.

"Listen, Mom," he says, blowing great burping bubbles up through the shake, splashing him and the table.

"Can you believe it? Milkshakes in the tropics!" A woman appears at the consul's side. Shane giggles as another bubble erupts onto the table.

Helen skips the scolding, as she wipes up with her napkin.

"My name is Laura," the woman offers before the consul can react. She gives him a nod. "You could wait for the rainy season to pass to get an introduction out of John here. My husband works for the Canadian High Commission."

Helen extends her hand, offering a smile instead of an explanation of her circumstances. "Helen, and milkshake man here is my son, Shane."

"Are you here because of the Air France incident?"

Helen is surprised by her quick deduction. She nods.

"I suppose you'll be in Paris by tomorrow morning. Lucky you. Breathe a little extra of that crisp autumn air for all of us."

"Actually, well, yes, I hope to be. We are waiting to hear that the flight arrived."

"But wasn't that hours ago?"

Helen looks at the consul, who puts his beer down and apologizes. "I was waiting to get more solid news. I'm sorry."

Laura frowns. "Is something wrong? My husband said everyone made it safely."

"Yes, I am afraid Ms. Burke's husband was not on the flight that went to Paris."

Helen's breath catches in her throat. She finds herself looking for help from Laura, who was until this most intimate moment a complete stranger. Laura touches her shoulder lightly and then turns to Shane. "Come here, honey, I have something to show you." She leads him carefully out of hearing range.

The consul continues. "I didn't want to give you bad news that was baseless or give you false hopes."

Helen looks away. She watches Laura show Shane a parrot at the bar. She guides his hand to pet it, and he laughs as the bird squawks in French. The consul is preparing to be the first official to tell her that Lewis may be dead.

"He and a Congolese man, a government official, were the only two missing, as far as we can tell. We believe that the official was murdered." The consul lowers his voice. "You should prepare yourself for the worst, I'm afraid. I'm waiting to hear what the other passengers have to say. Right now, we don't know where he is."

He can see that she is furious. "I merely wished to be accurate and complete in my report to you. I hope you will understand."

Helen's voice comes with a struggle. "In the future, Mr. Corbeil, please don't spare my feelings. I would prefer to be able to trust you."

Helen cannot keep the tears back now. The consul gives her a moment to compose herself. When she looks up, he hands her a napkin to wipe her eyes.

"Go home," he says softly. "We will find out everything we can. We will contact the group that was holding the airplane. We will compel them to account for an American citizen. If he is alive, he will be returned to us."

"I'm not going home, sir."

Helen gets up without expression and goes to get Shane. Laura has him in her lap. The parrot seems to watch Helen's approach.

"Mom, it's singing to you!"

Helen tries to smile as Laura lifts him into her arms to carry.

"I can walk, Mom."

She puts him down.

"I'll find out what I can," Laura says gently.

Helen has trouble opening the door. She is trying not to cry in front of all these strangers who have turned to watch her struggling with the door. Finally she realizes she must pull instead of pushing, and she is out on the street. The hot sun dries her tears quickly. If Shane understands what is happening, he is hiding it from her. She waves for Kalala. She knows what she needs to do.

FEFELE—LA FIÈVRE—FEVER

A FATAL WEAKNESS HAS begun to claim Lewis. Like a man banished to a tower, he has not been able free himself from the kakba. At midday, a bird lifts out of the trees just below him and flies close enough that he can see the bright yellow of its eyes. He stands when it circles over his head and then it glides away.

A subtle shift of temperature suddenly releases the moisture from the saturated air. The rain comes down in buckets, and without the canopy overhead to shelter him, he is instantly soaked. At first it feels good to let the cool water wash over him. Then he thinks to take off his shoe to catch the rain to drink. The wingtip is filthy; still, the water is welcome. By the time the rain stops, he is shaking, and he realizes his mistake. He cannot afford to misjudge this way. What an odd thing, he thinks, that homo sapiens have evolved to the point that they can die of exposure even in the tropics. What would his last thought be, crossing the edge of death, out here, a man who has lived his whole life successfully adapted to the concrete life of the city? Would it have any claim on the rational? Would he go out kicking, with blood and skin in his claws as any animal would, carrying the fight to the last spasm? Or would he just quit, give in to the alien mother, this earth, and weakly die?

Lewis stares at the green ocean of trees. Their arms reach up, as if promising to catch him—or urging him to fall. He suspects that his consciousness would be the first to bail, to seek relief, make the claim that the fall, some final grace, would be like flying. It would recklessly deny even that brutal slap of reality, the quick and dumb violence of suicide.

His thoughts are interrupted by a sound. At first he is not sure he is even hearing it—a low, mechanical hum, subtly oscillating, *wop, wop, wop,* a subtle pressure on his ears. He has to listen carefully to hear it. He jumps up, looking around like a madman. A helicopter! He is sure of it. He yells, raises his hands. He still cannot see it, but it has to be. It's unmistakable now.

"Hey! I'm here! Down here!" He screams, searching the sky for the machine. Just above the trees, faint in the shifting haze, he can't make out the shape at first. Then as the sound grows, he sees it—a military helicopter, the same green as the forest. It's not heading in his direction but passing him slowly on a diagonal.

He waves his arms and shouts more desperately.

"Come on! Here! Here! On this goddamn rock!"

He loses sight of it, and then even the sound is gone. He feels betrayed. He drops his arms. He waits.

Nothing.

The forest has won. He has made the wrong decisions, turned back too many times. He cannot compete, and the forest will have his life for it.

Whether he sleeps or not, he cannot tell—his nightmares and waking thoughts have become too much the same. Before him the night air shifts and undulates in shades of blackness, until he begins to imagine a spectrum of color that includes hues he cannot name and a kind of seeing that is the same as blindness. It occurs to him that there are different kinds of miracles. The plain miracle of being rescued by a helicopter, that is purely acceptable in fact. Then the familiar kind of miracle, a faith healing or a coincidence that challenges credulity, the kind that he has never believed in, the kind of miracle that is explainable only outside the realm of the senses, that without that simple barrier might seem ordinary and mundane. Then the elusive miracle of grace, like a touch in sleep, that eases the soul. And he wonders, as another mosquito settles and draws his blood, which he will be given.

———

Shane sits on his bed, beside the window, listening to his mother breathe. He can tell that she is having a nightmare. He slips from the cot and tiptoes quietly across the room to the sound of her. He moves slowly because he is still unfamiliar with the layout of the room, though Helen has been careful to show him and keep things in order. The light plays softly on his face as he moves in and out of shadow. In his hand is a small stuffed animal, a deer. The pupils have been worn out of the now plain white discs. He lays it on her bed and climbs up. He rests his small, cool hands on her bare arm, and her breathing begins to ease and become more regular.

———

In the morning Lewis wakes to the insistent chatter of colobus monkeys. He looks across the treetops at them. They are playing, chasing each other through the flimsy branches, like clowns with long tails and white faces. He smiles at this respite from the night, the release back into day and life. Even as the sun melts the high clouds, its equatorial heats burns the forest and makes it steam, creating new clouds. The sun forces him down from the kakba. The shade does not feel cool, but it is a kind of shelter.

His hunger has an edge now that clears his mind. Near the base of the rock, there is something white in one of the holes where the elephants dug, some kind of tuber, like a yam. He digs it out and brushes away as much of the dirt as he can, then takes a bite and waits. There is no bitter taste, no obvious poison, and after a while his stomach still feels all right, so he eats the rest. He digs up more of the roots and eats until he is full.

He feels a sense of control that he did not have before. He sits and takes stock of his wounds, looking to see if anything can be done. Flies and sweat bees swarm the red skin where he pulled the leech off his calf. He touches it with his hand. It's heating up with infection. Otherwise, he feels lucky; there are insect bites all over his arms and neck, but they seem okay. His clothes are a shambles. His white shirt is stained and torn in several places, as are his pants. His dress shoes are soggy but holding up. He laughs to think that the salesman was right; they are well made, worth the extra money. His socks are rotting on his feet. They will have to go soon. He rubs the wound on his leg with a wet green leaf to clean it. Then he pulls his pant leg down. He stands up and plans a march.

At least now he knows which way he must not go. He puts the kakba at his back and walks for three hours in as careful a line as he can manage; then he forces himself to rest. He sits quietly and picks up his book, hoping that its carefully articulated voice will soothe his terror and somehow bring him back to sanity. He reads aloud the tale of another man's fight with this forest, without giving meaning to the words, as if they were a meditation, a psalm written to ease his fears.

Then Lewis gets up and walks for another hour. The rush of carbohydrates from the tubers is fading, but he still feels reasonably clearheaded. He rests again, without reading, absolutely still, barely breathing. He cannot waste energy on fidgeting. He rests like a predator, so quiet that a tiny antelope walks hesitantly into the clearing less than five yards away without noticing his presence. The delicate animal, hardly bigger than a large domestic rabbit, trembles and pokes among the bushes, nibbling, and slowly takes a few tentative steps closer. Lewis remains still. He can feel the air moving almost imperceptibly against his face. The duiker cannot smell him. Lewis can see the glass of its eyes, and its tiny hooves pawing at the damp ground, the wetness of its nose. When it is only two yards away, he lunges. It tries to leap away, but miraculously he catches a leg. The duiker squeals and thrashes; the strength of the small creature surprises him. He gets a grip on its neck and then with both hands he begins choking it. The antelope's miniature hooves strike his leg, tearing his pants and cutting him. Its eyes are wild. He tightens his grip and holds it away from his body. He can feel his hands cutting off its air, its desperate tongue trying to swallow.

Soon his arms and hands burn from the exertion of maintaining such a fierce hold, but the duiker is no longer moving. He lays the small, limp animal down in front of him. Though his hunger was strong enough to make this kill, now he doesn't know what to do. He tries to tear into the hide with his nails, but they are too weak to break the tough skin. He picks the duiker up and sinks his puny, dull canines into the soft underbelly and pulls and tears until he makes a hole. His mouth fills with blood, and he retches and spits it out. He tries again, this time tearing a piece of the flesh from under the hide. It is virtually impossible to chew raw like this. Then he imagines the parasites and worms that undoubtedly inhabit the flesh of any forest animal, and he spits the gob of meat into the leaves and wipes the blood from his face.

He picks up the book, and blood smears the cover. It has nearly fallen apart. The pages are soaked and filthy. He lays it back down in the spongy bed of leaves by the wrecked duiker; Stanley's black eyes stare up at the canopy. Lying next to the antelope, the book looks like a shrine. Lewis wonders how long this reliquary will keep before some real animal comes to claim his kill and tramples the book like nothing more than rotting forest leaves. The exertion should have made him hot, but instead he feels chilled. He gets up and walks away from the poor ruined animal. *Some predator you make,* he thinks. He stops once, knowing he should go back and reclaim the meat. But he doesn't.

Dinner with Laura and her family is a relief to Helen. The food reminds her of home—pork roast, potatoes and green beans. After they eat, Shane plays with the three boys in an upstairs room while the adults wait for coffee. Ntumba, the nanny and maid, brings it with sugar and UHT milk. Helen spoons in too much sugar, relishing the sweetness like a temporary rescue from her anxiety. Mark, Laura's husband, seems relaxed, less officious than his American counterpart. He's been trying to bring up the subject of Lewis's disappearance all night, first waiting because of the kids and then just trying to find the right timing. Finally the silence that accompanies the arrival of the coffee provides a cue, and Mark launches into what sounds like a prepared statement.

"There are such limitations to what a government can do in this situation, you know, an outside, ex-colonial—or what do they call us—a 'neocolonial' government. No one seems to believe . . ." Mark pauses. Helen can hear Ntumba dropping silverware into the kitchen sink and filling it with water. "This is hard to say, harder to hear, I know. Please bear with me. First of all, no one seems to think Lewis was killed with the Congolese official. But where could he have gone? That area is covered with nearly endless tracks of rainforest; a lot of it has never been logged. That's part of the problem up there. The armies get themselves so mired in the muck that they can't even have a proper fight."

"Mark, I don't think this is helping," says Laura.

"I just don't know the answer. At least, I don't know a good answer. Frankly, I think your government is hedging its bets. I know if it was us, we'd like you to leave, quietly wait for us to find some proof, some solid information, one way or the other. It'd be best to keep you out of the way, long enough for it not to be of media interest. There's no positive spin on this for them, especially now. It just makes their job a pain in the ass."

Ntumba brings more coffee. Mark sets down his cup.

Helen tries to smile, or at least to keep from gasping for air. "I'm sorry, but that's exactly why the journalist is coming. Because the media *is* a pain in the ass."

"I don't know. I don't know that going in there will do any good, either."

"If I wait here, I'll find out nothing." Helen pauses. "That's what you've been saying."

"It's a long way to go to come to the same conclusion."

"I don't see that I have a choice."

Mark scoots his chair back and crosses his legs. "This fight has been going on in different forms since independence in the sixties. Mobutu kept it in check for a while, with a lot of French and American support, not to mention Belgian paratroopers and South African mercenaries. But these guys won't quit. It's probably true that there's just too much to grab—diamonds and gold. The U.N. thinks so. Just stay away from soldiers. They've got their own set of rules."

"I don't know, Mark. Do you think anyone can even get up there now?" Laura asks.

"The cease-fire makes things more predictable, as long as it lasts. And things are not nearly as bad up north in Equateur as they have been in the east, in Katanga. I've heard that the ferries are running again, almost as far as Kisangani. But things can change suddenly. The closer you get, the quicker you may have to get out."

Helen is quiet.

"Shane could stay here with us, at least." Laura lays a hand on Helen's.

"No. I can't leave him." Helen looks at them bravely. "I can keep us safe. They won't bother a foreign journalist, it could mean too much trouble." She turns to Laura. "I have to do this."

KALALA IS WAITING BY the car in exactly the same spot he was three hours earlier. They drive through streets without streetlights; most of the houses are dark, too.

"Why are there no lights?"

"Who knows, Madame? There is a big dam for power, but it is not always working."

The moon is three quarters full, and it lights the hills and the empty buildings and shimmers in the palms. Shane falls asleep in her lap as they drive back to the hotel.

She thinks of the storm that put the power out in a beachhouse they rented three summers ago. She remembers hearing Lewis swearing downstairs. It was late, and the wind was showering the windows with sheets of rain. Branches of trees scratched at the glass like animals desperate to get inside. She lay in bed, trying to keep covered, drifting in and out of sleep, so that she was losing her sense of ordered time, until it seemed that he could have been down there for hours.

She was afraid he would wake Shane, who was only three and sometimes had trouble sleeping through the night. She was about to get up, wrap a blanket around herself and find her way downstairs along the wall. She could just make out the frame of the door by the deeper shadow of its opening. Then there was a barely perceptible glow that grew into a bright light in her eyes.

"You wouldn't believe where I found this goddamn flashlight."

"Shhh, honey, Shane is actually sleeping. And do you have to shine that in my eyes?"

He turned it away, the light on the walls highlighting his silhouetted shape. He seemed too angry for something so unimportant.

"So what are you going to do with it?"

"I'm going to put it by the bed where it belongs."

"That's why you got up?"

"Yes," Lewis said, too loudly. "In case Shane wakes up."

"Shhh. Come on."

Lewis sat on the edge of the bed. He put his hand over the light so that the room dimmed except for a faint, warm glow. Helen could see the shadows of the delicate bones in his hand.

"He's not going to wake up."

"He might."

Lewis waved the flashlight, and the light went out. He

unscrewed and tightened it without success, then he banged it into his palm. "Damn it."

Instead of hushing him again, Helen rolled over and buried her head in the pillow.

"This was a bad idea." His voice seemed loud without a face to connect it to.

"What?"

"Coming to this broken-down shack."

"Why? Just because of one day of rain?"

Lewis was sullen. She couldn't see him, but she could hear his thoughts as though he were shouting.

"It just feels like he's missing all of it—the ocean, the sky."

"Lewis, that's not *all of it*," she whispered. She couldn't keep the impatience out of her voice. "You always have an excuse to be away somewhere, work, whatever. If you had more time with him, you wouldn't see it as such a *big* problem."

"You make too little of it."

"Because there's nothing to do about it. It's what happened."

"Helen, don't tell me it's nothing. It's your whole life."

"This talk doesn't do any good."

He was silent for a moment. She imagined that she could actually hear his jaw tighten.

"What am I supposed to do?"

"You could help a little more." She regretted it immediately, half prayed that the comment would just be lost in the dark. Instead it was burdened with all the arguments like this that they'd ever had. Helen felt a chill spreading over her as if one of the windows might have finally blown in. "I'm sorry. I don't feel like fighting."

He didn't reply, but she heard him scoff.

"Please say something."

His hand had been lightly touching her leg. He pulled it away.

"We are lucky to have him,"she said.

He let out a heavy sigh. She struggled with her impulse to yell at him and her desire to be smarter than that. There was no sense in it. When she decided to reach for him she was not sure where he was, and her hand found the bed empty.

"Lewis?"

"I'm here." She heard the regret and resignation in his voice. She found his arm.

"Come here."

The whole bed moved as he pulled himself over to her.

"You're cold."

Helen found his face first with her hands, his scratchy two-day beard. She could see the faint glimmer of his eyes. They seemed damp. She found his lips and kissed him. His hand slipped along her side. She thought of fifty things to say, to try to help, but then it seemed better try to fix it this way—silently in the dark.

———

Lewis collapses in the ditch, only dimly conscious in the hallu-cinatory haze that has enveloped him. The fever has come on suddenly, as if it had been waiting to ambush him. The elation he felt at discovering a road sustained him long enough to get through the twisted bush to the edge of the soft red clay, but now as he lies shivering in the shallow ditch, unconsciousness steals the victory.

He passes the night in fits, mostly horrors of his own making; but occasionally he sees with startling clarity the stars in the narrow gap that the road cuts in the trees, and they reassure him. He imagines Shane passing his hands, those awkward child's fingers, over his eyes. When he tries to speak, Shane whispers to him to be quiet. Listen. The hum of insects in the bark of the trees and the frogs rioting in the ditch seem to fall quiet, too.

"Crawl away from the road a little, Daddy," Shane whispers.

Then in a flash, Shane is gone, and over the trees there is a rushing light and laughter, sibilant in the hissing wind. Out of the light appear almost human shapes, which hover, trembling, and seem to descend as if they might pick Lewis up, but suddenly they rush away, disappearing beyond the dark trees. Something is crawling over his extended hand, something with many legs. In a flash of adrenaline he picks it up and throws it away to the bushes, and it makes a piercing scream, so loud he must cover his ears. He scrambles into the muck of the clay road.

"Not here, Daddy."

He drags himself across. Shane is laughing as if it is a game of tag.

"Daddy. Daddy. That's the way I used to crawl. Remember, Daddy? When I was a baby."

He slips into the other ditch and crawls up into the low bush that thrives where the forest has been cleared for the road, free from the tyranny of the grand mahogany and blackwood lokoko.

"Sleep, Daddy."

He lies back in the vegetation, which embraces him like a cradle. He feels a light weight like an infant lying on his chest. The child's hands gently grip his sides, rhythmically tightening into tiny fists and then relaxing with his breathing, and Lewis falls asleep.

THE MORNING OPENS with a deep, thundering roar. Lewis's body aches, and the fever has not released him. With a great effort he lifts himself to look toward the sound. He can see, maybe four hundred yards away, the first vehicles of a military convoy. They move slowly, half-mired in the red gumbo of the road. He hears the rusty bearings of the wheels screeching under their burdens. The men who walk alongside the vehicles are silent, carrying their rifles like children playing soldier. The foremost of the green metal machines is armored, and a few of the more privileged fighters ride on its flanks, stoned and red-eyed from smoking *mbangi*. The machine is pocked and dented where artillery has struck the armor. Behind them is a long line of transport vehicles, a mismatch of army vehicles and private cars that have been commandeered along the way. They look more tiresome than fearsome, as though they're looking for any place to stop and unburden themselves.

Even through the veil of his fever, these do not look like rescuers. Yet he nearly stands and calls to them anyway. He'd be happy to be a hostage now, but his weakness and delirium keep him from it. In a dream of what happens, he does stand, weakly, and yells in English, but they do not hear him. The convoy rolls by slowly, inexorably, and though he can see the mud stick in the tires and hear the men slowly talking, hear the drink and smoke in their voices, he is invisible to them and his shouting is silent. When he wakes they have passed, leaving only the trampled brush and even deeper ruts in the muck.

He slips again into unconsciousness, oblivious to the insects that have already begun to feast on him. A group of Mona monkeys approach him tentatively, chattering and egging each other on, afraid to get closer than a few yards before they retreat. A harrier eagle circles overhead, but eventually it, too, moves on. When the rain comes, it washes the clay from his arms, and then the sun comes out and dries him, and he steams like the bush around him, melting and folding into the landscape.

From down the road a young boy approaches. He walks as though he has a long journey ahead of him, but he has no bags, just a short stick in his hand, a straight piece of root with a gnarl at the end, a club. His feet are bare and red in the muck. He wears worn pants and a T-shirt so faded that the message cannot be read above the faint image of a Pepsi logo. He looks about ten, but his body seems too slight for him.

He stops near the spot where Lewis lies, as though he can sense some difference in the buzzing of insects, a piece out of place. He searches until he finds the body and doesn't seem surprised to see it there, cast aside. There is nothing that unusual about a carelessly discarded human body here. He walks up casually, and he is genuinely surprised to see a white man. He takes a couple of steps back so that he can see down the curve of the road to make sure that no one is around.

The man appears to be dead, but he cannot see a wound, any sign that the man might have been shot, and there is no trampling of the grass to suggest any kind of struggle or that the body was dragged or dumped there by a passing convoy. He barely manages to roll Lewis over onto his side. His body is limp, not stiff with rigor mortis nor bloated by the tropical heat. If he is dead, it has not been for long. The boy checks his pockets and finds his wallet and passport. Inside on the driver's license is a picture of Lewis, though it only vaguely resembles this face. He studies the document for a moment, then carefully returns the wallet and passport to Lewis's back pocket.

He leaps away when Lewis moans and extends an arm, reaching for something in a dream, something that just slips from his grasp. The boy sits down at a safe distance, trying to decide what to do with the man. A live white man is too valuable a thing to simply abandon. Such a thing has to be good for something. He waits patiently to see if Lewis will move again, and when he doesn't, the boy gets up and covers him with brush until he is well hidden, then covers his own tracks back to the road and returns the way he came.

———

Helen feels out of place on this side of the barricade at the airport, waiting for arriving passengers. She stands out among the Congolese greeting family returning from abroad and the drivers holding name placards meeting European businessmen and mining engineers. Shane is with Laura for the afternoon, playing with her boys. She misses having his hand in hers, and she finds herself looking down for him. By the time the journalist gets out, almost everyone else is gone.

She might have guessed that whoever it was would be held up because of his journalistic credentials, but she never imagined that he would be so young. No wonder he was questioned. Kalala takes his backpack from him and dumps it in the trunk. He doesn't think much of this boy-journalist, either.

"How was your flight?" Helen asks.

"Shitty. They don't allow CD players."

Helen is unsure of how to react.

He sits in the backseat with a dramatic slouch and a great sigh. Helen tries to remind herself not to prejudge him. Who was she expecting, after all? Hemingway? Though he is an American, he has a British name: Ian.

"I'm supposed to give you a message from Dan." He finds a folded piece of paper inside his backpack and hands it to her. It says simply "Good Luck. Be Strong."

"Do you know Danny?"

"No, my editor does. I was the only one she could find who'd been to Africa before, or was at least crazy enough to admit it."

"You've been here?"

"Not here exactly. East Africa."

He asks Kalala something in French. Helen picks up a few words of Kalala's response: generals, dangerous, thieves.

"Interviewing already?" she asks.

"Just trying to get up to speed."

"What'd he tell you?"

"He says this whole war is about mining, how much the generals can get out before peace sets in. That's pretty much what you hear about it. One of the most lucrative minerals they're getting out is called col-tan. It's especially valuable right now because they absolutely have to have it to make cell phones. They dig it out of the muck in the rivers."

"But that's not in the north? Where the plane is?"

"No. More east. Different rebel group, different acronym. But there's gold all over, and in some places diamonds. This is a rich part of the world."

Ian rolls his window down, and the air blows his long hair back. Helen takes a closer look at him. He doesn't really look that young. He might even be thirty-something.

"What I haven't figured out is if there is a peace deal in place, why did they hold on to the plane and the passengers so long? It looks like bad faith," Helen says.

"Everything's negotiation. Maybe it gave them an edge with the U.N. They could pretend to be helping out. Especially if no one calls it a hostage deal. The threat would be obvious. They must have gotten something they wanted to let them go."

"So it's going to be harder to bargain now."

"Yep."

"Those big generals aren't looking for Lewis."

"They have to believe that there's something in it for them."

"If the state department feels some pressure and those generals get the idea that the U.S. has decided to make a real effort to find him, that should make it worth something."

Ian rolls up his window, and it's quiet in the cab.

"Excuse me, but I have to say this. . . ." Ian clears his throat. "That all depends on everyone buying that he's still alive."

When the boy returns several hours later with a wooden cart fitted with a pair of bald car tires, Lewis is still at the side of the road. He pulls back the branches and leaves that cover Lewis, aware that all his efforts may have been wasted on a corpse. He wheels the cart as close to the body as he can. Then he kneels near Lewis's head and pulls out a small gourd that has been wrapped with the spotted skin of a bush cat. When he opens it he holds it at full arm's reach, as if the gourd contains some deadly poison. He waves it under Lewis's nose. He gets no response, though he prods the body with his foot. He looks up and down the road to make sure no one is coming and tries it again. A hawk swoops overhead, laboring with its broad wings, trying to get some elevation. The boy stops his work and waits until the bird leaves, as if it might be spying on him or thinking of claiming the body.

He reaches into his pants pocket and takes out three small antique vials and considers them, trying to remember the instructions that went with each. This is not something that he has tried to do before. He has only watched his grandmother attending a sick child in the village, marveling at her way of doing her work as much as at the power of her medicines. He opens the smallest vile, and some of the bright green concoction spills onto his hands. He opens Lewis's shirt and spreads the gooey substance on his chest and then wipes the rest off in the grass. For a third time he slowly waves the small gourd under Lewis's nose and then pries his mouth open and allows a few drops of the medicine to fall on the swollen tongue.

Lewis coughs and heaves. He rolls onto his back and opens

his eyes. The boy caps the vial and prepares to run. Lewis tries
to sit up, but he doesn't have the strength and the medicine has
the power to reanimate him only for a few minutes. He collapses and moans, mumbling deliriously. The boy contemplates
the difficult next move. He was counting on some cooperation
from Lewis to get him onto the cart. So before he lapses into
unconsciousness again, the boy drags him over to it by the
shoulders. All Lewis has to do is half crawl up into it. But that
seems about as possible as Lewis's flying away into the blue sky.
The boy is stumped by this part of the problem. He tries encouraging him in Lingala and then in French to get up, prod-
ding at him with his hands and showing him the cart. He
explains to Lewis that if he does not get himself into the cart, he
will have to leave him; that because of the rebels most everyone
who could help him is gone, chased off to live in the bush or
conscripted, and though his grandmother is strong in her craft,
she can't lift a half-dead white man.

They sit that way for at least an hour or more. The boy holds
on to the hope that the green goo he has painted on Lewis's
chest will eventually begin to work and transform his near
corpse so that he can lift himself onto the cart. But Lewis does
not move and the boy knows his own strength well enough,
and he eventually leaves him and walks back the way he came.
He leaves the cart, too, which stands mutely next to the dying
man, like a donkey guarding its fallen load.

IT IS LATE IN the afternoon by the time the boy returns.
With him this time are three young children, five and six years
old, maybe seven. The boy gives them some direction, and the
two youngest take a foot. The girl takes the other foot, and the
boy takes Lewis by his arms. Together they drag him a few feet
closer to the cart, and the boy manages to get Lewis's head and

shoulders on the edge; then he runs around to the feet to try to help there. He lifts, and together they attempt to shove the giant white man forward, but the cart rolls instead and Lewis's head slips off its precarious rest and falls back onto the ground with a dull thud.

Undaunted, the children try again, this time with a rock blocking the wheel. With their small hands, they take a firm grip on his front half and load him more securely before moving to the feet. It takes all of their strength to move his dead weight forward, but they manage it. Once he's on, they arrange him so that he won't fall off, and then they tie him down with sisal rope like Gulliver. Lewis's knees are tucked up to his stomach, his head is bent forward to his knees, his arms are folded close to his body. He looks like the pale fetus of a giant. Dusk falls and the clouds descend. The children bounce and roll him down the narrow road, into the gloom.

KOLALA—LE SOMMEIL—SLEEP

IAN SAYS THERE IS a ferry that will take them upriver, but he hasn't found a guide willing to accompany them. He seems ready to try it without one, but Helen knows they are going to need help somewhere along the way, from someone local, so she tries to find Malik's grocery. The number written on the scrap of paper is only partially legible, and it turns out there are many grocers on this street. Even Kalala is losing his patience as they pull up to the fifth one in two blocks. Shane waits with him in the car.

The store is crowded floor to ceiling with European goods, and the aisles are so narrow that to get to the rear she has to back up and wait to let a shopper and her child come through. Her attempts to communicate with the clerk are unsuccessful; her French is about as inadequate as his, and the man ends up smiling but holding his hands up as though she might be robbing him. She tries to return the way she came, but the aisle is blocked by two large women. She takes the aisle along the wall, and is about to ask another clerk who is kneeling on the floor, stocking shelves when she discovers she has found Malik. Until this moment she hasn't even considered the probability that he will tell her just what everyone else has—that it's a bad idea.

"You have come for help?"

"I didn't think I would find you. There are so many shops."

"But mine is the finest, *non?*"

She smiles. "I need to go to the interior, upriver, to where the plane made its landing."

His face is serious. "Why do you come to me?"

She realizes that while she trusts him because she needs to, he has no reason to trust her.

"Because everyone says that I cannot go. I am at my wits' end."

Malik stands up and brushes off his apron. His calm face encourages her.

"Do you know how I can get there?"

"It's not possible."

"Of course." She exhales the words. This dependency is exhausting.

"You must take a boat, then you might get a ride, but in the end you must walk. No one will drive you, not for money, because they know that the rebels or the government soldiers will just take the car."

"I would pay someone well to be a guide."

"Not me, Madame. I have responsibilities."

Helen puts the piece of paper with the name of his store, which she has been folding and unfolding, back into her purse. She tries to compose herself to be gracious about letting him say no, even though there is so much at stake.

"I'm sorry for being so pushy. I hope you understand. I have to do this."

Surrounding Malik is an approximation of all the material blessings of the West—blue laundry soap and fashion magazines and food in boxes and bags, with names that promise more than food. He has something to lose.

"I will find someone who can go, but perhaps you will wish you had waited. Perhaps you will wish you had gone back to your comfortable home." His look is serious. He means it.

"Thank you."

"I have been to the U.S., you know." He knew it would surprise her. "Everyone wants to go there. I thought I did, but it made me uncomfortable." He laughs. "But look at me. I was born in the Congo, not in Kinshasa, in Shaba. I had a different life then. I think it must be easier for me because I didn't fly here. I had to walk. I know what the ground looks like between here and there, every hump of sand and mud."

He picks up a pile of magazines in his arms.

"It will be good for you to walk. You think?" He smiles. "It is what you must do for love."

————

Lewis can just make out the old woman seated in the doorway of the dark hut. The air is thick with smoke from a small fire that smolders a dull orange in the center of the dirt floor. A faint light from outside, the first splinter of dawn or the last gasp of dusk or perhaps the moon, lingers on her ancient face. The room smells like earth, like muddy water, the heavy scent of roots and fungus. Lewis closes his eyes again. He dreams of water, of a river pouring through the jungle, cool, clear and deep. He pulls with his arms to the depths of it, where it is dark and cold, where he drinks instead of breathing. He has the sense of looking for something at the river's bottom, something that fell from his hand—maybe a ring or something made of a precious metal or a stone, and when his mind wanders and he no longer cares if he finds it, the water pours into his lungs and begins to choke him. He coughs himself awake. He can still feel a bit of fluid harboring in his chest, stealing his breath.

The woman turns to look at him, and he thinks he should conceal his wakefulness from her, but she has caught his eyes. She says something he cannot understand. He tries to answer, but his voice does not respond. The old woman gets up from her spot, and she brings him water in a sack made from animal intestine. She holds his head while he drinks with his eyes closed, and the water explodes with color over his thickened tongue. It is sweet like springwater, but he can also taste the earth in it, and something else, a medicine perhaps. She lowers his head and tests his forehead and neck for the fever; it still rages. Her hands are miraculously cool and then painfully hot.

"*Lala,*" she whispers. Sleep.

Lewis slips back into dreams. A hotel room in Paris. The room is grand and expensive. The tall, narrow window perfectly frames the Eiffel tower lit in the distance, and he thinks of when he went with Helen. They stayed on the left bank, and the room was small. The elevator barely fit two, and the streetlight that shone softly through the window at night made Helen's skin glow along the arc of her legs, her hands tight in the pillow. But now he has the uneasy feeling that he is supposed to be waiting for someone, not Helen, and although it was his idea, he is having second thoughts. He gets up from the bed stiffly and walks down the golden hall from the room to the bar.

All the women are young and well dressed, listening to dapper, confident men who lean over their drinks, pleased with their own monologues. Lewis sips his scotch, trying to quell a nagging sense of apprehension. He lays his hands on the marble counter, and the moisture of his palms leaves a faint impression there before it fades.

The noise of the street clamors in behind a tall, dark man silhouetted against the light inside the portico. He enters the bar with the air of someone who is expected. As he moves into the light, Lewis can see that he is dressed in skins and feathers. Scars tattoo his bare chest, and in his right hand he carries a human head. He holds it casually by a clump of wet hair.

Lewis looks for an exit, getting ready to run, when he sees the window again and realizes that he has not moved. He is still sitting on the bed. And now he thinks he should have looked closer to see whose head it was. He closes his eyes to see again, to remember—a young woman with dark hair and fine gold earrings.

There is a knock on the door, and she comes in without waiting for Lewis to respond. She leaves the lights off and walks over to where he sits on the edge of the bed and kneels before him with her hands in his lap. She takes his hands and puts his fingers in her mouth, sucking each one and looking up at his eyes.

"What do you want, Lewis?" He can hear the thickness of her lips in her voice.

His gold ring clicks on her teeth as he tries to pull his hand away. Suddenly it is dark. He looks up at the trees that have trapped him, and the teeth bite down. The ape reaches to grab him, shrieking with his severed fingers in its mouth as Lewis backs against the tree, holding his bleeding hand and looking desperately for an escape. The ape grabs a branch, holds it over his head and runs at him, screaming.

Lewis wakes yelling or with the feeling that he must have

been; even with his eyes open, he cannot see. He screams until his voice is hoarse and barely human. A light comes into view, just a spot of it at first, a dim yellow point. Finally, as it comes closer, the glow fills the small hut and restores his vision. Suspended in the light is the face of the boy who has saved him. He does not speak but holds the lantern where he can see Lewis's eyes. He looks at Lewis as if he is meeting him for the first time, but the confidence in his face helps calm Lewis down enough to close his eyes again, and the boy is gone.

IN THE MORNING sunlight spills through the narrow doorway. There is no one else in the small hut, and he can hear a rhythmic pounding outside and children's voices. He is lying on a low-slung hammock only a few inches off the clay floor, which has been beaten and polished by bare feet. He can smell the dust and ash in it, mingling with a myriad other scents from bottles and vials and bowls of herbs and dried leaves and murky liquids. He lays his hands over his face and closes his eyes as tightly as he can, hoping to test the reality of what he sees, but when he opens his eyes and lowers his hands, the room changes only in subtle ways: the light dims slightly on the earthen floor as a cloud veils the sun, or there will be a momentary pause in the tapping or a subtle increase in the wind rushing in the trees outside. And then for a while a bird settles in a tree somewhere nearby and calls at odd intervals. He is too weak to sit up, but his delirium is easing, and he welcomes even the most mundane details as evidence of that. He thinks of Helen, relishing a memory that is not a nightmare, that comes to him under his control.

The first time Helen ever undressed for him was in bright sunlight. The window was open, and a warm breeze blew through her hair. She unbuttoned her blouse and unhooked her bra, smiling at him. He sat on the bed, unsure of where to rest his hands. She slipped her skirt off, and her underwear, and stretched her arms over her head like a cat. Then she laughed and ran at him, knocking him into the pillows, knocking the breath from him. Later, in the evening light, he tried to read, and she worked a crossword puzzle lying away from him on her stomach, the soft light from the lamp caressing the small of her back.

"What do you want, Lewis?"

He set his book in his lap.

"From this? From me?" She wasn't looking at him, not making too much of the question.

"I don't know. Do you?"

She smiled, laid a hand over her heart and in a melodramatic way announced her list. "I want love, passion, trust, truth, intimacy, sex and flowers on a regular basis."

He laughed.

"And healthy children."

In the morning, Helen drank her coffee. She seemed serious. Her mood was as still as the air in the room. She kissed him, and he held her and whispered, "I want you. That would be enough."

After she left, he worried that he had gone too far. But then he opened the windows, and he felt like laughing.

The boat is so rusted and dilapidated, it seems risky to board it even at the dock. There must be three hundred people trying to get on, and the noise, the general chaos, is deafening. Their guide is nowhere to be found. Ian is impatient; he knew this, he knew that the whole thing was another one of those damn promises, a yes that means no, because no one wishes to disappoint.

Besides that, it appears that having a ticket is merely the badge
of a rube, and the pretense of a reservation merely elevates the
bearer to a higher requirement of bribe. The boat was meant to
leave the preceding day, and they waited for two hours only to
find out what everyone else seemed to know without notice—
that it wasn't leaving.

Shane sits at the edge of the wooden rail, where the scent of
fresh creosote overpowers the smell of dead fish and the proto-
zoa that make a foam in the brown waters. His feet hang over
the edge as he listens to the dull sound of waves washing
against the hull and lapping at the pier. He presses his hands
over his ears, anticipating, from the faint hiss that precedes it,
the blast of the steamer's whistle. After the deafening noise
rings out up the river, Ian turns to Helen.

"How does he know?"

"What?"

"That the whistle is about to blow?"

Helen shrugs and looks at her son. Strangers, especially here,
seem to expect him to be sentient because of his blindness.

"This is the part of Africa I cannot abide."

"What's that?"

"The constant waiting for nothing to happen."

She barely hears him. Two boys have approached Shane on
the dock and are trying to get his attention, puzzled, not yet
comprehending his blindness. One has a large bird of prey in
his hands, an African kite with a yellow beak. The hawk hangs
upside down, held by its feet, and flaps weakly when the boy
lifts it up.

"*L'épervier!*"

Helen looks at the wretched bird. It is pathetic hanging from
the tight grip of the boy's relentless hand, its beak open as it

pants for breath. It is certainly near death, but there is still a
fierceness in its eyes.

"Shane, don't touch that bird."

"*Madame,*" the boys say. "*Achetez le! Achetez le! C'est un
bon marché!*"

"*Elle ne veut pas l'acheter.*" Ian answers for her.

"What do they want?"

"They want to sell you this bird." Ian tries to wave them
away.

"No. No. Come on, Shane." Though Helen and Shane walk
away, the boys follow with their captive.

"Will they eat it?"

"*Est-ce que vous mangez l'épervier?*"

"*Oui.*"

Helen shakes her head.

"*Voulez-vous que nous le laissez?*"

"Did they say let it go?" She turns to the boys. "*Oui.
Laissez-le.*"

"*Cent francs. . . . Bonne chance pour le voyage!*"

The bird flaps weakly and turns its head, so it seems to be
looking right at her as she digs through her purse for the hundred francs. Her hands are shaking as she hands over the dirty
money.

"You shouldn't do that," says Ian.

"What's a hundred francs, a dollar?"

The boys ceremoniously lay the bird on the deck, dramatically untying its feet, and then run off with their money. It is so
weak it merely lies there, barely making a sound, like distant
wheels on gravel. Ian walks over to the bird.

"I don't think it can fly."

Shane pets it, which it endures briefly before flapping and

half limping to a place in the shade to hide. The bird peers at Helen from the shadow of an old crate. She is glad for her hat. The sun is merciless, getting hotter by the hour like coats of thick paint. Ian watches Shane, who is listening intently, trying to find where the bird has gone.

"If your friend and his guide don't show up, I don't think you should go. With the boy it isn't safe." Ian says.

"We don't know that, do we? How it is."

"I'll go alone," he says. "I'll stay two weeks, tops. I'll come back then, no matter what I've found."

Helen sits down. He's right. It's crazy even with the guide, though at least then she could communicate, know what she's getting into, stop at the point where it seems dangerous—if she has not already passed it. She looks down at the barges. So many children are there, and for them it is routine. They will go.

"Okay, Ian. Let's give him another hour."

She turns her head to get her face out of the sun. Even Ian sits down. More and more people pass by. She looks into every face until she thinks she couldn't recognize Malik. She has nearly given up when Ian spots him.

"Is that him?"

Malik comes down the long dock over the silted water. He wears a wide hat, and surprisingly he is alone. No guide. He has a light bag in his right hand. Helen stands and straightens her long skirt, takes off her sunglasses and blinks in the brightness.

"Where's the guide?"

"It seems the guide must be me after all, Madame."

"Really?" Helen says, relieved, suddenly even cheerful. "Are you sure?"

"Why not?" He beams. "I could not find anyone who wished to go. They say it is not possible." He laughs. "We may not get far. Have you found your berth?"

"We've been waiting."

"Oh, you mustn't wait. I hope there will be something left."

Malik takes Shane's hand, and they follow him to the boat, swept up in his buoyant mood, as though they were embarking on some adventure. Any doubts Helen had disappear, but as they wait in line she turns back to the dock for a moment, just in time to see the two boys she paid return and chase the poor kite from its hiding place. Triumphantly they lift the bird in the air again, wave to her and run off into the crowd.

Tickets and bribes for the controller, and they have a tiny compartment in first class for Helen and Shane. Malik will sleep in second class, and he takes Ian, grumbling, to find a room. The boat pushes off with a reluctant but mighty heave, into the fat current of the river. Traveling steadily day and night, it will take four days to get to the town the consul told Helen about. She stands with Shane on the bow, where the diesel smoke is blown away, and stares at the increasingly sparse scattering of buildings along the bank until they disappear into the wildness of the bush.

DJAMBE—LE POUVOIR—POWER

AFTER TWO DAYS, LEWIS is strong enough to crawl to the door of the hut. He pulls himself into a patch of sunlight and rests against the clay walls of the small house. The village, at least in the total number of dwellings, is much bigger than he expected. Most are mud huts built over frames of empty cans and chicken wire, but there are also a few buildings made from concrete blocks with tin roofs. The village seems abandoned— almost half of it has been burned. If he could stand, he would get up and explore, but even sitting up makes him dizzy, and he can feel the fever latent in his limbs and neck as if it is waiting to pounce on him. There is a wooden bowl with food in it next to his hammock, the same thing that was served on the airplane after the emergency landing. He digs his fingers in and eats greedily. He can feel his stomach receive the food, and its sugars and carbohydrates tickle his blood.

He passes in and out of sleep, moving when he is awake to

stay out of the slowly advancing patch of sunlight. About noon, halfway between sleep and wakefulness, he sees the movement of someone coming. He ought to go back into the hut, but he's too exhausted to move. Within a few minutes the boy arrives with his grandmother. She clucks at Lewis, apparently not pleased that he has dragged himself out of bed, and the boy helps him back to the hammock and gives him water.

"Where is everyone?"

The boy looks at him. He obviously doesn't speak English. He gives Lewis a coconut, open at one end and filled with coconut milk. Then the grandmother passes directly into his mouth a pungent liquid that numbs his tongue, and he washes it down with more of the coconut. He hears children playing outside, but there is no sign of anyone between the age of this boy and his grandmother.

"Was the village attacked?" Lewis suggests, pointing toward the burned huts and showing his fists.

The boy nods.

"How long ago?" Lewis asks, then realizes he must think of a way to communicate this with sign but comes up with nothing.

"Where are all the people? People?" He gestures with his arms to the emptiness of the place, and points at the two of them. The boy points to the forest. He takes the potion from his grandmother and urges Lewis to be quiet and rest, and then he hands him another vial to drink from. The strong taste of it lingers in Lewis's mouth. For the first time he notices the boy's T-shirt, the faded Pepsi logo. He almost chuckles at the irony of it.

"What's your name?"

The boy doesn't understand. So Lewis points to himself. "Lewis." He feels a bit like Tarzan, but he doesn't know how else to do it.

The boy smiles and lays a hand on his own chest. "Kofi."

SOMETIME IN THE NIGHT, Lewis opens his eyes. He dimly sees Kofi and his grandmother, sleeping across from him, and the small shapes of two younger children. He feels strong enough to stand. Whatever it was, a bout of malaria or yellow fever or typhoid, or something unknown to Western medicine, it has retreated, at least temporarily. When a cloud dims the feeble light, he is startled to realize that he has been seeing by starlight. The cloud passes, and he sneaks quietly outside under the palms. He looks up to find that even the starry sky is unfamiliar. He cannot find a constellation he recognizes. He sits down against one of the few larger trees that escaped the burning of the village and closes his eyes. The air, though still warm, feels cool to his lungs now that the fever has passed, and he slips into a calm sleep.

He doesn't wake until the sun burns through the dawn haze and begins to dry the dew that has settled in the grass around him. His leg has fallen asleep because of the wallet and passport in his pocket, and he leans to one side to take them out, then rubs his calf to restore the circulation. He flips the wallet open, grimacing at his own image staring at him from the driver's license. He thumbs through the business cards and credit cards and then sees Helen's picture. He has to catch his breath to keep from dropping it, struck by the sudden awareness of the terrific distance between where he is now and where this photograph was taken. He looks up at the village. Some of the younger kids are up and playing a game with sticks that looks like a mock war. They all want to be on the side of the attackers, and they argue about who will be the victims. He looks at Helen's picture one more time and puts it back into his wallet.

Kofi emerges from the hut with a yawn. He stretches and then looks around for Lewis. He asks him with hand signals if he can walk. Lewis stands and nods. Then Kofi yells something to the children. They put down their sticks and begin searching the village, gathering cassava, plantains and yams. Soon the grandmother is up, too. She has a bag for her medicines. It doesn't take long to get ready; there is so little to bring. Kofi waves for Lewis to follow, and the group begin walking down the road, slipping in the ruts left by military vehicles. He is surprised by the cheeriness of this band of refugees, who chatter as if they were merely out for a morning stroll.

Besides the grandmother and the young children are about a dozen others who did not or could not flee into the jungle after the first attack. Mostly they are orphans, or too old like the grandmother, but among them is a pretty girl of fifteen or sixteen who has stayed in the village at a huge risk. She holds a radio/cassette player in her free hand as she helps the younger children keep moving. She lifts one of the youngest on her back and carries him down the road, her long legs stepping nimbly along the muddy track.

———

The forest looms at the brink of the river as if pushed from behind by the relentless growing of the jungle. Birds call into the opening, the relief provided by the waterway that braids among low islands in a confounding proliferation of channels. Monkeys perch in the branches that lean out over the water, their tails hanging in curves like upside down question marks, until the boat approaches and they race, squealing, into the canopy to avoid becoming dinner. Helen and Shane spend most of each day in the bow for the faint breeze it provides in the heat. Before them, amid the barges, children are washed in the brown water, food is prepared, and the passengers trade, among themselves and particularly with the river traffic, which enthusiastically paddles into the ferry's path. Fish, live crocodiles trussed with rope, birds, unlucky Mona monkeys, and a few chimpanzees piled up like old coats are all traded for every colored plastic item imaginable and for broad machetes and guns so old that some of them might actually be muskets. At night there is dancing, and because the batteries in the boom boxes are on their last legs, the music has an eerie warbling sound that drifts away across the sullen water of the river.

Every morning Malik strolls among the barges, looking for bargains and treasures, and he always comes back with a bag of mangoes or guavas or sweet red bananas. This time when he finds Helen and Shane in their usual spot, he has a young monkey. It clambers into Shane's hands before Helen can intercept it. Shane cuddles it like a teddy bear, but Malik registers her shock.

"I'm sorry, Malik, it might carry disease."

"Ah. . . . *Celui-ci est apprivoisé*. He doesn't bite."

It climbs onto Shane's shoulder and makes its claim, ducking its head to hide from Helen as though perceiving that she is the enemy.

Shane laughs. "Can I keep it, Mom?" He judges from her silence that there is room for negotiation. "Just for the trip. I can let it go when we find Daddy," he offers.

Helen looks at the monkey, and it tilts its head curiously at her. She knows what she should do, but instead she gives in. He has to get a few perks out of this ordeal. She reaches out to pet the monkey, and it peeks around Shane's shoulder, ready to make a truce.

"What does it eat, Malik?"

He holds up some bananas, which he brought for just this outcome.

"Of course." She smiles.

THE CURVE OF THE WORLD • 129

IAN SPENDS MOST OF his time on his own. Despite the rumble of engines he likes the view sternward, watching the river churn behind them. In the evenings he drinks beer with Malik, and they speak French. Occasionally he remembers Helen and shifts to English, especially when he thinks he has a particularly compelling observation to make.

"There's no news here," he says. "It's all too familiar: jungle rebels, corrupt governments, atrocities, crushing poverty, and the only thing anybody cares about in Africa anyway is that the gorillas and elephants are getting murdered—the filthy 'poachers' are messing up the white man's petting zoo, spoiling the Big Safari. The nineties were supposed to be the decade of democracy. Nobody even noticed. I think you have to be a decent potential market to warrant the West's support for democracy. What do you think, Malik?"

"Have another beer, Ian," Helen interjects, with a look of apology to Malik.

"I think it's true. We can't afford to buy, so we are not news in America or Europe. Not big enough news." Malik smiles at Ian and raises his beer.

"Whatever news is!" says Helen. "Who can pretend to really understand another culture enough to tell their story?"

"News *is* a cultural interpretation, of events, of facts," Ian pronounces. "It's always naming who is in power."

"But it has real effects, in a real world," says Helen.

Ian shrugs this off.

"Perhaps you have noticed that the white man's *evu* doesn't work so well here," says Malik, half-laughing.

"*Evu?*" Helen asks. "What is that?"

"It is a word in the Maka language, Madame. It means a kind of power, like witchcraft. Like *djambe*." He studies Helen for a moment to make sure she is comfortable with the subject. "*Djambe* is like a crab or a rat that lives in the belly." He slaps a hand on his stomach. "It's a source of power, but it is ravenous. It must always be fed."

"It's greed," Ian offers.

Malik shrugs.

"Then what is the white man's *evu*?" Helen asks.

"That is the question, isn't it? Some people think it is the power to enslave people, make the factories, get things for yourself instead of the village or your family."

"That's too simple, Malik. How do they have such power?"

"*Djambe le mintang*. The whiteman's sorcery. It is the way the 'big man,' the man in power, constructs the world. Like you said, the man who names it." Malik waves his hands in the air. "And it's all the symbols, too: a logo, a fetish, talisman, spell, slogan . . . *et la différence, c'est quoi?*"

"One is superstition, the other is—" Ian starts.

"Like Tom Cruise, no? He has it. *Djambe*."

"That's just PR, an image."

Malik smiles. "Like a Nike logo on your tennis shoes, a charm hung around my neck. Maybe it is you who are catching up." He puts a hand to his gut. "*Djambe* is powerful."

Helen laughs, "Like the Coca-cola Lewis sells: sugar water with a logo."

"Ah, then your husband is *un féticheur*," says Malik. "Congratulations!"

Ian leans back with his beer. "So what are we worried about? He can take care of himself."

Malik laughs. Helen smiles and gets up and walks to the rail. Below, dinner fires glow quietly in the haze and smells of burning meat. A group of men are gathered on one of the pontoons, gambling. She thinks of Las Vegas, all the pale gamblers serving slot machines and rolling dice. One of the men stands up, triumphant, yelling and then nearly spilling overboard along with his palm wine.

The boat is nearing their destination, and she can feel a steady pull on her heart now. As they round each broad bend, she looks up from the turmoil of the brown water with dread and anticipation.

Lewis trails behind as the small band of refugees approaches an encampment by the stagnant pool of a small river. The road is arched over with great stands of bamboo that tower almost fifty feet up from the sandy soil, like the gates of a great castle. It is an unhealthy place. Where the river ends and the road fords the shallows, a pirogue is sunk and decaying. An impromptu market has already been set up, though there is very little to trade, and most of the people end up begging a little cassava and a few plantains from those who have them.

Kofi's grandmother builds a small cook fire, and because she doesn't have any kind of pan, she lays the plantains directly into the fire to cook them. The children have traded some of their cassava for a chicken. The girl ties its legs so that it cannot escape.

When the plantains are charred, the old woman hands the largest to Lewis. Though she has carried it all the way from the fire with bare hands, it is still too hot for him, and he ends up dropping it into his lap, where the heat is even more unwelcome, and frantically brushes it to the ground. Everyone laughs as he picks it up, blows the dirt off and gingerly peels the steaming fruit. Kofi sits down next to him with his own.

"*Malamu?*" he asks in Lingala, touching his stomach.

Lewis takes a bite of the warm food. Kofi sits comfortably on a small wooden stool he has somehow managed to trade for.

Lewis wishes he could think of a way to thank him, something more than just saying it.

"*Merci.*"

Kofi smiles broadly, though he assumes that Lewis is referring to the banana.

"When do we go?" Lewis tries in English.

Kofi shrugs. He does not know.

"I must go"—He presses a hand to his chest and then makes a sign for walking with his fingers—"to the big city." Lewis tries a sign for city, but it ends up looking like a sign for mountains.

"I must go."

Kofi nods, and indicates that they will go together.

"When?"

Kofi signs, *In the morning, after sleep.*

Lewis nods. He likes this boy. It's hard to imagine what's in it for him.

Sometime in the night his stomach begins to riot again. He crawls into the bushes and heaves until he is afraid he may be bleeding. By morning the fever is back. Kofi sits next to him with a bag, prepared to leave, but Lewis cannot stand. After a while Kofi disappears and returns with leaves and roots from the forest. The old woman prepares them over a small, smoky fire, and Lewis chokes the medicines down. He's trapped in a dream of reaching for something, searching for a door, then striking at it with his hands, but he cannot make it yield, cannot exert any force against it. Every attempt is dulled by the weak, cotton thickness of the sleep.

Lewis loses track of days. He spends most of his time leaning against the gnarled roots of an old tree, and time rushes by, like some kind of bullet train. The sky pours overhead, night and day, moon and sun. He thinks that even if he becomes blind with this disease, the world itself will not be changed.

Somewhere in the midst of his delirium the rebels raid the encampment. Through the stunning whirl of his fever it seems distanced, the way it would be on television at home, happening to someone else. Lewis hides himself under a stand of bamboo, where his dirty clothes make an ideal camouflage.

The rebels elect an older man, one of the few men they can find to speak for the hundred or so refugees, and they yell at him and threaten him. They seem to be working unnecessarily hard to create any kind of pretext for their violence. It would be easier if they were simply outright sociopaths, cold blooded but predictable—if they would just get on with it—but there must be just enough humanity left in them that there is still some terror in this for them, too.

Finally one of the young men works himself up enough to step forward and butt the old man in the stomach with a rifle, and another pulls out a machete, threatening to make an example of the elder now crumpled at his feet. Everyone runs for the bush, and the line is crossed. They attack with machetes and knives, young boys in uniform chasing old people and children, like some cruel game of tag. Perhaps the worst part is that there is an *idea* behind it all, to send a message—to flood the cities with refugees who have been horribly marked.

The hopelessly one-sided attack is over in less than twenty minutes; most of the rufugees have run off unharmed. Yet the rebels stay on into the night, tearing the place up. Occasionally they search the periphery of the camp for those who might be hiding. Kofi keeps his hand on Lewis, pressing him under a cover of banana leaves and quieting his urges to cry out. Several times they are nearly discovered. A boot lands by Lewis's hand, and in the heightened world of his fever he feels the heat of the soldier's leg and smells his body, which nearly gags him. Lewis is surprised that he has felt so little fear during the attack.

Perhaps it's the possibility that getting caught might help him. At least he'd be back where he started. But there is something in Kofi's eyes, the tight grip of his hand, that tells him what a risk this is for the boy. They press their bodies into the leaves and hold their breath until the soldier is gone.

There is little to take, and eventually the rebels lose interest in the camp and the convoy rattles away into the quiet hum of insects. What was once a squalid refugee camp is a chaotic mess of pots and dishes and scattered clothes. The sun is well up before anyone comes out of hiding. Kofi's grandmother is not among them. Kofi searches for her along the edge of the clearing, calling her name. It is only when his voice is hoarse and reduced to a whisper that he gives up. He sits by the river with his bare feet in a stagnant pool of water. Lewis cannot see his face, but he imagines that the boy must be crying from the way his body seems to tremble.

His face is emotionless when he comes over and stands near Lewis. He stares vacantly at the mess before them, as though trying to decide what course to take now. He drags Lewis to the old tree and props him up, then brings him water and food, which he lays within reach. Then he takes Lewis's wallet and passport from his back pocket. He tries hard to tell him something, but Lewis is only vaguely aware of it. His conscious registers just one particular moment—Kofi stopped on the road, picking up a stick and looking back at him one last time before walking away.

———

The steamer arrives in the river town on its own schedule, but once again everyone seems to know about it, and there is a great crowd at the dock clamoring for a place on the downriver trip. Helen is impatient to disembark, but the docking itself takes more than an hour. There is a lot of discussion about how the barges are to be disconnected. Ian gazes over the tops of the coconut palms that line the river.

Shane's monkey has run off somewhere to hide in the boat or on one of the barges. Malik lays a hand on the boy's shoulder. "I'm sorry. I think the monkey has decided it's best to stay on the boat."

Ian turns to Helen. "The little beast might be right, you know."

"Perhaps." Helen turns away from Ian.

"He could be anywhere out there," he says.

"Losing an American, a white man, is not like losing an old shoe. People will remember if they saw him. And if he finds the government troops, this is where he will end up."

Ian looks down at the swarming dock and the town beyond, which seems to cling tenuously to this small clearing at the edge of the forest. "I hope they have ice."

Shane leans over the bottom rail on the upper deck, feeling the sultry breeze rolling off the river. The small port is loud, mostly human voices: men shouting as they untangle the mess of barges, laughing at their work; children calling out for their mothers or yelling in their games; women still at their trade bartering or gossiping in rowdy groups. He feels the water still urging the boat downstream, and the low rumble of the diesel engines stubbornly resisting; he hears the water lapping against the shore, and farther away, an absence of sound—the haunting stillness of the forest.

The town is smaller than they expected. Most of it hugs the river and disappears into the thick snarl of regrowth that borders the deeper forest. Their cab winds its way through the potholed streets. They pass a scattering of old colonial buildings along the dirt main road, and beyond them, upriver, a haphazard suburb of mud brick houses with rusted tin roofs. There are only a couple of hotels; one is notorious for the expatriates and prostitutes that have taken it over as a sort of second home; the other, possibly as a consequence of the popularity of the first, is nearly vacant, so that is the one Helen chooses. They drive through a dilapidated white arch into a small courtyard. Once it would have been almost luxurious, but the air-conditioning doesn't work anymore and the cold water barely trickles from the showerheads. There are only three places to eat in town, and Ian gets sick the first night and is reduced to subsisting on a liquid diet. After putting Shane to sleep in her room, Helen finds the journalist collapsed in the bar.

"I don't think you should be eating the ice, Ian."

"I think you like it here," says Ian, as he picks up his glass and gives a weak toast to the trees leaning over the courtyard.

"It's not bad, but I would rather not be here at all," she says.

"Most wouldn't." He tilts his glass and discards the last cube of ice. "Be here."

"You don't think so?"

"Nah. They'd let the 'officials' handle it."

"I don't know."

"Obviously you're an exceptionally dedicated wife."

"I'm a dedicated mother." She lets something of the uncertainty of her relationship slip into her voice without meaning to, and Ian hears it.

He takes another gulp of his drink while he considers it. "A dedicated mother?"

"Look. . . . Never mind."

"You know, that makes me think of something that has been confusing me. Do you live in New York or Spokane?"

"Both. Well . . . Spokane. I've been taking care of my mother."

"So you're separated?"

"No."

He grins. This is the part of journalism he likes best—the in-consistencies in people's stories, the way "facts" are colored by agendas. He chuckles.

"And now you're out here in this godforsaken bush, against everyone's advice, looking for him because you are a 'dedicated mother.'"

Helen doesn't answer; she's angry at having let this slip. She gets up.

"Don't go. I'm sorry."

She stands there for a moment, looking at Ian. "How could you ever expect to understand what I'm doing here?"

Ian looks down at his glass.

Helen regrets her tone. "We're supposed to meet with some of the local police tomorrow." She turns to walk away.

"You know, you're right. What the hell do I know?" He seems sincere. "Obviously it's more complicated than that."

Helen stops. She shakes her head.

"Or maybe it isn't," he adds.

She hopes Ian cannot see that she is shaking.

"So you're still in love?"

Helen scoots her stool in to put it away and lays a few coins on the counter for the bartender.

"Of course I am."

———

Kofi comes to the Church of Christ Mission late. It's night, and the generator is off. He finds a place to sleep in the schoolroom, by the half wall that is open to the outside. Sometime in the middle of the night it rains, and the deluge is deafening on the tin ceiling. When the sky clears, a bright moon casts a deep shadow on the boy's face. He looks even younger than his ten or so years. Bats come and go from the rafters all night, scrambling noisily along the beams, emitting their soft, sibilant calls.

Kofi is up before it is fully light, leaning against the door of the school, watching the yard for signs of movement. A dog is the first to make an appearance. It looks almost too well fed to be recognizable as a dog in Africa. It trots across the bare dirt yard without noticing Kofi. Half an hour later, behind the loose chickens, a young girl comes out of one of the low huts. She's barely eight, and she has her baby sister strapped on her back. She begins sweeping the dirt with a short broom made from thatching. She makes an arching, overlapping pattern that looks like the scales of a fish.

Kofi becomes so mesmerized by her work that he doesn't hear the groundskeeper come from the other side of the school until it is too late. He turns to run, but the big man is quick and grabs him.

"What're you doing here, boy? Prowling for something to steal?" he shouts in Lingala.

"No, sir."

"You're with the rebels."

"No, sir."

"Then I'll keep you for them. I'll turn you in for stealing."

"I haven't stolen anything."

"That's only because I caught you first."

The man, whose hands are like a vice on Kofi's neck, drags him across the yard. The girl stops her sweeping and watches until they pass, and then she carefully sweeps away the footprints and drag marks in her work. The man slams Kofi into a shed and locks the door with a padlock. Kofi hears him walk away and go inside one of the main buildings.

He slumps against the interior wall without bothering to try the door. His eyes slowly adjust to the dark room. There are bags of seed, jugs of insecticide and citronella torches leaning in a corner. And right by the locked door there is a machete. Kofi studies it for a moment, amazed that the man would have left him here with such a weapon. He takes it down, testing the blade with his thumb. It's dull, but it could still be useful. He sits back down and lays the blade behind him, out of view.

It's stiflingly hot, and eventually Kofi drifts off into a kind of half sleep. He does not dream, but gathers the hours into his unconscious in brief snatches of sound—the sweep of the girl's broom, a distant motor, and then the steady call of a bird in a tree just over the shed, like an alarm.

There are only a couple of seconds' warning, the voices of the man and the girl, before the door swings wide open, and Kofi has to rely on instinct to respond. He jumps up with the blade, swinging it in a wide arc as he leaps at the man, who blocks the blow with his arm. The collision sends the dull blade flying from Kofi's grip, and it clatters into a corner. Kofi gets a close look at the deep gash as the man's arm tightens around his neck.

"So you've come to maim me, eh, boy?"

"No, sir."

Out of the corner of his eye, Kofi sees the girl running toward the house.

"You must have a sharper blade for that, you know, boy. My arm is still strong."

Kofi kicks wildly in an attempt to get free, but the man only tightens his grip, and Kofi begins to lose his air. The girl runs back, leading a woman by the hand.

"See what I have here," the man announces to her. "I have

*one of those boys who go around cutting off people's arms.
What should we do with such a one?"*

Kofi feels the woman's eyes on him.

"He's just a boy."

"Look at my arm!" the man bellows.

*"You shouldn't have locked him in the shed with a machete,
foolish man."*

A little air slips back into Kofi's weakening body.

"Bring him inside, and I will see to that cut on your arm."

Kofi sits on a chair with his bare feet on the wooden floor. He
looks up at the one window, which is stained glass; Jesus hangs
on a cross like a villager caught and maimed by rebels. Kofi
slips his hand into a pocket to make sure that he hasn't lost
Lewis's wallet and passport. At a long, narrow table, the woman
pours water over the cut on the man's arm to clean it.

"He can't leave the mission. It isn't safe," she says.

"He may not stay."

The woman pinches his wounded arm, and he cries out. Then
she leaves him and walks over to a medicine cabinet for antibiotics and gauze to dress the wound. Kofi watches carefully;
the cabinet is full of Western magic in ampules and vials, bottles and needles. All of it is white and clean, purified of anything
living, the opposite of his grandmother's earthen cures. The
woman shuts and locks the cabinet, slipping the key into her
hip pocket.

When the man's arm is bandaged, he grabs Kofi roughly by
the neck again and leads him to a field of cassava. In his hand
he has the same dull machete that wounded him. He stops Kofi
and turns him around, glowering with his bloodshot eyes.

"You may run away if you like." He lets go of Kofi's arm and
even gives him a push.

Kofi is silent. The man raises the machete, but Kofi still does not move.

"*I have my eye on you, boy.*" The man brings the machete down as if he might hit Kofi with it; then he hands it to him. "*Use this for what God intended it, and you may be fed tonight,*" he says, and leaves Kofi to work the field.

Makanisi—La Mémoire—Memory

THE POLICE HEADQUARTERS IS a flimsy shack down by the dock. The fetid smell of the river, that brown soup of fish and mud, wafts over the two policemen sleeping in plastic chairs out front. They look up but don't say anything as Helen and Malik walk past them through the open door. Malik has had misgivings about this errand. He says that talking with the police can be too much trouble. Ian is staying behind at the hotel with Shane, using the excuse of making arrangements to fax his office. Apparently he had problems in Kenya, something to do with failing to salute the president's motorcade, and he says that in the Congo the police have a much worse reputation.

The sergeant sitting at the desk hardly looks intimidating to Helen until he has her passport in his hands. He flips through it, taking his time checking the stamps, frowning and looking for something that seems out of order.

"Our airport is too small for Air France, I think," he says, without looking up, speaking in English for Helen.

Malik asks him if there is a strip anywhere nearby that might accommodate a jet in an emergency. The sergeant takes a map from the single drawer in his desk and unfolds it. It's so old that the names of towns are Belgian. Malik leans over the desk to point.

"Here? Isn't there a wildlife refuge up here now, *une réserve?*"

The sergeant shakes his head and waves over a vast area to the north of the town. "There is nothing here," he says, looking directly at Helen.

Malik shrugs. Helen senses that he came only to appease her.

"Has anyone seen a white man? Have you heard anything?" Helen cannot help asking the question, though the answer already seems apparent.

The sergeant laughs. "All this belongs to the rebels, Madame, to Jean-Pierre Bemba. No one must go here." He seems uninterested in the fact that her husband has disappeared somewhere in that "nothing." Helen looks at her passport, which is still in his hand.

"I guess that's it. We should go, Malik," Helen suggests, as casually as she can manage.

Malik turns to the sergeant. "Is there a fee?" he asks, pointing to the passport.

"For what?" Helen asks, a little irritated.

Malik ignores her. *"Enregistrer?"* he suggests.

"You should have come to see me straight away," the sergeant says, as if the problem is more complicated now because of their failure to report to him earlier. "Someone might think you are spies."

"We came as soon as possible. Perhaps you can you make an exception in our case."

The sergeant smiles, and Malik negotiates the fee. Helen gets her passport back.

IN THE OVERARCHING DIN of town, Helen tries to find some peace in its single garden, a cultivated bit of jungle where a semblance of European order still maintains a few small victories. She sits on an ornate bench in the shade of an ancient mubula tree while Shane piles rocks in a dry fountain nearby with a steady clicking progress. The sun shifts gently through the branches, and she can almost imagine a rustling sound to its movement. Then a gathering of clouds brings shade without making it any cooler.

Her thoughts wander from the obstacles she has already encountered in this small town to a simple memory of Lewis. So many times she found him awake early in the morning, sitting by the stove with a burner on for warmth, reading some airport paperback he'd picked up on a business trip. Sometimes it surprised her to see him, as though she had forgotten he was back.

"Did you get enough sleep?"

He looked up at her as from a great distance, slowly finding a focus. It was a familiar habit that gave her a moment to study him as he seemed to return to himself like an occasional visitor. Usually she could see his thoughts and reactions as they formed and prepare herself. Was his face set in a frown or the suggestion of a smile? There was something disquieting in this awareness of him, a sense of responsibility for him during these moments when he seemed to have lost himself. He yawned and stretched, and a faint scent of him, mixed with his coffee, drifted over like an invitation. She took the two steps closer to be kissed. His face felt scratchy and warm.

"Not enough."

"Not enough what?" It took her a moment to remember her question.

"Sleep."

Helen smiled and turned away. She easily sensed the other possible meaning in his words, one that would have been obvious at an earlier time, would have been the only meaning. Not enough sex. But she wasn't going to suggest it. It was unusual that Shane was still asleep. But then Lewis's hands thought of it, in a somnambulant, automatic kind of way, a step ahead of his consciousness.

"Shane will be up any minute," she whispered.

"But he's not up now," he also whispered. Lewis stood quietly, slipping his hands up under her robe. "Got a minute?"

"Not even."

He released her, and lightly kissed her neck as he took his coffee to the sink. "Yeah, I have to take my shower."

She watched him walk away. He didn't seem angry or frustrated. Though she appreciated not having the pressure of hurrying that into their morning, it disturbed her to see him give in so easily. He should be a man about it. He should pout.

Helen made Shane's oatmeal, and the steam rising from the bowl dampened her face. She covered his breakfast with a piece of foil and walked quietly up the stairs to his room. He was still sound asleep, his body so relaxed he looked melted into the covers. She heard Lewis turn the shower off and step with bare, wet feet onto the tile. She eased Shane's door shut so that the latch made only the lightest *click*.

The bathroom was warm and humid. Lewis was still wet, leaning over the sink to wipe the steam from the mirror. Helen hung her robe on the door.

"We've only got a minute."

She kissed his damp neck as he stepped back to make room for her. His body was warm from the shower. She turned to the mirror and laid her hands on the wet marble of the sink. Lewis was looking down as he pressed against her back to kiss her shoulder. She guided him with her hand, and they both looked up at the same moment, surprised by the intensity of their reflection together in the fogged mirror. His arms tightened around her and she didn't take her eyes away from him in the mirror, and in this gaze they created a world that was complete and indistinguishable from the physical press of their bodies. The urgency of it felt as though it could burn away the slow ice of habit that had formed between them, like layers of the same problem frozen each over the last by dumb repetition, as if there could be in that moment, in their lovemaking, some fleeting opportunity. But what Helen saw in the mirror were two people who seemed paralyzed and a moment that was already passing.

Afterward he continued to hold her, and when she finally looked away from the mirror, he released her and sat down on the toilet, still out of breath.

"Mom!" Shane yelled from the hall.

She grabbed for her robe and quickly turned to put it on.

"Helen."

She looked back at Lewis impatiently. "Lewis, please."

Shane was already banging on the door. She opened it and picked him up.

"I couldn't find you."

"It's okay, honey. I was right here."

Helen shut the door behind her without looking back. As she walked down the hall with Shane, she had the dreadful feeling that she could have waited just one second more, two more little poundings on the door.

When Lewis went back downstairs, he was late for work. Helen was already putting a sweater on Shane, rushing to get him ready for preschool. They nearly bumped into one another getting through the door on the way to the car. Shane had trouble getting his seat belt on, and she was leaning over him, struggling with it, when Lewis walked behind her toward his own car. She clipped the belt and quickly leaned out the door.

"Were you going to say good-bye?"

"Of course."

He said it so confidently that as he walked back over, it made her wonder why she thought he would skip it. He kissed Shane's cheek.

"You look different," he said after kissing her, his face now smooth and cool from shaving.

She shook her head, not sure how to answer this, why she should look different, why, after making love, this good-bye should seem oddly formal. She let go of his hand and watched his car turn the corner and disappear in the morning traffic.

In his more lucid moments, when the fever ebbs in its cycle of intense heat moving into teeth-chattering chills, Lewis is aware of where he is. All the refugees, even those who were maimed, are gone. They must presume him dead or as good as dead. Without Kofi, his only hope is to be discovered or to ride out this fever and get up one day and follow the deep ruts of military vehicles. Each evening when the sun relents, he crawls to the river and drinks the stagnant poison that seeps there. His hunger has passed into something beyond simple hunger, a weakness and passivity. He falls back against the trunk of the tree, and it looms over him as if to whisper, *The world will have its way with you.* Its branches darken and seem to shake. *And if you let it, it will destroy you and remake you into something more willing to fight for itself.*

People have begun using the road again, passing with great loads on their heads. Women with children strapped to their backs walk by slowly, rarely giving him more than a curious glance. With each passing footfall, he asks himself where a sense of meaning comes from in a life like that—that endless routine of carrying the stuff of survival on your head to the market, bearing eight children. Or what life is like for that old man, who was once a young goatherd, who now leans on his staff, following the ten thousandth generation of goats? Was he ever tempted to throw down his staff and make a mad run for the bush? Lewis looks back up at the tree arching over him, at the splinters of sky exposed there. What about his own life? Did his father or grandfather ever stop at some quiet moment, in an empty house or in the alley taking out the garbage, look up at a star-washed sky and yearn for his soul to take flight?

In his wildest hallucinations he has become the tree. He can feel it growing into him, the vines taking root in his chest, invading everything. He raises his arms like the branches and stretches till he can see over the canopy of the forest. In the distance, he can see the silver form of the plane stranded on the narrow strip of runway.

After three days, he has given up hope that Kofi will return. He senses a critical threshold approaching, a final opportunity. This bout of fever is subsiding like the last, and when it does, he will have to move or the next assault will surely kill him.

———

Kofi sits to a meal of yams dug from the ground with his own hands. There is nothing to adorn them, just the simple thing, baked in a fire so it can be eaten. No matter how he tries, he cannot avoid the man he wounded, the boss, whose name is Mr. Bokasa. His protector, Bokele, whispers a prayer for the food. Kofi knows that he cannot stay indefinitely. Eventually, Mr. Bokasa will find an excuse to take revenge, beat him, or run him off. It is a hard refuge he has found, and though in the immediate storm any refuge is tempting, somewhere in the far south, in the city, he has an uncle who would take him in if he could only cross the roadblocks and checkpoints that now divide the country.

Mr. Bokasa stands up from the table. *"Get up."*

"Yes, sir." The chair nearly tumbles over as Kofi pushes it back.

He has Kofi work by lantern light, peeling and preparing a mountain of raw cassava with a short knife. The boy hacks each tuber with the knife to peel it and then passes it onto the pile, which smells sweetly of cyanide and clay. By the time he blows out the lantern, everyone else has been sleeping for hours. He walks, exhausted, to the shed where Mr. Bokasa has given him a bed.

On the way he passes the kitchen. The door has been left open, and it rocks back and forth in the breeze, banging against the jamb. He goes over to shut it, first peering into the room. Food has been left out on the table, not just sweet potatoes but packaged goods: flour and honey. Next to them, hanging from the back of a chair, is a bag. All he would have to do is slip in quietly, bag the food and run off. He could get a long way before light, which is still a few hours away. Somewhere in the house, Mr. Bokasa is snoring.

It's an obvious trap—but he is tempted. If he is quick enough he might just get away with it. He tests the screen door with his hand; it is not latched, but the dog could be anywhere. He decides to walk around the house to find out where it is. Quietly he shuts the screen and leaves the door as he found it. He completes a circle of the house without encountering the beast. It must be sleeping with Mr. Bokasa tonight.

He comes back to the screen door. Mr. Bokasa must have rolled over, or Bokele pushed him in his sleep, because he is quiet now. Kofi listens for the dog, perhaps his nails tapping on the wooden floor as he trots from one room to another, but it, too, is still. Kofi slips in through the screen. He leaves the door open so it will continue to bang lightly in the wind, and he tiptoes silently across to the table.

He lays his hand on the tomatoes, which look redder than blood in the dim light that spills through the kitchen window. He pulls a chair out, slowly so that it makes only the faintest sound, which must surely be covered by the softly banging door, and he sits down and stares at the food, trying to decide what to do. In the corner he notices the medicine cabinet with its colored bottles, liquids and pills. It is locked tight, and he could not possibly jimmy it open without waking the whole house. He should just take the food and make a run for it, quickly, while there is still a chance.

He digs in his pants for the wallet and the passport that he has kept hidden from Mr. Bokasa. He lays them on the table and flips the wallet open. The picture of Helen slips out, and he picks it up, staring at the strange white woman. She seems angry, and he is afraid of the photograph. He tucks it back in behind the picture of Shane. He carefully studies Shane's blond hair, the painted white wall behind him and the furniture, the details of a different world. He takes the driver's license out and tucks that into his back pocket. He hears the dog behind him too late. It walks up to his leg without barking and sniffs. He feels its hot breath on his bare calf. Kofi does not look down, and after a minute the dog walks away and goes to the door. It scratches at the screen. Kofi puts the wallet and passport back into his pocket and is just about to sneak over to let the dog out when he feels Mr. Bokasa's knife against the back of his neck.

"What are you doing here?"

Kofi doesn't answer.

"You are trying to steal my food."

Kofi shakes his head. *"I want to trade."*

"Trade? For the food you were going to steal?"

"No. For medicine."

Mr. Bokasa turns him, still holding the knife. He looks into his eyes. *"What do you have to trade? Eh, boy?"* He laughs quietly. He doesn't want to wake Bokele.

Kofi doesn't say. He stares back, and Mr. Bokasa can tell that there actually is something. He is intrigued.

"First let me see if you have the medicine."

"For what?"

"Malaria."

Mr. Bokassa studies him. *"Not for you?"*

Kofi doesn't answer.

Mr. Bokasa waves his knife at him. *"You stay there."*

He goes to a closet next to the cabinet and shuts the door behind him. In a moment he reappears with a key. He holds it up for Kofi to see, as though there were some magic or power in the key that the boy should respect. Then he goes to the cabinet and unlocks it. He takes out bottles of pills, holding them up to find enough light to read the labels. Finally he brings the right medicine and sets it on the table.

"What are you trading? Give it to me. Be quiet or I will kill you now. Bokele does not like a thief."

Kofi takes out Lewis's wallet and passport. *"I will trade this."*

He holds them out, and Mr. Bokasa suddenly grabs his hand. He takes them.

"What good are these to me?"

Kofi stares back at him defiantly. He knows as well as this man that these are valuable things. The passport would be easy to sell. It's an uneven trade.

"I will catch you, and before you can say a word, I will kill you for stealing this medicine."

He lets go of Kofi's hand and pushes the bottle of Mefloquine across the table. Kofi grabs it and runs. Before the door slams shut he hears cabinet glass breaking, and a moment later the dog barking and Mr. Bokasa yelling, *"Thief! Thief!"*

Kofi runs until his legs give out. Then he crawls into the bush and waits for light.

Helen's mother sounds as if nothing is wrong, though her voice is thin and distant over this post office phone so ancient that it belongs in a museum.

"Miriam is an idiot."

"She's not there, is she, Mom?"

"No. She's out. You were only going to be gone a few days, Helen."

Helen looks out the window at the impossibly unfamiliar scene, the dirt roads and the white buildings with their wainscoating of red mud from the rains, the crowds of people and their burdens. It's a place she's certain her mother could never imagine.

"We've had to go up river, Mom, to get closer."

"How is Shane?"

"He's fine. He keeps telling me how close his dad is."

Shane is building a fortress in the dirt of a planter just outside the door of the phone booth. She wishes her mother could see him. She might worry less. He looks as content as he ever has, happy to let the days drift by.

"Helen?"

"Yes."

"What if Lewis is not alive?"

"I don't know, Mom."

"You can't go through the whole jungle looking for him."

"No." Helen watches a spider slide down the dusty window by her booth. "If we don't hear anything in a few more days, I'll come home. I promise."

She hangs up. She gets Shane, and they walk down to the river. Her stomach feels empty, tired of the food, and she is weary of the bed she has been sleeping in. Three days and they still have heard nothing, other than that it is suicide to try to pass the government roadblock. Refugees trickled in for a while, and then that stopped. Malik and Ian go out to find someone who may know something more, "an unofficial source," says Ian, but no one has seen or heard anything of a white man. There may be nothing to do but wait; the news may have to come to them.

The riverbank is strangled with hyacinth. Helen sits on the roots of a tall tree and watches Shane throw rocks as far as he can. He listens carefully for each *ker-thunk* of the landing.

"I think Dad is swimming in this river." He throws another rock, but it lands in such a tangle of weeds that it does not sink. "I can't swim."

"No. Someday, maybe." Helen lays a hand on his shoulder, but he shrugs it off.

"I don't want to go home yet," he says.

As she helps him get ready for bed, he still seems worried. It's easy to see it in his face. Perhaps because he is a child or because of his blindness, he does not consider hiding his expressions, and it disturbs Helen to be aware of these emotions she might not normally be meant to see. She tucks the mosquito netting under his mattress as if she were carefully wrapping a package. "Don't lie awake worrying," she says. "We'll decide this tomorrow."

She goes outside to sit in the small, dilapidated courtyard, where she can still see their door and window. Lizards curl in the shadows, and legions of bugs are drawn to the bare bulb that hangs under the eve. She looks straight up at the sky, at the stars and the brightly lit moths that dance before them. *What am I doing here?* she thinks. In the distance, through the trees, she hears a night bird calling. It does not repeat like most bird-calls, but changes with each new vocalization, and it sounds somehow desperate, as if it is trying to chase the night away, to bring an early day. She wonders if it will it be enough to know that she has come to the end of the line, that she has gone as far as she can go. She passes her hand through the soupy air, swinging at a mosquito, which dodges her in a drunken, heat-syruped dive for the ground.

She is accustomed to her memories coming when they are summoned. She feels in this a critical sense of self-control, that these remembrances do not ambush her, suddenly looming when she turns a certain corner of her thoughts unprepared. But there is another kind of memory that she cannot control, that dwells in her unconscious mind at some constant, higher level of priority, barely submerged like the sleeping rocks of a river's cataracts. Encountering one of these memories is like finding home in the middle of a nightmare; yet it can unfasten the reality of the present moment, laying claim to a more significant precedence. In this chair, this night, in a place where nothing smells familiar, with evening wandering as if lost in the thick currents of air, there is no anchor for her thoughts to protect her from such usurpings. They become more vivid than the present.

"You are going to be late," She said quietly to Lewis, who was holding on to his pillow as if it were a life preserver. The morning sun was already burning away the frost on the windowsill.

"No."

"No?"

He rolled onto his back and stretched his arms to the headboard. "I can't go in. I'm going to tell them I'm sick."

She sat next to him on the bed. "What are you going to have?"

He looked at her, as if seriously considering it, taking stock of his ills. "Consumption."

"You mean tuberculosis?" she said, enjoying the joke.

"No, more old-fashioned. Like I need to spend my winters in a warmer climate, like Lisbon or Athens. In my case, I think it's some kind of brain-consumption."

Helen dumped a pillow on his face. "Yeah, well, I have to get Shane off to school."

Before she could get up, he took her hand and sat up without letting it go. "I can do that."

She looked down at his hand. "So this disease is not *that* debilitating. You can drive."

"Oh it's debilitating, definitely, but I can drive. Yeah, no problem."

"You really aren't going to work?"

"Nope. Not today."

Helen watched him help Shane into the mini-van and buckle his seat belt. He started down the driveway and then remembered his coffee on the roof, which had managed to stay perched there. He had to stop and lean half out of the window to reach it.

"Do you know where you're going?"

He made a face at her.

The house seemed oddly lit when she went back inside, as if the sun were suddenly coming from a completely different and impossible angle. She took her coffee outside. The quiet of the morning distracted her as she tried to read a novel. When Lewis came in through the gate, he looked like a boy up to some kind of mischief. He contemplated his surroundings like someone who had just walked off a plane in a foreign country.

"So this is what I am missing every day."

"This is it."

"It's beautiful."

He walked over and sat by her at the small outdoor table under an elm tree. The trunk was more than two feet thick, and the branches reached over most of the yard, encompassing everything in their sheltering embrace.

Lewis exhaled.

"Is something wrong?" Helen asked.

"No. Nothing." He shook his head. "I'm not going to call."

She didn't respond, but he felt the need to explain.

"I can't face it," he said melodramatically with a grin.

She laughed. "You're safe here."

"Yep," he said, looking up at the sky. "This is where I want to be. It feels easy."

"What does?"

"Life." He gestured with his hand as if it were an element making up the very air. *Love,* she thought.

Lewis stayed home a week. He took Shane to school and he brought him home, carrying him in on his shoulders. He waited when she had work to do, sitting in the yard without reading, or slept—he slept a lot—and he took her to lunch when she was done. And though the memory reverberates now in her mind, she cannot remember how it ended—what happened when the day came when he returned to his work and their routine. Or how they drifted apart again after that. She sits up in her chair, a little nauseated, as if the wandering of her thoughts has produced a kind of motion sickness.

"Madame, you should go inside." She hears the voice and turns. Malik is standing behind her, hands in the pockets of the wool suit he wears regardless of the heat, his face calm and quiet.

"I will, soon."

"You were thinking?"

"It is hard to know what to do."

Malik sits down next to her. "We may not be able to find him. Perhaps it is not possible this way."

She looks at Malik. It's the first time he has expressed any doubts.

"I was in Rwanda in 1994. I don't think I've told you this. I was a teacher there. I ran when everyone had to run. I was lucky I heard them calling up the attacks on the radio early."

Helen looks at his eyes. There is no fear there, no sadness, nothing to suggest that the experience of that terrible genocide was any more real for him than it was for her, reading about it in the newspaper. He seems to view his own experience from a distance.

"I was a suspect because I am Congolese, a spy. In one village my friend's uncle was very angry; he threatened me and wouldn't let us stay. He wouldn't trust his own nephew. I only wanted to get away to Tanzania. And I could see it. Just there, that hill." He gestures with his hand at the night as if the hill were there now. "But sometimes you must wait. If I had run, if I had not been patient, I would have been killed. I waited three and a half months." He sits down next to her. "You cannot always have what you simply must have."

Helen takes a deep breath. "Why are you helping me?"

He shrugs and looks away.

"You have a business."

"A business is not always so good, you know, Madame. A man is lucky to make a little. And then I have my wife's family. They think I have more money than I do. They think I am cheating them by hiding it. Or they worry that I have got it by witchcraft. Then they think I should sell my car to buy something for them. I am happy to be away for a little while."

Helen straightens up. "Do you think I'm wasting my time?" she asks.

He looks at her, amused by this thought. "How do you waste time?"

NKISI—LE REMÈDE—MEDICINE

SHANE DREAMS OF HIS father swimming. Overpowering everything is the sound of rushing water, a deafening roar that shakes against his eyelids. He hears his father gasping for breath, arms pulling frantically in that tumult of hissing serpents and thundering birds. But the current is powerful and he is getting weaker. Rocks loom beneath the surface like shadows, holes in his vision. And then he gives in and turns his feet down the current, his arms over his head like broken wings.

"See my magic," Shane says. He holds his hands out as if conjuring something in the air, as if he sees lights there, some flicker of nerves he interprets as magic.

"Of course I can see the magic," is his father's only answer. "Watch for the rocks! Take my hand."

Shane wakes without knowing if his father has survived—if he swam to the shore and pulled himself onto the dry, air-drenched rocks and remembered how to breathe again, heaved the brown water from his lungs. Shane cannot sleep, and after he lies there awhile, awake as day, he yells for his mother. And Helen lightly caresses his face until he falls asleep again.

———

When Kofi finds Lewis again, it is late. The evening sun is beginning to cool. He was worried that Lewis would not be there or that he would already be dead, and then he would wish he had stolen the food instead. He sets the vial of medicine next to Lewis, and the sound of the cap snapping open rouses him. He is too weak to react to the return of his savior. He closes his eyes, takes a breath and then opens them.

"For me? *Pour moi?*"

Kofi looks down at Lewis's lifeless face. *"Oui."*

"Pourquoi?"

Kofi does not answer. He has maybe four or five of the capsules in his hand. They are old, and some of them have been fused together by humidity. Kofi believes that Lewis will know what to do with them, and he puts them in his hands, which are trembling so much that Kofi has to tighten Lewis's fist over the pills to keep him from losing them.

Lewis looks at the bottle, but the instructions have been mostly worn off, and in any case, what little he can make out is in French. He looks at the pills and decides that Kofi's guess is as good as his.

"Water?"

Kofi returns with a leafful, and Lewis takes the pills. He falls back against the tree, feeling the water spread into his limbs and the bitter, poisonous taste of the medicine on his tongue. Kofi sits and watches him as if he expects the medicine to begin working immediately. Lewis closes his eyes, waiting for the signs of poisoning; but the drug seeps into his blood without obvious effects, and the sun reddens and quits.

Lewis doesn't wake until the morning light crosses his eyes. Kofi is standing over him. He waits while Lewis eats a few charred pieces of yam he has found in an old fire ring.

"*Ebongi tokende,*" he says in Lingala, then tries French. "*Allons-y.*" He makes a sign to leave.

Lewis stands for the first time in almost a week. Dizziness nearly puts him back on his knees, and he has to reach for the tree to support himself. When he feels steady enough to stand on his own, he checks to make sure he has his wallet and passport. Kofi notices him find the empty pocket. He points to the medicine, and tries to sign that he made a trade. It takes Lewis a moment to understand, and before he can respond, Kofi turns from him.

"*Ebongi tokende,*" Kofi insists, and starts walking without looking back. Lewis pushes himself away from the warm trunk of the great tree. He has more strength than he thought, enough at least to follow.

They walk for three hours before stopping. The red road runs virtually straight to the horizon, where it ends like a gun sight notched in the forest. In the enormity of this scale, each step seems a futile and ridiculous act of faith. Kofi hands him two more of the pills to swallow, and Lewis takes them, still sure that he will soon die of either an overdose or the disease. He follows Kofi's feet in the mud rather than looking up at the pale sky or the unnerving swath of the road. His feet slip without throwing him off balance. There is something perfectly relaxed in his posture, like a palm tree in a great wind.

"I must sit," Lewis gasps.

Lewis collapses in mud, and Kofi moves off the track and sits in the coarse grass. He keeps a careful eye on the road so that they will not be surprised by a military convoy.

The forest is oddly silent here, or relatively so, compared to the cacophony he was accustomed to in the uncharted tangle of it. The monkeys scramble into the bush ahead of them, and the birds fall mute as they pass. Only the hum of the insects is unaffected. Why *has* Kofi come back for him? It is obviously dangerous for him to be on this road, and he had to stop frequently to allow Lewis to catch up. He shares the little bit of water he can carry, and they have no food, so he will have to beg for two.

"*Pourquoi?* Why?"

Kofi turns to him with a stern gaze that is mature beyond his years. Whether he understands the question or not, the answer is the same, something that is either too complicated or too obvious to put into sign language. Lewis is suddenly humbled and amazed that this young child is his rescuer. At home he might have leafed past an ad with the photograph of a boy like Kofi, something for an international relief organization, and his thought would have been that it is the boy who needs to be rescued.

"Thank you. *Merci.*"

Kofi looks at him, puzzled.

"For rescuing me. For coming back for me."

Kofi smiles, though he cannot understand more than the tone of it.

"For the medicine." Lewis points at the small bag Kofi carries with his walking stick. "*Merci.*"

Kofi nods, and then he stands up. He reaches a hand out to help Lewis stand. His arm is strong, but Lewis is heavy, and Kofi can feel how weak the fever has made him.

After a few hours they turn off the main road, onto a track

that has seen much more foot traffic than trucks or tanks. It meanders down a gentle slope as if made by someone who was daydreaming. Lewis thinks he hears the distant murmur of a village and the crying of a child.

The younger children run out to meet the white stranger, shouting with anticipation until they are close enough to see his ragged clothes, his haggard face. They have never seen a white man like this, and they fall silent and back off. Kofi approaches a woman who is pounding *fufu*. She has a long pole to knead the dough, which a young child turns over with nimble fingers between downward strokes. The woman stops when she sees the white man, and the child looks up with wide eyes.

Lewis tries to follow the conversation from the responses of the woman. She is not happy to see them. The children watch from a distance as Kofi pleads with her; she points down the road, and Lewis begins to assume that they will have to leave. As the two talk it over, more women show up from the nearby huts, and an old man hobbles out to join them. He yells at Kofi and threatens him with a club. But Kofi stands his ground, saying something and pointing to Lewis. The old man shouts some kind of challenge, and he looks at Lewis as if assessing him, doubting the assertions that have been made. The children hide now, as if they expect some kind of bad magic. Something about the village is not quite right; it's more than its ruined huts, more than the absence of young men; it's something in the way the huts themselves stare out at them. The old man waves his club bravely at Lewis and directs a few words to the general gathering, and then he stiffly walks away.

The woman goes back to her work, and except for the children, the village ignores them. Kofi sits down near a pen that might have once held goats or pigs, but now the fence is falling down. Lewis sits next to him, glad to feel earth beneath him.

Kofi offers him water from the clear plastic jug that he carries. Only a couple of swallows are left, and Lewis uses the tepid, muddy water to wash two more of the pills down. Across the wide path that weaves among the huts, a young woman eats her dinner. She whispers something to a boy of about four, who brings a wooden bowl to Lewis and Kofi and runs away as quickly as he can. He parades this act of bravery in front of the other children, his small chest thrust outward.

Lewis eats greedily with his hands. He is grateful to be done walking, grateful for the food and even the musty water. Exhaustion and the minor improvement in his health have produced a sense of satisfaction.

The young woman finishes eating. She drinks something, and then sits back against the slender pole that supports an overhang on the front of the earthen house. She stares steadily at Lewis, rarely lifting her gaze, as though he must represent some inscrutable truth. Or maybe it's just that he is a break in the routine, and she is still young enough to be curious, like the children who steal between the huts to get a glimpse of him and then run away.

Kofi eats his food slowly and then gets up without explanation and goes off into the village. The sun has dipped into the trees, and the shadows are getting heavy. The woman has barely moved; her body is so relaxed that she looks as if she might melt into the red clay. There is nothing to take her away, no chore or duty to occupy or worry her, just the easy experience of time and whatever her thoughts might be as dusk gathers its heavy robe. She is dressed in a wraparound skirt and a light-colored thin shirt. She must be nineteen or twenty. He can see the brightness of her eyes even from across the path.

She lifts her hands from the dirt and brushes them off as if she might get up, but instead she tucks her bare feet under her and rests her hands in her lap. She has a calm, open face, and a softness to her jaw and heavy lips that unnerves him. He has the ridiculous thought that if she were in Europe or America she would be discovered and paid for her beauty. He would even like to photograph her. Then that feels insulting and stupid, and he is left with the plain fact that he is aroused.

She lies down where she is, on a woven grass mat. He watches her without looking away, the frankness of their visual exchange muted by the faltering light. He can almost hear her breathing, urging him to cross over to her, to lay his hand on her arm or slip it under the shirt to her breast, to let her legs wrap around him and pull him down. He forces his eyes closed to stop these thoughts, and in that darkness the vision is different. This could be Helen. It sounds like her, he can believe that it smells like her, and there is a madness in him that is willing to insist on it. His heart panics. *Touch her. Let her save you. Let her lift you out of this nightmare.*

It's reassuring to hear a child begin crying again. He abruptly opens his eyes to an approaching light. He sees Kofi, or recognizes his form, next to an old woman who is carrying a kerosene lantern. The young woman across the road quickly gets up and disappears through the door of her house. The old woman chatters in a raspy voice to Kofi as they approach, and with every step the child, off somewhere in an unknown part of the village, seems to scream louder.

The woman laughs when she gets near enough to see Lewis, as if she has caught him at something he should be ashamed of. She holds the light close to his face. Her body has a strong, disturbing smell to it. He is relieved when she moves away.

Kofi shows her the bottle of pills, and without hesitation she pours them into her hands and then licks from her fingers the fine white dust. She puts the pills back with contempt and hands the bottle to Kofi. Lewis notices for the first time that Kofi seems afraid of her, though she is so physically frail that the boy could probably kill her with the slightest blow from his stick. She motions for Lewis to stand up, and he follows as she leads them through the village.

Kofi turns when she is a few steps ahead and whispers a warning to him—"*Ndoki*"—and points at her staff.

A few people are still out, and in a couple of candlelit stalls soap and biscuits are being sold. Several older men lean easily in the shadows, drinking palm wine. The fermented sweetness hangs in the weak breeze. Lewis and Kofi continue to follow the old woman through a section of the village that was burned. It is so dark that Lewis knows that if he were to lose sight of her, he would have to wait for the sunrise to find his way. The shadows of the charred frames and collapsed walls of the huts dance with the swing of the lantern; and without anything else to see, the smells become stronger—burned thatching soaked by rain and already molding, the dung of animals or their remains and the rancid smell of human garbage, mixed with other strong and frightening smells that he cannot identify. Lewis stumbles over something that is vaguely soft and heavy, and then to keep from falling again he lays a hand on Kofi's shoulder and lets him lead, closing his own eyes to avoid the mad gamboling of the shadows.

Finally they come to the woman's hut. She lays two mats on the dirt floor and then retires to her own bed, which is made of piles of old clothes and looks more like a nest. From across the room Lewis sees her eyes, still open. She is looking directly at him. Kofi lies down on his mat next to Lewis.

"*Kotala ndoki te, ti tongo,*" Kofi whispers in Lingala.

"What?"

"*Ne regardez pas la sorcière avant qu'il fait jour.*" Don't look at the witch, not until it's light.

Kofi looks away from the old woman and covers his eyes. "*Ndoki.*" Witch.

NDOKI—LA SORCIÈRE—SORCERESS

"IT'S NOT A STORY, more like an AP bulletin, but I can tell you what I've been able to find out."

Helen lays her hands in her lap a little formally to receive the news from Ian. It's late in the evening; the bar is empty except for the three of them. A breeze wanders through the room, making it some fraction of a degree cooler than it was, just enough to offer some respite. Her hair is pulled up so the breeze can cool her neck. Malik leans forward in his chair as though he's anticipating something big.

"The plane landed on a strip less than seventy kilometers from here, barely inside the area controlled by the rebels. It's surrounded by mostly virgin jungle; actually, it's supposed to be a wildlife reserve. They built the runway for one of Mobutu's ministers who came up once for a ribbon cutting ceremony— supposedly to encourage a little eco-tourism, a nod to the environmentalists in Europe to distract from the real logging and mining rape-and-pillage story. Anyway, the point is, it's on the other side of the government roadblock, which has effectively become a border. Nobody is getting out across those roadblocks, though thousands of refugees are piling up trying. It's pretty grim. They have no food for these people, who have already been hiding and starving in the forest for months. The government accuses them of collaborating with the rebels, and will probably let them starve or try to chase them back into the bush."

Helen looks out the window to avoid his eyes. "They'd let you go the other way. Cross into the rebel area, I mean, right?"

"They might. But who knows if you'd get back."

Helen stands up. "Malik, you'll take me there? At least to the roadblock?"

He wants to say no, but instead he says yes.

Ian sits back in his chair. "Perhaps you don't take this seriously enough, Helen."

"I believe I do."

"What if you do get across? How are you going to get seventy kilometers to that airstrip, and why, besides? That's the one place we know he isn't." Ian pauses. He looks at Malik for some help. "Unless he's not alive. You can't hire a vehicle to take you because the rebels will commandeer it. Are you and Shane going to walk?"

Helen is still standing, rigid and pale. She remembers what Malik said about walking, what she must do for love.

"We came all the way upriver, but he's not here and no one has heard even a rumor of him. This is the end of the trail. You can search forever and not find him. Or you can wait here forever to see if he'll just show up." Ian stops. He's said enough. His voice softens. "But I can't. The boat is scheduled to leave for the capital on Friday. It may be the last one out for a while."

Ian gets up and wanders to the bar to get another warm beer. Helen sits back down. Until now it has been a matter of principle that she can do what is needed to find Lewis. The idea that there is no such thing as "can't" has kept her going. On some level she still believes what her mother told her when she was in kindergarten, that she can do anything—as if she herself would be the only obstacle life would offer. Now she may have to leave, not only without Lewis but also without any more to tell Shane than what she could have learned if they had stayed in Spokane.

"Malik, if you will take me, at least I will have gone as far as I can go. There is still the chance that he could have somehow made it as far as the roadblock, or that maybe somebody there has seen him or heard about him."

Malik lifts his hands as if to shrug it off as a fated thing, the will of God. "Of course."

———

Lewis opens his eyes. The *ndoki*'s body is still. She must be asleep, though her breathing is raspy and uneven. Kofi is sleeping with his back to her, one hand laid palm outward over his eyes, as if he is protecting himself. Lewis remembers his warning and starts to look away from the woman, but then he thinks he can see, just faintly, a light hovering over her. It is so elusive that just as he is convinced he isn't seeing it, her body convulses and the form seems to rise from her and rushes out through the loose thatching of the ceiling.

He quickly closes his eyes and the blankness is reassuring. It should be a place that belongs solely to him, safe from this phantasm, but then that faint light invades even this sanctuary. Whether this is a nightmare or a waking hallucination, a trick of his eyes or a betrayal of his imagination, he is seized by it like a small animal trembling in a predator's mouth. The light shifts and changes, and when it is close enough, Lewis can see that it is the *ndoki,* though she appears to him as a young woman with wildly braided black hair. She is charging at him on the back of a leopard. He is surprised that he has not tried to run. The leopard's breath is hot and damp. It opens its mouth around his leg and though it does not bite him, he feels its teeth against his skin.

She seems out of breath. Her chest rises and falls, and he cannot look into her eyes. By the force of her will he climbs onto the leopard behind her and holds on by her waist as the cat takes two bounds and is then suddenly flying over the jungle. The night sky is bright with stars, and he finds himself exhilarated. The witch's hips shift, and she turns to him. Her mouth is wet and red, but when he looks into her eyes, they do not belong to the young woman. They glower back at him ravenously. Below them is a gathering of some kind, an unnatural light in a clearing. The leopard drops down to land so fast it's like falling, and Lewis prepares to hit the ground. He opens his mouth to scream, but his voice is impotent.

Then the *ndoki* takes his hand, crawling with him under a tangle of wet, twisted roots. The ground is dank and slick with mold and algae. With hands like an animal's claws she holds his ass and draws him in. Inside her he can feel something, a snake curling around his penis, scratching him with its poisonous fangs. He hears laughter—not hers, but that of a great crowd of people, an audience. And then, drowning everything else out, there is the child, crying.

IN THE MORNING, the *ndoki* is gone. The hut smells of burned hair. It takes Lewis some time to recognize the source of it. Just outside the small, dank room there is a fire; the breeze occasionally ushers a puff of smoke into the room. Next to the fire is the body of a monkey, its hair matted with blood. Its hand lies close to the flames and must be the source of the smell.

Kofi is up already, sitting on his mat and watching Lewis wake. He raises a hand to his mouth to silence Lewis. He seems very tense and alert. Lewis looks back to the fire. He can see only the old woman's back as she picks up the small monkey and lays it whole in the coals of the fire. The flames leap up, consuming the hair, then smolder down into a sour, pinguid smoke.

Lewis signals to Kofi, silently asking if he will eat the monkey. Kofi raises his eyebrows and nods. The *ndoki* pokes her head in the doorway, and she says something and points to the monkey roasting on the fire. Lewis turns away from her face, revolted by his dream and terrified to connect with her glance. He follows Kofi out of the hut, and they sit close to the fire and wait for the meal.

The scene around him will not conform to anything remotely realistic. The entire area has been burned, the huts are skeletons of framing and charred clay brick, roofless and bare to the sky. The trees are black and twisted, as if contorted while trying to flee in the final moments of the conflagration. The gray sky is low and close, like the tight, wet air. He struggles to insist that this is merely the transformation of a normal world by fire.

When the monkey is cooked, Kofi eats his share. Lewis cannot touch the meat. He is too disturbed by the almost human hands and feet left in the flames. The *ndoki* seems amused by his reluctance. Over them a tree hangs low with sticky white flowers. Lewis realizes that they are the source of the awful sulfurous smell, the sappy blossoms of a canthium tree. The *ndoki* holds her staff in her weathered hand and chews the last of the monkey.

Malik tells Helen it isn't a good day to go to the roadblock. His reasons seem vague, and Helen cannot make sense of what he is telling her. She senses that even her good friend is now stalling. Shane has been antsy the last couple of days. He lifts her arm and climbs into her lap, and she catches herself feeling irritated by his fidgeting. She lays her hand gently on his shoulder to calm him down.

"Where's Ian, Malik?" Normally he would be sitting at the bar having his late breakfast beer, making notes in his journal and swatting languorously at the burgeoning fly population.

"He went for a walk this morning." Malik avoids her eyes.

"A walk?" She senses something amiss.

"Madame. I did not wish to bother you."

"Bother me? What's going on, Malik?"

"Ian went to the roadblock."

"Oh, good."

"Not good. There is a problem."

"What's wrong?"

"The soldiers are detaining him."

"Detaining him?"

"They have him at the school where they have set up their headquarters. They have hurt him a little, but I think he will be okay."

"Damn it." Helen lifts Shane from her lap and stands up.

"Where are you going, Madame?"

"To get him out."

"No."

She looks at him, puzzled.

"It will only make it worse. It will cost more money," he says.

"I don't care about the money."

"Of course not, Madame. But the soldiers do. If we go now, they will only send us away and beat him more. We must wait."

"Malik? How can this be?"

"He has a big mouth, your friend."

Helen sits down, but then stands again. "How does it work Malik?"

"Tomorrow I will go there and tell them I have no money but will offer them a little. They will tell me he is a spy, that it doesn't matter about the money, and they are going to shoot him."

Helen presses her hands over Shane's ears, but he pushes them away.

"Shoot who, Mom? Ian?"

"No. No, Shane, they won't really shoot him."

"Then maybe Friday, I can go back and offer a little more. If I have enough, they will let me have him. They will be bored, and they will want their money."

"What about the boat? It won't really leave on Friday, right?"

"You see, Madame, sometimes the schedule works in your favor."

Helen smirks and turns away from Malik. "Shane, let's go for a walk."

"Where will you go?" Malik asks.

"I don't know—nowhere." She takes Shane's hand. "Don't worry, Malik, we'll just go down to the river."

As THEY FOLLOW THE long trail upstream, Shane is restless, and he hangs on her hand. After half a mile a large clan of red monkeys runs across their path. They shriek and throw things at one another and then scramble up the fat trunk of a tree. Shane stops to listen, smiling at the noise. Then the monkeys become quiet, and Shane turns his head, hearing each one settle in its spot. Suddenly there's an especially loud scream as one of the monkeys makes a surprise attack on another. It is part of the play, but the second monkey loses its grip. It grasps desperately but cannot catch a strong enough branch, and it falls perhaps thirty feet to the hard-packed dirt path right in front of them.

Shane frees his hand from his mother's before she can react and hurries to where he heard the animal fall.

"Don't touch that monkey, Shane," Helen shouts as she tries to stop him, but she is too late. He has already laid his hand on the shoulder of the injured animal. The monkey is still breathing, but he seems to be unconscious.

"Let go of him, Shane. He may bite."

The frightened monkey makes a lurching move to escape, and Shane reacts by grabbing its leg. The monkey bites. Shane yells and lets go, and the animal scurries into the bush, where it thrashes around and after a while finally quiets and does not move.

"Shane, I told you not to. You have to listen to me. You have to."

Helen looks at his hand. The bite is dull and bruised, like a human bite except where the canines have punctured, but it is not bleeding. Shane is shaking, and he is not going to be consoled. She picks him up and heads back to the hotel, holding the hand in hers and cursing herself for her stubbornness, for pursuing this as far as she has. She can hear the reproach of all those who warned her it wasn't safe to bring Shane. She feels vain and stupid.

Shane is still crying when she passes a small group of huts, a family farmstead. The children run to the animal fence, which is made of heaps of dried thorny bushes. They stare at the

176 • MARCUS STEVENS

crying child in amazement, and then the mother begins to laugh at him, and the children join her, jumping up and down and pointing at him as he wails. Helen frowns at them, but it only serves to heighten the entertainment. They are not used to this kind of public display. What has this boy to cry about? Helen hurries on. If she could leave this very moment, she would. She would welcome a privileged helicopter sent by the American government to lift her above the heads of the trampled masses. She would do anything to be gone.

Malik helps them find a doctor, who cleans the injured hand. Since the doctor speaks mostly French, Malik translates as best he can the warnings about the myriad diseases Shane may have been exposed to—symptoms of fever and vomiting and rashes, convulsions, headaches, the whole gamut that she must watch for. His biggest concern is rabies, and he says they are lucky that he has the right medicine, hypodermics of thick, pink serum. He injects Shane's small hand and wraps it in white bandages that reassure and seem to heal with their very color.

"The boat will not be here for another couple of days," Malik tells her without her asking.

What the *ndoki* wants is Lewis's saliva. She spits in the dirt near her feet, and then indicates that he is to do the same into a wooden bowl she has given him. He is not to drink the concoction swimming there, though it smells of coconut milk and mango, palatable, even good.

He is reluctant to do it. He feels violated by this request for such an intimate part of himself. He looks to Kofi for an explanation or a way out, but Kofi expects him to do it. This must be their part of the deal, their payment for the meat and whatever else Kofi has arranged with the sorceress. He points to

Lewis's stomach and holds a fist in a way that seems to signify power. Lewis spits into the bowl. The *ndoki* grins. She indicates that he must do more. He spits until his mouth is dry and tentatively hands the bowl back to her. She takes it, and before Lewis can react she drinks the mixture, keeping her eyes fixed on him.

She takes something from the folds of her dress, a small bundle no bigger than a marble, on a twisted bit of string. She hangs it over Lewis's head, scratching the nape of his neck with her fingernails as she ties it on. He is unsure whether this is meant to heal or protect him. Then she gives him something in a small gourd, indicating that he is to drink it. He looks at Kofi again and takes a big swallow. Instantly his whole face is burning. He prays that he hasn't just been poisoned. The immediate effect, along with the smell of the dying fire and the charred remains of the monkey, is to make him only weaker and sicker. He stands abruptly as she moves away. He's going to leave now, with or without Kofi. He takes a few unsteady steps. But Kofi is waiting for something else from the *ndoki*. In her hand she has something Lewis assumes must be a root, twisted and black. She ties it up in a bundle with waxy leaves and Kofi takes it. As he gets up to leave, she addresses Lewis.

"*Sala keba na mai,*" she warns. Beware of the river. She touches her chest to indicate the talisman she has tied around his neck.

"What?" asks Lewis.

"*La rivière,*" the *ndoki* hisses.

MOTEMA MAKASI—LE COURAGE—HEART

LEWIS AND KOFI WALK with the sun at their back for the rest of the morning. About noon they hear an explosion not far ahead, then the brittle crackle of automatic weapons fire. They hide in the bush for an hour before continuing cautiously up the road. A mine has exploded, completely destroying one of the rebels' vehicles, and they've left it where it is, still hot from the fire, its tires melted and charred.

"*Nous l'approchons,*" Kofi signals. We are getting closer.

For the rest of the day they do not see or hear a living thing, beyond the aching hum of insects. The clouds in the sky are high and thin. Finally in the distance they hear a sound like a colony of birds, and after a while they come to a large gathering of refugees that marks one side of the roadblock. Kofi leaves Lewis at the outskirts to look for food, but he comes back with nothing. They sleep on the road with the rest and wait for morning.

Malik brings Helen coffee. He has gotten into the pleasant habit of bringing her a cup in the mornings. She's not sure where he finds it, but she has even gotten used to the UHT milk, though now the unfamiliar taste only serves to remind her how much she wishes to be home. Malik looks carefully at Shane's hand; the bandage is still bleached white, and he seems safe. Shane takes the mango Malik offers and eats it with his left hand, not bothered at all by the strings that lodge between his teeth or the juice dripping to the floor.

"How's Ian?"

"He's okay. He's not happy, but he has learned to keep his mouth shut."

"Did he tell them he was a reporter? Show credentials?"

"No. At least he is smarter than that. They might have killed him. Right now he is just a kid, one who smokes too much marijuana."

Helen turns away from him. "Shane, please don't get that bandage dirty. It has to last." She sighs and looks back at Malik. "Have you heard anything about the boat?"

"There are only rumors. Still the same. Are you packed?"

"Yes."

"I will see what I can find out about the boat."

Malik seems relieved to be going home, too, and he rushes off leaving the door slightly ajar. A gecko slips in through the crack and runs up the wall to find a corner to hide in. Helen watches and wonders what dangers this small reptile has just escaped and what sort of haven he has secured here. The parrots that are used to being fed in the courtyard make a racket outside the window, perturbed that no one has yet come down to eat and share breakfast. Out beyond the courtyard the traffic is already insufferable, and the reek of diesel rises with the heat from the pavement.

Helen looks down at her hands. She lays one over the other to keep them from trembling. She closes her eyes and sees her mother's yard, lightly covered with a spring snow. She reaches out to touch a pink-blossomed cherry tree, and a hundred red-winged blackbirds scatter, calling and spreading in the sky like words of black ink. It will be good to leave, to feel the thrust of the jet's engines lift her from this continent, where everything is a struggle, as if the very heat has brought the force of life to such a boil that all it can do is choke itself with competition for every scrap. Some snow and ice and silence will be a welcome relief—a world more stone than riot.

"I'm hungry, Mom."

"You just had a mango."

"I want real food."

"Real food?"

"Fruit Loops!" he announces, and Helen cannot help but smile.

"When we get home."

"But I don't want to go."

"It's time."

"No, Mom."

She is surprised. The way he's been acting, she had assumed the opposite. His expression is so earnest, it is easy to forget that he is just seven. He still gets mad, throws tantrums, but it is unusual that he doesn't want to leave. Any child wants to be home.

"Shane."

He walks over to her. She finds a cloth to wipe his face, and he braces for the job.

"It's time. We can't go any further. Your dad . . ." She stops. His face is open, waiting for anything, trusting her. "Your dad might have been hurt out there. I don't know. He may have . . ." She stops again. "It's a very dangerous place, and I don't want you to get hurt again. He won't be able to come home with us right now."

"Who will help him?"

She doesn't have the nerve to declare Lewis dead without proof, no matter how convincing the circumstances. "I don't know. We just have to wait and see, and we can wait at home."

Shane can read her tone; he can tell there is something more to it and that it is very serious.

"I keep dreaming about him."

"Oh?"

He squeezes her hand tight.

"Bad dreams."

She holds him and brushes his hair back from his face. If he could see her eyes, would it make it better or worse? Could he see her fear, or would he be reassured? Can he tell anyway, just from the way she holds him? She starts to pick him up.

"I can walk, Mom."

———

The roadblock seems completely arbitrary. There is no obvious logic to where it has been set up, but it creates a definite line. Where Lewis stands with Kofi, hundreds of refugees are camped along the swath cut in the forest by the road. On the other side, beyond the soldiers, there are only few people, and beyond that the road is empty. There are massive concrete barricades, which could not be easily moved. No one is traveling this way.

"Allons-y!"

Lewis looks at Kofi, confused.

Kofi tries sign language. He expects Lewis to lead. Perhaps they will let a white man through—a white man with the right attitude. Then Kofi takes something out of the waist of his pants, a small card and a sheet of paper. Lewis takes the card. It's his driver's license. It's a little worse for wear, but there is his picture, staring back at him from another life.

"You kept it."

Kofi hands Lewis the paper. It's a flyer, some kind of religious tract, on stationery from the Church of Christ Mission. It's in English. Lewis looks to Kofi, puzzled. Kofi is anxious and growing impatient; he indicates that Lewis should wave the paper at the soldiers.

"But this is just a religious pamphlet."

Kofi looks at him, desperately imploring him to understand.

"They won't be able to read it," Lewis argues. "It's English, not *français*." He looks again at the neatly typed paper. That's the point. "Okay."

He walks the hundred feet or so into the crowd, pressing for a way through. It seems impassable. "Shit."

"*Allons-y!*" Kofi insists. He pushes aggressively at the people in the back of the line, shouting at them in Lingala. At first they won't budge. But when they see Lewis, they grudgingly move aside. The further the two push into the crowd, the more yelling it takes and the more resistance they meet, until finally the people ahead won't move for anything.

"*Allons-y.*" Kofi begs Lewis this time. He's acting as if his life is at stake.

Lewis yells at the man in front of him. "Get out of my way."

Lewis shoves the man hard. He holds the paper up. "Let me through. Get the hell out of the way." The crowd begins to yield again. Kofi stays close behind Lewis.

"Move!" Lewis is surprised to find he has the strength to push and shove. They are almost through the crowd when he sees a white man just on the other side of the barrier. He's talking to the soldiers.

Lewis shouts, but the man does not hear him.

He pushes harder, but the people are pressed so tightly together that it is difficult for them to move even if they wish to. Lewis and Kofi shove themselves a few more yards forward. The man is still there.

"Hey!" Lewis raises himself above the crowd, waving his hands to get the man's attention, but there is too much noise. Lewis pushes with a growing sense of panic. When a small man in front of him digs in, Lewis hits him in the center of his back with his fist and pulls him out of the way. He gets a few feet closer. He is clawing his way through now, shouting, enraged. He looks again for the white man, but he can't see him.

"Hey! Get out of my way!"

He nearly starts a brawl. Suddenly a soldier forces the barrel of a gun into his chest and yells at the crowd. Lewis almost stops, but the instinct for survival has taken over. He moves as if he is going to hit the soldier in the face. He holds up the paper and driver's license as if they were diplomatic credentials.

"Put that fucking gun down! Let me through."

The soldier backs up behind the barricade, and the crowd has moved away from Lewis. He is in a no-man's land between the two sides.

He shakes the paper again. "I am a goddamn American ambassador. Now move the fuck out of my way, you motherfucker."

Two more soldiers rush over and point their weapons at him.

Lewis walks straight up to them as if the soldiers whose fingers are set to the trigger do not exist.

"Let me through." He shoves the paper into the hands of the closest soldier, who takes it and looks at it carefully. Now Lewis is afraid that the young man *will* be able read it. He might understand English, at least enough to know what it is. In a second the ruse will be up, but he tries not to lose his nerve, maintaining an attitude of disdain and impatience. Next to him Kofi stands with a proprietary air, like his personal aide de camp. If Lewis could see himself in a mirror it would be all over.

"*Restez ici.*" The soldier walks away, taking the paper and Lewis's driver's license with him. So he can't read it, but he's going to find someone who can. Lewis should never have gotten them out.

"Let me through." Lewis tries again, but the soldiers hold their ground.

In a moment the soldier returns with a superior.

"*Qui êtes vous?*" the sergeant demands.

"I don't speak *français. Non parler . . .*"

"*C'est quoi ce papier?*" He waves the paper at Lewis.

"Let me pass," Lewis says again, but he can tell that it isn't going to be that easy.

"*Qui êtes vous?*" the man insists again.

"I don't speak French." He points at the driver's license. He is losing some of the attitude. More soldiers have come. There are at least six weapons pointing at him now.

"American. . . . américain." He tries it as if it is some kind of password.

The sergeant hands back the paper and license and waves him away.

"*Personne ne peut passer.*"

"You have to let me through."

The sergeant turns and walks away. Lewis is defeated now. He stands in disbelief, half tempted to run for it but certain that these soldiers will fire at him on reflex.

"*Allons-y,*" Kofi says again, but even he has lost his conviction. Still Lewis stands his ground, defiantly holding his papers.

Then behind the soldiers he sees someone making his way over and hears shouting in French, and he can just make him out over the heads of the soldiers—the white man. He is speaking rapidly to the sergeant and gesturing at Lewis. Then he walks right past the sergeant and through the soldiers to the barricade. Suddenly Lewis realizes what he must look like, his filthy clothes in tatters, his beard and haggard face, a street beggar at best. No wonder the sergeant was not impressed.

"*Qui êtes vous?*" the man says quickly as the sergeant catches up with him.

"I'm American. I don't speak French."

"You are American? *Mon Dieu!* What are you doing here, huh?"

Lewis raises his hands and is about to answer, but the sergeant is now shouting at the Frenchman. The Frenchman shouts back and holds his passport in the seargent's face, making some kind of threat. The sergeant asks Lewis for his papers again. Lewis steps forward to hand them over. The sergeant then makes a show of studying them and hands them back. He nods.

"*Venez avec moi,*" the Frenchman says. "Quickly. Come now."

The soldiers have lowered their guns. Lewis begins to follow the Frenchman. Kofi follows, too. But as Lewis passes the first soldier, the man raises the butt of his rifle and knocks Kofi to his knees. Lewis turns to him. Kofi is gasping for air.

The Frenchman pulls on Lewis's arm. "Come, right now."

Kofi struggles to get up, but already the soldier is standing between him and Lewis. Lewis grabs at the soldier to get Kofi, and suddenly all of the rifles are up again.

"He's with me," Lewis says.

"Who is he?"

"I don't know, but . . ."

"Leave him, then. It is not your business."

The Frenchman pulls on his arm, and Lewis allows himself to be pulled another step away.

"These boys are everywhere, expecting favors," says the Frenchman.

Lewis hesitates.

"We must leave right now, before things change."

Lewis walks away. Behind the soldiers he sees Kofi stand up. They knock him down when he tries again to push by. And the last Lewis sees of him, he gets up stiffly, clearly hurt, and the soldiers push him back into the crowd.

"You look terrible."

Lewis looks at the white man blankly, stunned by the release from his ordeal. He sits in the front seat of the Frenchman's Land Cruiser, swallowed in its hot upholstered seat and the icy blast of air-conditioning. He is nearly delirious. A fly beats against the windshield, stupidly looking for an escape. Lewis closes his eyes. When he opens them and looks outside, he meets the eyes of a group of children who have gathered to stare at him. They peer through the window as close as they can physically get to it, pressing their hands against the warm metal of the vehicle. It might at first be possible to make the mistake that these poor children are merely begging, looking for some kind of rescue, a hand up, but then what he sees in their eyes is only curiosity.

"You need a beer, my friend." The Frenchman blows the horn and then pulls away out into the dirt road. "The town is not far from here, though the road is terrible. But they all are."

KOKENDE—RETIRANT—RETREAT

IAN LOOKS MORE ANGRY than hurt. The bruised cut on his face is healing with a rainbow of colors. It cost twenty thousand francs to get him out, much of the cash Helen had with her. Malik wanted to wait another day. He said they could have got him out for ten thousand, as if there were a market price for something like this and, like tourists, they paid too much.

Shane scoots across the seat of the cab. He stops in the middle, next to Helen. She presses his hand into hers to offer some comfort, but it's her hands that tremble. Shane squeezes it four times. *Do-you-love-me?* He has to make a couple of attempts before she gets it and answers with three squeezes: *Yes-I-do.* Then two: *How-much?* But Helen is distracted by a question from Malik.

"Straight to the boat? *Oui?*"

Helen looks directly ahead. Some part of her would go to the roadblock, just to look into the forest beyond it, just because they have come so far. But there is no question of that now. Shane squirms next to her, and she remembers her part, answering with a single tight, long squeeze of this hand. *I love you this much.* She looks at his injured hand, the white bandage, which is already filthy with the red dirt.

"Yes, Malik, *allons-y!*"

They drive through the dirt streets that lead like a maze to the river. When they get close to the boat they are jammed in traffic. Most everyone is on foot; men push carts, and women carry huge loads on their heads. The cab presses into the crowd, bumping into people but making little headway.

"What is it, Malik?"

"A lot of people are afraid of a fight."

"They don't trust the cease-fire?"

"You can never know how it will go. Besides, the government troops are terrible looters. They are afraid that before the pullout the soldiers may decide to take something for themselves."

Ian straightens up. "It's just a question of who will do the taking. That's why it makes so little difference. It's business."

"*Oui,* a business. Is not government always a business? Were you never arrested in America?"

"No."

"*Non?*"

"Okay, once, for pot."

"And you paid a fine, *non?* You gave them money to let you go."

"Yeah, but I got a receipt." Ian laughs.

"Oh well, yes. Good for you."

Helen looks out her window at all the people elbowing the glass of the cabs. Even though this simple cab isn't much, she feels insulated, already privileged. "I can't see how we're going to get through if we have to get out and walk. We have too much luggage."

"Don't worry, Madame." Malik opens the door to get out— he has to push people out of the way to do it. Ian gets out behind him. "I'll come with you. I'm ready to get out of this cab." He struggles to keep up as Malik disappears into the throng. Helen marvels at his ability to move through the crowd.

"Why aren't we moving, Mom?"

"A lot of other people are trying to get on the boat, too." For an hour they creep along. The driver leans on the horn and inches forward.

"When does the next boat leave?"

The driver looks at her but doesn't answer.

She remembers to try French. "*Quand est-ce que le bateau quitte?*"

He recognizes the word for "boat" and points ahead.

"*Quand?* When?"

He shrugs. She realizes that it is not just a problem of communication. No one knows.

Shane sits up. "It's night at home when it's day here."

"Yes."

"I'll bet it's snowing."

It takes another hour to reach the area near the dock, and the morning is heating up. Finally the cab can make it no further. Helen's heart drops. There are enough people to fill the boat four times.

"What is it, Mom?"

"There are too many people, Shane."

"It's okay. We can stay. My hand is much better."

"You're such a brave boy."

"I had another dream."

Helen smiles.

"It was about bats. It was scary. There were bats everywhere. They sounded like water in the air. *Whoosh, whoosh!* A boy was hunting them, he had a special bow, and he had a secret spot where there was a waterfall. He climbed in a tree and shot the bats with poison arrows. And they fell in the water. They were funny in the water all wet. Bats can't swim, can they?"

"No, I don't think so."

"But then it was scary again, because there were so many bats in the water. They made a bad noise, and I was afraid to fall in." Shane stops. He is scaring himself in the retelling of it. "Do you think that Dad is in a place like that?"

Helen looks at him. He has asked her so many times to give him a place to put his father. Trusting her to know.

"What do you think?"

"He *was* in my dream." Shane's voice is soft. "He was sick."

It's tempting to say something, invent a temporary lie to relieve him. But before she can respond, Malik pops his head in the door.

"We have a berth; you must come now."

Behind him Ian looks out of breath. Malik gives instructions to the driver so he will deliver the bags, and he hurries Helen and Shane out of the car. He is in a triumphant mood.

"Oh, this was close, Madame. We nearly did not make it. They were holding a first class cabin for a very wealthy merchant. But I convinced them. It was expensive. The boat is full; I hope it will still float. And there are more barges than ever."

Malik ushers them through the crowd. What would her chances be, she wonders, if she did not have Malik, or if she did not have money, the equivalent of a year's income here, at her disposal to bribe a captain? They press by a woman with a child wrapped in a cloth tied to her back. The child is awake but dazed by the heat. Her eyes follow Helen as she passes. To get this far, Helen has had to get used to cutting in line. She holds on tight to Shane's hand.

On the top deck the captain leans against the rail, overseeing the boarding. He turns to greet them, encouraging Helen and Ian to take advantage of the bar, which has miraculously been stocked with ice. There is even a faint breeze this high up, though the direct sunlight still burns without respite and shade is in short supply. Ian finds a bar stool, glad to be inside. Helen gets a Coke for Shane and one for herself.

On shore they have cut off the flow of new passengers. The decks of the barges are crowded beyond capacity. Several men work at the dock, untying the great ropes that secure the barges to shore. The boat is so encumbered that it can hardly budge, though its engines bellow and shake the whole vessel, but the flotilla finally pulls slowly out into the current. They will be taken downriver, like a raft of army ants on a flood, trusting the captain to keep them clear of the shoals lurking in the brown water. Smoke billows from the stack, and Helen wonders if they will clear the shallow point downstream. She looks back to the town and the jungle beyond it, which fades into a green haze. She has a sudden pang of regret, an intuitive feeling that she has made a mistake.

Then there is screaming below, and she peers over the rail; one of the barges is hung up on a shoal. The inertia of the ferry is so great that she feels only the slightest shudder as it rips away from the flotilla. Several of the men attempting to keep it tied on are pulled into the water. Though they manage to regain the separated barge, it is drifting. With no engines to guide it, eventually it will get hung up on an island downstream, stranding its hapless passengers. They seem to have thought of this, and many jump off to swim for shore before the barge can be sucked into the main current.

Out of the throng of people watching from shore, one woman catches Helen's attention. Perhaps it is because she is dressed in red. She stands on the beach at the base of a tall green palm that reaches up to the crown of the forest canopy. She seems small and insignificant beneath it. The boat begins to round a bend in the river. Helen looks down at her nearly empty glass, takes the last sip of her Coke and turns away from the view of the forest.

———

Lewis cranes his neck to look up at the dry blue sky. "Why are all of these people wet?"

The Frenchman hadn't noticed. "Swimming?"

"In their clothes?"

"Ah. Some disaster with the boat, probably. It was leaving today." The Frenchman leans on the horn to clear a path. "Things are a mess. But at least there are still a couple of decent hotels."

They drive through the crowds who did not make it onto the boat and on across the small town. When they pass the first hotel the Frenchman winks at Lewis. "The other hotel is not quite so new, but it is much better." He smiles as if this might be some kind of joke. Lewis looks at the crumbling white arch of the entrance as they pass; it's hard to imagine that this is the newer hotel.

As they continue, Lewis tells his story. It sounds preposterous to him, hearing it aloud, and he half wonders if the Frenchman will believe it.

"I have no money. Nothing."

"Ah, what does it matter? You will pay me back when you

can. I must help a man who has come so close to death and escaped."

Finally they come to an old Victorian building with weathered paint atop a low hill. In the distance the river shimmers like a poisonous snake. Lewis gets his own room. It isn't much. He should have known that there would be no phone. He sits on the bed for a long time, in a state of shock, trying to find the energy to go find one. When he closes his eyes the scene at the roadblock instantly appears—the mass of people, the sergeant, Kofi at his side, the rifle butt knocking the boy to his knees. He opens his eyes to the bright room, afraid to close them again. There is a knock, and the Frenchman pokes his head in. He hands Lewis a razor and shaving cream.

"You will need clothing, too, *oui?* Maybe they don't fit so well." He laughs.

Lewis takes the clothes with a quiet thank you. The Frenchman stares at him, as if trying to comprehend something inexplicably foreign about Lewis despite their common whiteness. It is a long, awkward moment. Lewis should say something more, but he doesn't, and finally the Frenchman shuts the door.

Lewis decides to get cleaned up before going to find the phone. The water pressure in the bathroom is barely adequate to fill the tub with vaguely warm, rusty water before it quits altogether. Still, Lewis manages to wash and shave. He dresses himself in his benefactor's outfit, which is clean but looks even more alien than his own ruined clothes. He stands in front of the mirror. The man he sees there is a stranger, neither the man he once was nor the man he has been. He lies on the bed and, without meaning to, falls asleep. He does not wake when the Frenchman comes to get him for dinner. He does not wake that night. He doesn't even move until the sun is on its way down the next day. A stray fragment of light from the dirty mirror in the bathroom falls on his eyelids, and for a second he's afraid he is still in the forest.

He wakes slowly from this dreamless sleep, and then he gets up and goes in search of a phone. It is late enough that he finds the Frenchman with a few other white men among smoldering mosquito coils in the bar. Besides the African bartender who leans at the far end, no one else is there. Beyond him through the doors, which have been left open to gather what breeze they can from the nearly motionless air, there is an empty pool, cracked and bleached by the sun. Normally these men would be working, mining or prospecting, but the uncertainty of the cease-fire and the threat of renewed fighting have temporarily put them out of their regular work. One or two might be involved, in a small way, in selling arms to one side or the other, nothing big, just a sideline to pay for some beer and some company in the African dusk. They are involved in a debate, though there is no real disagreement, more of a diatribe, really, on the lousy way the Africans have been running things.

"This is Lewis, an American I found wandering in the jungle yesterday morning," the Frenchman says, laughing.

There is a pause in the conversation to gulp a bit of the yeasty foam, and for a moment it is quiet. Then they manage a few half-hearted greetings. The men seem genuinely stunned by the combination of the beer, the stupifying heat, and the drone of their circular debate.

"Is there a phone?" His question is an interruption.

"Who knows?" one says, and they all chuckle at what apparently is a joke.

"Sit down, man, have a beer. You must be starving. We have some burgers coming," one thunders. "You may as well. There's no boat for a couple of weeks now, and Marty's airplane is confiscated. We're stuck!"

The man slaps Marty on the back, and they all laugh. Lewis gets the impression that confiscating airplanes is a regular thing here. He accepts the offer of a beer. No one asks Lewis to explain himself. Perhaps there is an unspoken code in a place like this, to leave out the details of what a man is up to. He is happy to skip the story. Soon the beer, just the one, is making Lewis very sick, and he's not ready for the food when it comes, dry meat and greasy fries. When he excuses himself, they hardly notice.

The woman at the hotel desk has little to do since the last boat nearly emptied the town of foreigners, but she isn't going to give up her job, so she guards the position.

"Is there a phone?"

She looks at him without expression, expecting him to figure out that he is going to have to speak French or some version of it.

"Telephone?" he asks with what might pass for a French accent in a high school drama class.

"*Oui.*" She points to a room that appears to be a business office.

Lewis sits at the desk, which is adorned only with the phone and a well-used fax machine. He picks it up optimistically, but there is no dial tone. He clicks the receiver button a couple of times to no effect, then goes back to find the woman at the desk.

"No dial tone."

She gives him that impatient look again. Despite the obvious fact that she has nothing else to do, she seems to have no time for his language problems.

"*Problème,*" he tries, afraid that it might be Spanish, not French. He holds his hand to his ear in an attempt to sign that there is no dial tone.

She reluctantly abandons her post and accompanies him to the office. She picks up the phone, observes the problem and clicks the receiver button as he did and then hands it to him. There is a dial tone. He is overwhelmed by the promise of it, the pure potential of a connection to the rest of the world.

"*Merci*," he says, but she has already left.

A phone. He holds it for a moment in his hand as he tries to remember the country code for the U.S.—one, of course. He dials, and though the ring is unfamiliar, he braces himself for Helen to answer, praying that it will not be the answering machine. But then a prerecorded voice comes on in heavily accented French: "*Vouz avez appelé un numéro de téléphone qui ne plus est en service. Veuillez vérifier votre numéro et essayer de nouveau.*"

"Shit."

He sets the phone down, but when he picks it up this time there is no dial tone again. He clicks the receiver button, even shakes the phone, hangs up, picks up the receiver until he gets a tone again, and is grateful for that. He dials again.

"*Vouz avez appelé un numéro de téléphone qui ne plus est en service. Veuillez vérifier votre numéro et essayer de nouveau.*"

He tries again but gets the same answer. He sits staring at the phone, ready to plead with it. He approaches the woman at her desk again.

He just holds his hands up in the air. "*Problème.*"

She frowns. He points to the phone.

"*Vouz avez appelé un numéro . . . ne plus est en service. . . . essayer de nouveau.*" Lewis stumbles through a rendition of the recording he has been getting.

"International?"

He nods—it seems obvious.

"*Vous devez régler la communication avant de le composer,*" she explains. He doesn't understand. She reluctantly translates. "You must pay first."

Lewis has no money. He has no choice but to approach the men in the bar and beg them for it. He heads for the lounge. The bitter smell of European cigarettes and an air of racial superiority wafts down the hallway. The conversation fades into a few chuckles and then silence as he stops at the table without sitting.

"I have been stranded here. I have no money. I have to make a phone call."

They don't respond immediately, as if the statement does not automatically translate into a request. So he makes it. "I need to borrow some money. I can have it wired as soon . . ."

"No one is wiring money into this godforsaken place, eh." The Canadian chuckles.

Lewis stands there, impassive.

"I need money. Enough to call the States."

They are silent for a moment longer; whatever gloom had been chased to the shadows by their gaiety ebbs back into the stale room. Finally the Frenchman speaks up. "We must take a collection for our Yankee companion. I must somehow get my clothes back, *non?*"

They laugh. And as Lewis stands there, they pass around an empty beer glass. Most contribute something. The Canadian and the Frenchman are generous. A Rhodesian man who has drunk himself to the point of silence pointedly passes the cup without adding anything. He seems sullenly hostile; perhaps it is because Lewis is American. The last of the men hands Lewis the glass. They all stare at him as though he's standing there in his underwear.

Then the Canadian breaks the silence. "Good luck, then."

Lewis walks out with the beer glass in his hand. He takes it to the front desk, ignoring the woman's surprise at his choice of wallet. He holds up three fingers. *"Trois minutes."*

She answers so quickly that he cannot understand. He hands her the glass so she can take the money out. She takes most of what is there, leaving a few coins that are virtually worthless. *"Deux minutes,"* she says.

He sits at the phone and goes through the ritual of clicks and shakes that produce a dial tone. He dials and gets a steady beep this time. No recording, but no ring, either.

"You must help me," he begs the woman. He borrows a pad and pen and writes the number down, but even after she tries it several times for him, the call does not go through. She gives up only after she has become somewhat frustrated herself. She apologizes and returns to her desk, gets his beer glass, puts the money back in and hands it to him.

"Essayez demain," she offers. "Tomorrow."

Lewis cannot leave the phone—the betrayal of the technology threatens his sanity. He can look at the wilderness, or up at the wide sky and expect contempt, expect to be cast down. Accept it. But this phone is connected to real copper lines that are carrying a million, trillion frivolous messages, as they *always* have for him. He is tempted to smash the phone, to beat it into insignificance. A phone seems like a simple enough miracle, so little to ask for now that he has been delivered from the forest, now that he has made it. Just a call. A wire.

THE WHITE MEN ARE by the pool. They have drunk enough by now that they might even imagine it to be full of water—even the man who lies at the bottom, passed out in its feminine curve, still gripping a beer. These men chose to be here. They did not leave on the boat when they could. They are not afraid, certainly. They know how little things will change for them whichever way it turns out, and perhaps even the in-convenience of recent events has landed them in just the kind of limbo they are looking for, a kind of purgatory and the oppor-tunity or excuse for a binge.

They are not alone. There are four or five African women among the nine of them. They sit in laps and lean hips to chairs, drink and laugh, casually waiting for the real work. No one no-tices Lewis arrive and sit in one of the cushionless, peeling lounge chairs. They are too stunned by the alcohol to speak. They fade slowly as the night gets late. The men with women wander off first, and eventually the others depart, some with a bow or a wave. The last is the man at the bottom of the pool. He stands and looks around him as if he ended up in the bot-tom of this pool as a result of some practical joke. He leaves the bottle to the company of the broken glass already there, climbs up and staggers off.

Lewis cannot sleep. He lies on his lounge chair, bathed in the scent of citronella, and stares at the clearing night sky. The stars seem particularly far away. A brick wall behind him separates him from the town, the diesel cabs and *tro-tros*. The wall was made by a man, now retired on the Rhine, who saw the right time to get out. Lewis is grateful for the illusion of civilization. It's like a hand held out, at least; though the reach is short, there is some promise in the theory of it.

On the second-floor veranda one of the women comes out, straightens her blouse and quietly knocks on another door, which opens to receive her. After perhaps an hour, another woman comes out of a room on the third floor. She shuts the door quietly, as if she has sneaked out. She digs through the man's wallet, takes what she finds in the way of cash and then tosses the wallet at the door. She walks a little way down the

veranda, and then she stops and leans out over the railing, looking directly over Lewis, at the town beyond the wall.

She does not move for a long time, trusting all of her weight
to the feeble rail. As Lewis watches her, he cannot help imagining her fall. The rail buckling suddenly, giving way, its bolts
rusted out by the humidity. She falls like a heavy bird, slowing
her descent with arms outstretched. When she hits the cement
there is no sound to it. When finally she notices Lewis by the
pool, staring up at her, she casts down a look of open disdain,
takes her bag and disappears.

The madness of this time of night is what the sleeping man
avoids. One thought is keeping Lewis awake, and it will not let
go of him. He can close his eyes, but he can't escape it. He hears
the Frenchman's words.

"These boys are everywhere, expecting favors."

He cannot rid himself of the haunting thought that if he had
kept a tighter grip on Kofi's hand or had the courage when the
moment tested him, he could have brought them both through
the roadblock. Kofi saved his life, more than once, and the
weight of the debt startles him. The irony, the part that is keeping him awake, is that no one will blame him for walking away.
In fact, no one needs to know about Kofi at all, if he wishes. He
is the keeper of his own story. Tomorrow or the next day he
can find another phone, someone to assist him, and slowly the
privilege of his birth will descend like a deus ex machina to save
him. A few hours of sleep in the hushed cocoon of a jet and he
will be home, as if nothing had ever happened. Though the
house will be empty, the door will open smoothly on its hinges.
The lights will come on, inspired to brightness by some abstract
and distant power. The house itself will rescue him with a tech-
nological life that is nearly flawless, serving him like a slippered

butler, with ice and food, TV, e-mail and electronic music. And Helen and Shane will be a mere two thousand miles from him, a single domestic American plane flight away.

Still the image of Kofi consumes him. It's as if he let go of his hand in a lake, let him slip under the water to drown, and he cannot convince himself of the convenient thought that it happened by accident or because of forces beyond his control, that there was nothing he could have done, not even to save Kofi's life but merely to help him—just once—when he needed it.

KOLINGA—L'AMOUR—LOVE

HELEN HAS NO PLANS to stay in the capital any longer than necessary. Ian has already left. When she saw him off at the airport, his face looked tired and changed, but he tried to smile and make a weak joke. At the top of the ramp he waved as though he was waving at all of it—the whole of Africa.

The American consul is relieved to hear that her trip upriver has caused him no further problems and that she will be leaving. As if to confirm it, he asks for her flight information and offers to see her through passport control. He makes promises to keep the search open, and needlessly checks that he has all her contact information in the U.S. He seems hollow and fake, smiling with excessive sympathy like an undertaker. No one believes that Lewis is still alive. His own report assumes that Lewis was killed by the rebels when he foolishly tried to run from the plane. His body would have been dumped somewhere in the thousands of square miles of rain forest, unrecognizable after a week. The report is already on file with the state department. In a soft, casual business voice, he offers her a copy, if she needs it, for insurance purposes. He has so much difficulty speaking in an appropriately hushed tone that he ends up hissing like a snake.

Helen has the day to get her things organized. Laura has taken Shane with her boys to see the gorillas at the zoo. After her visit at the embassy, she walks past a large, open stadium built with truckloads of ex-colonial guilt money in the sixties. Right in the middle of this overcrowded city, the stadium stands completely vacant, surrounded by a fence and rarely used. She thought a walk back would be a good idea, but her hotel is on the opposite side, so she must detour the perimeter of the whole complex to get there, turning a half mile walk into two. She keeps the fence on her left, the traffic, jammed and shimmering with fumes that quickly give her a headache, on her right.

It's the hottest part of the day, and she neglected to wear a hat. When she can clearly see the hotel, she notices a hole in the fence and a clear path cut in the grass. Ahead of her the road curves away from her destination. She decides to take the shortcut. She feels a bit conspicuous, ducking through the fence in clear view of all the traffic, and for an awkward moment her blouse is caught on the wire. She looks back at the stopped cars, but no one is watching her except one of the boys selling toilet paper. He waves at her, and she waves back, feeling a bit stupid. She unhooks her shirt and takes a few quick steps into the park. She feels suddenly vulnerable, alone in such a wide-open place, but it's also liberating after the boat ride down the river, where every square inch had at least one claim on it. The farther she walks in the stadium grounds, the quieter the traffic becomes behind her.

In the middle the grass is short, barely grass at all, and when she nears the arch of the stands it turns into gravel that pops under her shoes. Just the sound of fifty thousand feet on this gravel would be awesome. She stops. A faint wind pushes gently against her back, as if urging her away. She never imagined leaving this way, under these circumstances, never thought of leaving alone—of Lewis dead. Without the evidence, without the phone call, the knock on the door, without some sign, it is impossible to choose the right moment to accept it, to say, *Beginning now, he is dead*. She stops. Going even a step forward feels like a confirmation of it. She expected this feeling when the jet door shut on them and they pulled the ramp back. Instead, here it is now, right before her, created by her own wandering.

Lewis is dead.

Lewis is dead. And the last thing she ever did was to leave him.

The sky over her head is pale blue, and the empty stadium seems to echo her thoughts. This stone has heard so much shouting at political rallies, seen the concentrated dreams of people dashed and stolen so many times, heard so many children condemned to death, how can her loss matter? All she wants now is to feel his hands hold the soft part of her arm, to feel his kiss and his arms gathering her. She wants to extend those moments when a kiss meant everything it should mean, when his eyes seemed like a blue fire and she could yield and know that her choice was right. She is crying when the boy runs up from across the field. He has three or four rolls of toilet paper in his hand, as though he were sent on cue, to give her a tissue.

"Madame! Madame!"

She waves a hand at him, automatically fending off the sales pitch.

"Madame, vous ne devez pas être ici!"

"Excuse me?"

"Venez vite. C'est une mauvaise place."

Though she only vaguely understands the words, the tone is clear; she is not supposed to be here. The boy is already racing toward the opposite fence. She tries following him at a brisk walk, then has to run to keep up. She looks over her shoulder to see who they might be escaping, but the stadium is still empty. The boy scrambles through a hole in the fence where it abuts a shantytown of improvised shacks and open sewers.

"Par ici!" He waves for her to follow.

He heads down a narrow alley, and she loses him after a couple of turns and slows to a walk, picking her way carefully, looking for a path that will lead to the main road. When she gets the hotel in view again, rising out of the palms, it's still about a quarter of a mile away. Though the road seems to be to her right, she heads straight for the hotel rather than get lost trying to find it again. Women look up from their smoky cooking fires, and the children are so surprised to see her they don't even get up to follow. Everyone stops to stare as she walks by. They are not used to seeing a white woman in this part of Kinshasa, especially a tourist.

She comes to a small market, a row of low, open shacks selling meat. The red flesh is piled in carts and hanging flyblown and exposed to the heat and humidity. The butchers hack at it with dull knives, breaking pieces at the joint and lopping off small hunks for patrons. One of the men comes out of his stall kicking a dead rat toward the fouled gutter. She gags and almost turns back, but the hotel is less than two hundred yards away now, straight behind the meat market.

She cuts between a couple of stands and starts down the shallow slope behind them. Then she realizes her mistake. This is where the trimmings and offal have been tossed; the ground is muddy with blood, which seeps in rivulets down the hill to a canal that she will not be able to cross. She turns back and slips, falling onto her knees. The blood stains her hands and clothes. She gets up in such a panic that she nearly slips again, and then she sees that she is not alone. Leaning against shacks and sitting in the mess behind them are half a dozen people. It's as if they, too, have been cast aside, like useless garbage. Their limbs are twisted by various diseases, leprosy, elephantiasis, and they gaze at the intrusion dully. She looks at her hands, as though this might be something that she wrought. Her stomach wretches and she vomits. She looks up weakly as a butcher comes out from behind his shop and stares at her. He is strikingly handsome; his arms are lean and strong.

"*Pourquoi êtes vous ici?*" he angrily demands. Helen gets up to run, and he shouts at her. "*Vous ne devez pas être ici. Va-t-en!* Go, go, go."

Helen runs away from him like a thief through the crowded market. She doesn't stop until she comes to the red carpet that pours from the hotel entrance under the cold stare of the doorman.

AT THE BATHROOM SINK she splashes water on her hands and then her face until it finally runs clear. Then she undresses, throwing her soiled clothes in the corner of the white room. She sits in the tub until the water is cold, disturbed only by her trembling breath, which is still shallow and uneven. She closes her eyes and tries to force the vision of the meat stalls from her memory. Death is in the belly of the world, in every palm, looking over every shoulder. It threatens to suffocate her, sucking the air from the room.

With Lewis, Helen allowed herself to break her most sacred

rule of relationships. She had never let her days be dependent on a boyfriend's plans. She had not automatically held any time in reserve. With Lewis she hadn't realized that they took all of each other's time, until he was out of town and she had not been on a walk without him for several weeks. It was a Saturday, a warm summer day, and she could hear the clocks ticking in every room. They ticked out of sync, and she could hardly believe that she had ever lived with the sound. She went around and shut them all down, stopped the time at nine-o-seven. Then she drew a bath and sat listening to the crisp, articulated sound of the water pouring off her arms. She wanted to remake the vow, looking critically at her body in the distortion of the water. The conviction felt good, though another part of her thought *What is love going to be then, with all this held in abeyance?*

Now, in Africa as she stands up out of the water, she shivers with realization that she let it happen anyway, for twelve years of her life. Love. She steps out of the tub and wraps herself with towels. Her skin feels clean and her own again. Then she makes the mistake of closing her eyes, and she can feel Lewis's warm hands on her back and then her arms and waist, all the ways he needed to touch her, his breath against her neck, breathing in the smell of her hair. She sits cross-legged on the slick tile and cries until she is tired enough to stop.

HELEN DRESSES AND STOPS in the lobby to collect her tickets from the travel agent who has an office there. Malik is waiting for her in the café with a latté and crêpe filled with berries and whipped cream. She had almost forgotten that he would come by. She sits down, laying the tickets between them on the table. Malik picks them up.

"These are heavy," he says, and carefully sets them back down. "That's as it should be. They are going to take you far, across a whole ocean."

Helen catches his cheerful eyes, and she feels her body momentarily relax.

"Ian is already gone?" he asks.

"Yes."

Malik stands and takes her hand. "I wonder what he will say about us."

Helen just shakes her head.

"Someday you must come back, when the fighting is over, perhaps."

Helen nods to avoid saying something stupid, that he should come to America, too, sometime, that maybe he would like it better now.

When Malik finally has to go he releases her hand and calmly turns away. He stops at the door and waves. It's harder to leave than she thought.

KOSALA—AGISSANT—ACT

LEWIS GETS UP EARLY. It's still dark. He feels stronger than he has since he fled the airplane. Rest and some decent food have restored his strength. A few minutes after dressing in the Frenchman's clothes, he slips out of the room. It clouded over during the night, and the gray sky is barely beginning to yield to day. At the front desk the woman is asleep in her chair. In some of the collapsing buildings that seem to stagger down the shallow slope of the hill, a few people are beginning to stir. A boy of about fifteen pushes a cart up the hill and smiles at Lewis as he goes by. Lewis passes a small Christian church and stops for a moment to listen to the singers, the clear harmonies lifting into the trees. A little farther along he hears a distant drumming, and then a group of young school children march by, carrying their small stools on their heads. They stare at him as they walk by and then run on ahead, laughing.

When he gets to the edge of the town he stops. Even this

early, the day is in full swing, cabs and *tro-tro*s loaded with people and their cargo: baskets of cassava, tomatoes, plantains, guavas and live chickens. One of the birds is being held out the window by its feet because the car is too crowded to accommodate it. The dirt road races by only a few inches under its beak as it holds out its wings as if trying to fly. Lewis follows the progress of the ill-fated bird into town, catching a glimpse of the black bead of its terrified eye as it passes. The cab bounces out of sight into the bustling town.

He doesn't have a clear memory of what the distance to the roadblock might be, and there are no landmarks in this swath of forest, no signs. Ahead of him the road is empty. The trees stand like vagrants lining the path, and their branches seem to turn away from him in the wind. He feels hated, just for being a man, and suddenly what he's doing seems insane. He doubts his own presumption that simply because he has a white man's clothes, there is anything he can actually do for Kofi. He feels puny, and he would be happy now to take the hand of mediocrity if only it were offered, somewhere. He looks toward town, the smoke and noise, but he does not turn back. His resolve will have to be better when he gets there. He will have to confront the soldiers with courage, and he cannot fake it. They will run off a man with a weak heart.

He walks slowly; it must be midday by the time he first hears the noise of the roadblock around a shallow bend in the road. He stops. Beneath the murmur of the gathered voices is the rumble of heavy equipment, like the low roll of timpani. He takes a deep breath, and again he hesitates, takes three or four steps back and then stops himself. He closes his eyes.

He is not this kind of man. He never looked at the sheer face of a cliff and thought he should climb it, confront his fears, overcome them. He has always lived with his shortcomings like unwanted dinner guests, too polite to chase them away. His hands are shaking. The deep conviction of the night wilts in the brightness of the day. He does it again—walks to where he can just see around the bend and then turns back. Some part of him is screaming *Run, run, run. This is not your place. Go home. What are you doing here?*

But then he does it. He walks into full view of the roadblock, and he knows that now he must walk up like "The Big Man," the "superior white man," some blood descendant of Stanley or King Leopold. His breath quickens, but his shoulders hide it, and his face is strong as he closes the distance with an unexpected sense of calm. Beyond the roadblock he sees the camp of the refugees. There are thousands of them now. He hadn't considered that just finding Kofi might be the real challenge. He walks right up to the soldier nearest the barricade, who has his back to him. Clearly the young man does not expect anyone to approach from this direction, and he turns, startled. Lewis stops close to the soldier, closer than is comfortable for either of them. He can see into his eyes; this young man seems intimidated by his audacity.

"Arrêtez-vous!" The soldier shouts without the force he would have if Lewis were even a few steps farther away.

"Let me pass."

Lewis has decided not to even try French. The soldier doesn't respond, but he looks around as though he wishes someone more senior were there to handle this.

"Let me pass."

Lewis is too close for the soldier to properly raise his weapon, and when he takes a step forward, the soldier yields and moves back a step. Lewis does not wait for him to regain his balance. He walks by and through the barricade. It's an exhilarating victory, so easy. Then he hears the soldier move back into position like a closing door. Two more soldiers rush over, their hands ready on their weapons, waiting to see what the white man will do. His heart sinks; his choice is made now. Crossing back will not be done so easily.

He walks thirty yards without looking back before he stops. The refugees have ceased clamoring to get through. They have turned this spot in the road into one long camp, like a village with one grand, muddy boulevard. It's a siege, and if they do not starve first, they might finally pass. What has stopped Lewis is laughter. In his frame of mind he perceives it to be directed at him, but it is not. It is just an old man who has lost his mind. He sits on a small woolen blanket, his face streaked with dried tears. Exhausted from his crying, he is laughing a cackling, desperate laugh—and it might as well be at Lewis. Kofi is not here, just sitting waiting for him. He is an idiot, as much as this old man.

Lewis walks along the boulevard, looking for Kofi, determined now to complete this part successfully. But there are only women and young children and old men, as if someone neatly deleted a whole segment of the population, men between the ages of ten and forty. He passes a woman who sits by the temporary shelter of poles and broad leaves that she has erected against the rain. Her children are gathered in her lap. They do not squirm or compete for space as children usually might, but perch there with a dull kind of patience from so much waiting. She looks up at Lewis.

"*Que voulez-vous, mondele?*" she asks. When he doesn't respond, she shouts. "*Où allez-vous, le blanc?*"

Then she spits, and Lewis stops. He's beginning to wonder himself why he is here, and he sure as hell doesn't know where he is going, either. A few children come to beg him for food. He holds up his hands to indicate that he has nothing, but in these new clothes they do not believe him. He tries to shoo them away but the youngest keep following him. He tries to catch the woman's eye, as if he might explain himself somehow, but she has looked away, no longer interested.

The encampment is long, and by the time he nears the end of it he has an entourage. One of the smaller girls holds on to the pocket of his pants, making a sort of claim. He has not seen Kofi. It was foolish to imagine that he would still be here. He has certainly gone somewhere else, back to the bush to try and find his grandmother, or another village, or to the river. There is no way to know.

Lewis turns to look at the children accompanying him. Their youthful faces do not match their expressions; there is none of the excitement of children competing for a favor, just a serious desperation in their silence. If there were not so many, if he didn't need the money for the phone, he could give them some of the coins that came from his own begging. They keep pressing closer to him, and he has trouble turning around to start back toward the roadblock. He is beginning to worry about the child who has her hand on the pocket of his pants. He hasn't hidden his money, and now he is afraid that she might try to take it from him. He tries pushing her hand away, but she holds on firmly. He has to stop and grab the four-year-old's wrist and pull her hand away. The angry look he gets from the children scares him. He walks faster, with the parade following closely. Finally he stops and he tries to chase them away. He waves his arms at them.

"I don't have anything."

The kids back up a few feet, perhaps, but they aren't leaving.

He shouts. "Go away." It frightens a few of the smaller children, but they merely find an older child to hold on to.

"Go away!" Some of the women nearby look up at his shouting.

He turns and tries walking more quickly, but he could not outwalk even the youngest of these children. What a ridiculous mistake. He did not come all the distance from town and risk crossing the roadblock just to shout at these poor children. Kofi is not here. He has satisfied his conscience. He has done more than he could be expected to do. He shakes his head and walks faster, afraid that he may already have gone too far.

When he gets about fifty yards from the soldiers, he slows down. He doesn't turn to look back, but the children have begun to fall away from him, and by the time he has crossed half the trampled ground to the barriers, even the girl who was holding on to him has relinquished her claim. He approaches the soldier he pushed by with a plan: don't stop, no matter what they do. He has the Frenchman's clothes now; he can pass with impunity. Even if they raise their guns again, he is going to walk by them, make no eye contact, in no way acknowledge their authority to stop him. Without the crowd pushing at them it should not be a problem. They are not going to stop a powerful white man. Why should they? But when he gets to the roadblock, the soldiers do stop him. They seem angry at the cavalier attitude that got him across in the first place. Two of them stand directly in front of him with their rifles crossed. He tries to appear relaxed about it, forces himself to be calm, but his hands shake when he hands them his driver's license and a sheet of stationery from the hotel.

"Où allez-vous?

"Hotel Parisienne."

They study the paper critically. They have all the time in the world. They hand it back to him with the driver's license, and Lewis takes a step forward, expecting to be allowed to pass, but the soldier holds his hand up. He does it to stop Lewis, but there is a softness and casualness to the gesture that catches him off guard. He hesitates and then steps back. They are going to make him wait for an officer to come over. From a distance the man looks like the same sergeant he encountered last time. Lewis studies him closely, trying to decide if he recognizes him, but he realizes that even when he is close enough to see into the man's eyes, he cannot tell. He can only hope that if it is the same sergeant, he won't recognize Lewis now, shaved and dressed.

Lewis hands him his license. He watches intently for any sign that the man remembers.

"*Venez avec moi.*"

"What?"

"*Venez avec moi.*" The man points to an improved lean-to near the barricades.

Lewis follows him. If he recognizes Lewis, he isn't showing it. They stop outside the lean-to.

"*Restez ici.*"

The sergeant walks into the shed. There is a radio, and Lewis waits while he attempts to contact someone on it. The officer sits down with Lewis's license in his hand. Everyone is moving slowly, sitting or waiting, in no hurry. A couple of the younger soldiers sit by a smoldering fire, roasting a bush rat on a green stick.

Lewis turns away from the smoke and closes his eyes to protect them. When he opens them, he is looking at one of the transport vehicles parked on the refugee side of the barricades. Underneath it he can see the legs of four or five boys, sitting in a row. Without walking around the truck he cannot see their faces. The odds that one of them is Kofi are astronomical. Or maybe they are not. These legs look like they belong to boys

Kofi's age, but they are not moving, and he suddenly realizes with a sick feeling that they could be corpses. He looks over at the two officers, who are still trying to get the radio working. Neither is watching him, and the soldiers around him have lost their curiosity about the white man. Cautiously he takes a couple of steps to get a better view.

The first boy he can see is the right age, and he is alive. But it's not Kofi. Lewis can see no more than the arm of the next boy. To see any better he will have to pass a soldier who is sitting on a pile of spare tires. The man appears to be asleep. Lewis watches the officers for a moment, trying to judge their disposition, but it is impossible to tell anything. The snatches of conversation that he can hear are a mix of Lingala and French. He steps a little closer to the sleeping soldier, and he can see the next boy. Again his age is exactly right, but it's not him.

He turns his attention back to the officers. The sergeant is fiddling with his license and ends up dropping it in the dirt. He picks it up and looks again at the picture. Then he looks up at Lewis. He doesn't seem bothered that Lewis has left his assigned spot.

When he looks away again, Lewis takes half a step past the sleeping soldier, so that he can see the third boy. All he can see is his arms. He is leaning back on them in a way that seems familiar. Then Lewis sees the tattooing on one arm, a ring of cauterized scars just below the shoulder. It's not Kofi. He looks quickly back at the two officers. His license isn't in the sergeant's hands anymore. It's been slipped into a pocket and forgotten for the moment.

No one is guarding the boys, but they must be prisoners, probably conscripts; the age of combatants is being lowered on all sides of the conflict. Lewis isn't sure what to do. His own return is in doubt now. The officer who had his license comes over to him.

"*Pourquoi voulez-vous passer ici?*"

"I am an important person. I have a right to cross."

The man does not understand him.

"*Important.*" He tries with his best Inspector Clouseau accent, pointing to himself.

"*Rapporteur?*"

"*Oui*—No. *Non.*"

The man frowns at him.

"*Oui ou non?*"

"No. Let me pass."

"*Vous devez attendre.*" He signals for Lewis to stay put and walks away again.

"How long?" Lewis asks, but he is ignored. It occurs to him that all he needs to do is bribe this man. Money will allow him to cross. That must be why they are making him wait; but they have not really suggested it as far as he can tell, and he is afraid to offer. He has so little money that at this point, he thinks it would probably just piss them off. He cannot afford to start the negotiations too early. He looks over his shoulder. The children who had followed him are sitting at the edge of the camp, watching to see how the soldiers will treat the rich white man.

The sleeping soldier is awake now. He gets up and stretches, then leaves his spot. Lewis casually takes the few extra steps to where he can see the next boy in line. It's Kofi! He is staring down at the pounded clay beside him. He has a dull bruise on his forehead. Lewis steps back quickly. He doesn't want Kofi to see him before he knows what he is going to do. He could probably just walk over there: the soldiers don't seem to care where he goes on this side of the barrier. But then what?

Something makes Lewis look up at the sky, which has been getting gloomier while he has been waiting. The deluge comes abruptly, hammering the ground and bouncing back up in a reddish-brown mist. The children scatter and the soldiers move to the shelter, but the captive boys sit stoically in the rain even though they are quickly covered with red mud. Out in the open the sound is deafening. Inspired by the wildness of the downpour, by its chaos, Lewis runs over to Kofi.

"Come on!"

Kofi doesn't respond right away.

"Come on, get up!"

Kofi stands. Lewis looks over at the barricades. The rain is so intense, he can barely see that far. The soldiers don't seem to be paying any attention to him; they are still trying to get out of the rain. If he and Kofi make a run for it right now, they might just make it.

"*Allons-y!*" Lewis shouts. Kofi is right behind him as he heads for the barricades. The soldiers under the shelter look up. They have to shield their faces to see.

"We have to go *now*!" Lewis shouts, and he passes through an opening in the barricades. He does it deliberately, walking, not running; he does not want to get shot in the back. But as if he has set off an alarm, two of the soldiers come racing out of their shelter despite the pounding rain. They are angry, shouting at him and waving their arms.

"*Arretez-vous! Arretez-vous!*"

Kofi hesitates, despite Lewis's pulling hard on his arm. It gives the soldiers time to raise their guns. Lewis stops. He raises his hands and starts shouting back at them. "Put those fucking guns down!"

Lewis backs up, pushing Kofi behind him.

"You motherfuckers!" he screams, waving his arms at them like a madman. Then he turns with some burst of courage or absolute foolishness and walks straight at them.

"Fuck you! Get the hell out of my way!"

His rage is dangerous. Kofi has not followed him, and the soldiers still have their guns up. Lewis stops again and then backs up a few steps, but he does it with disdain, turning his back and walking away from them.

"Fuck." They are not going to make it. He is angry, not afraid. It's simply unbelievable that this might be how it will end for him, with all these witnesses but no one to tell the story. He turns to the soldiers again. He glares a last time, working hard to suppress the urge to run at them though it would be suicide. Their weapons are still up, but they have calmed down enough that he senses he might have room to make a move. He turns back to Kofi.

"Allons-y."

They walk away from the barricade, back toward the refugee camp. The rain is coming down harder. If the soldiers are yelling after them, there is no way to hear them. Lewis does not turn to look again. No matter what they eventually do, he has bought a couple of minutes with his audacity though he has ultimately cost himself the chance of crossing here—ever, with or without Kofi.

When they reach the first of the refugees' shelters, Kofi turns to see soldiers getting into a jeep to pursue them. The tires spin wildly in the slick clay, and the jeep weaves in their haste to get up speed. Now Kofi ducks into a gap between the huts, and Lewis follows. They run at the edge of the bush, parallel to the road. It is so slippery that Lewis falls several times, trying to keep up. The soldiers have the vehicle moving, and they are racing down on them. Lewis thinks he can hear the *pop pop* of handguns being fired. Just as the soldiers catch up to them, Kofi finds a small game trail cutting through the bush at the edge of the forest. He and Lewis claw and thrash to get to the more open forest.

Kofi is waiting for him, standing at the edge of a deeper gloom. It is quiet here, compared to the din of the downpour on the open road. Lewis stands and listens hard to hear if the soldiers have followed. They have not. Kofi turns and starts running, with Lewis close behind. Overhead the great arms of the trees have replaced the sky, and the rain falls in a fine, calm mist; the water runs down the trunks and branches and seeps into the spongy ground and tangled roots. Lewis lifts his feet high to avoid tripping on the creepers and vines that lay across the winding animal path, and runs again into the rainforest.

Mai Makangani—La Neige—Snow

Outside the Disney store in the Cincinnati airport, a large plastic Mickey Mouse grins at Helen and Shane like a modern-day Statue of Liberty, welcoming them home. A child comes out holding her bag wide open, so enthusiastic to inhale the contents that she does not watch where she is going and walks right into Shane. She apologizes sweetly, but her mother rushes over and grabs her roughly by the arm and pulls her away, as if to be out of hearing distance, and then scolds her.

"Didn't you see? That poor boy is blind?"

Helen keeps Shane close until they get to the gate for the last leg home. He sleeps all the way to Spokane. When they walk out of the terminal for their first breath of North American air, the wind blows a light snow into their faces. The car starts grudgingly, awakened from its long, cold sleep. They drive to her mother's house without speaking, listening to the tires spinning on the wet road and slipping in the dirty slush. In their summer shoes they step gingerly through the snow on the front yard. It takes a couple of tries in the chilling wind to get the door unlocked. Helen stops just inside the house. She can feel the wind on her back.

Shane pushes the door shut with a shove. "We're home!" he shouts.

The house does not answer back.

"She's probably sleeping, Shane."

"No she's not." The voice comes from deep inside.

"Hi, Mom."

Helen's mother makes her way slowly down the hall with her walker. Helen hugs her and helps her to the kitchen table, where she sits with Shane while Helen brings their luggage in from the car. Shane eats Fruit Loops for dinner, with plenty of fresh milk, and tells his grandmother all about Africa.

"It's time for bed, Shane," Helen says quietly, thinking that it feels good to dress him in clean pajamas and wash his face with a warm wet cloth. She tucks him in and then sits down next to him.

"It's nice to be back," she whispers with a smile.

Shane doesn't answer; he just reaches up for a hug goodnight. By the time she gets back to the kitchen her mother has fallen asleep. She lays a hand on her shoulder.

"Come on, Mom. It's late; let's get you to bed."

Her mother wakes with effort and silently accepts the help. She feels heavy and uneasy leaning on Helen's shoulder. It's a struggle to get her into the bed. Helen finds a chair and sits next to her mother, and before long she falls asleep, too.

She wakes sometime in the night in a panic. Her mother's breathing seems labored, but after Helen listens for a moment she seems okay. In the kitchen she finds some paper and a pencil and makes a list—the names, all the people she will begin calling tomorrow to tell that she came home without Lewis. The last entry reads "Life Insurance." It's something someone suggested she needs to do, but just seeing the words formed there upsets her. She lays her head on her hands and cries.

She doesn't hear her mother shuffle into the room, and when she does it is too late to cover up. Her mother limps stiffly to the table and sits down next to Helen. Her eyes reflect her fight with the pain, the injury that stubbornly will not heal.

"I should have stayed, Mom. I should have waited longer."

Her mother lays a hand on Helen's for a moment and then lets go. She moves back, trying to find a way to sit that doesn't hurt.

"When your father died, it was so sudden. That car hit him, and it was over like that." She looks down at her hands, as if they could help keep the memory at a distance. "They had his body for me to look at, to identify him. He had a big bruise on his face, but he was all cleaned up. He didn't look dead to me. I tried to believe them. The last thing I remember thinking was that I was mad at him for being late. I wondered if he was, you know, sneaking around."

"No you didn't, Mom."

"Yes, I did."

Helen frowns.

"Isn't that why you left New York?" Her mother whispers it.

"Mom, no."

"Don't look at me like that, honey. Something was wrong."

"It wasn't that. Really."

"I guess it doesn't have to be something that dramatic, does it? Sometimes it's hard to remember that it takes a warm hand now and again, a little extra care to keep it alive. A man will fool you. He'll try to give you the idea that he doesn't need anything."

Helen looks down at the table between them. Her mother continues.

"I don't mean to sound so wise. It's just something that has come to me recently. Far too late to be of any use." She coughs and clears her throat. "I'm sorry, Helen. I forgot what I was saying."

"About Dad."

"Yes, that's right. Finally, in his coffin your father looked dead. Didn't he? Do you remember?"

"I do. He didn't look like himself. I wish I hadn't looked."

"It's easier, though, that he looked like that, like he was made of wax and in a suit he would never have worn. Better than at the hospital. There you could still imagine him getting up, even with the bruises. But not in the coffin. Not like that."

Helen closes her eyes, trying hard not to see her father.

"You need to think of Lewis that way—in a coffin, all done up."

"Mom, please." She doesn't say that there is a part of her that is relieved, willing to accept any answer just to be over it. But the thought also makes her sick.

"It'll hurt a lot for a while, but then . . ." Her mother stops. This hurts her, too. "Oh, dear."

They are both quiet enough to hear the humming of the re-frigerator, the settling of the house on its foundations. Her mother notices the list Helen made.

"That's a good start. That will help."

She rubs her hip, which always bothers her more when she sits, and then she clears her throat again. "You and Shane are going to be alone soon. I'm sorry."

Helen stands and helps her mother up from her chair and then back to her bed. It's impossible for Helen to fall asleep again. After a while she stops trying and goes back to the kitchen, but she is afraid to turn the light on and wake her mother again, so she sits in the dark, waiting for it to get light outside.

She has so many images of Lewis, and not one is of him dead. Lewis at the door, winding down from work, or standing in an unlit kitchen by the window, sipping his too sweet coffee. His sugary breath kissing her good-bye. Asleep on the couch, his book yawning open like his jaw. Laughing with toothpaste in his mouth at some silly sarcasm she couldn't keep to herself. Sitting with her on a Saturday morning reading magazines, or going through bills. Lewis with Shane, lifting him from his crib and holding the child so tightly she had to warn him to be careful. And then the way he often looked at Shane, that unrequited gaze that yearned for some visual exchange.

It hasn't been light long when she hears Shane awaken. He patters down the hall to the bathroom, flushes and then emerges in the kitchen. Normally she is careful to make sure she announces herself, so that he isn't surprised. But she has been quiet all night, and she doesn't immediately speak. Shane walks in slowly, moving across the still room with a hand out, until he gets to the refrigerator. He gets his milk, though it isn't exactly where he expected it to be. After he has his bowl and spoon, he sits and eats his cereal, spilling half of it. For Helen it feels good to have him in a safe place. The bandage on his hand is clean and smaller. There are prescription medicines from Safeway in the bathroom, a red, syrupy spoonful to be taken night and morning to keep him from harm.

"Good morning, Shane."

"Hi, mom," he says between bites. He's surprised to find her up early. "Did you go to bed last night?"

"No."

"Aren't you tired?"

"Yeah."

He slides off his chair and wipes his milky mouth on the sleeve of his pajamas.

"Over here." She speaks again to give him bearings. He climbs into her lap and puts his hands on her face.

"Try to talk."

"I can't," she mumbles through his fingers.

He laughs.

"Don't worry about Dad," he whispers.

She tries to respond, but his hands are still over her mouth and her voice comes out muffled. He laughs so hard at the game that she goes along with it, making nonsense noises to keep him laughing.

IT TAKES HALF THE day to get through her list of calls, though she gets better at it as she goes. She begins to believe the explanation, the improbability that he could have survived, the near certainty that they will never know what actually happened to him. Her friend Margaret answered as if she'd been expecting her call.

"When are you coming back to New York?"

"I don't know. What for?"

"What for?"

Helen can hear the implication in her friend's voice.

Margaret softens her tone. "I can help you do it. We will— the book club."

"There's no body, Margaret."

"Helen. How long can you continue to keep that door open? It must be exhausting."

"Yeah."

"A memorial would be appropriate."

Helen tries to speak, but her throat is too tight.

Margaret fills the silence, guessing at what's bothering her. "We all have bad times, fights. Stupid things happen. People knew you guys better than that, Helen."

Helen sets the phone down for a moment and closes her eyes, breathing through her clenched fists.

"Helen? Helen?"

She picks the phone back up. "Yeah."

"Let's not do this over the phone."

"Okay. When I can—"

Helen is interrupted by her mother, calling from her room like a child. She hangs up and finds her in bed, lying on her back, her eyes damp as though she might have been crying.

"I need my medicine."

"For pain, Mom?"

"Yes."

Helen goes to the cabinet to get the codeine. She shakes the bottle, which is nearly empty.

"How many have you been taking each day?"

"I don't know, dear. Just a few."

"Have you been constipated?"

"No," she says, and Helen looks doubtful. "Well, yes."

"We need to be careful about that, Mom."

"I need the pain medicine. It's excruciating."

Helen is taken aback by the deep seriousness in her voice, the pain in the word itself; it is easy to treat her more like a child. "Okay."

Helen gives her the medicine and takes it back to its shiny cabinet in the bathroom. She stares at the collected potions there, so many colored pills. By the time she gets back to check on her, her mother is asleep again.

LISTENING TO THE INSURANCE agent argue the possibilities that Lewis is alive comes as a relief to Helen after all the calls she has made assuring friends and family that he is most likely dead. The insurance representative tells her she will need a Report of Death of an American Citizen, from the American Consul in the Congo, and since it is unlikely that she will ever get a local death certificate, she'll also need a Statement of Unusual Circumstances. She can just imagine Lewis's reaction if he knew his life is now summed up as unusual circumstances. When she is ready to file the claim, the company will find a local investigator in the Congo to make sure there is no fraud involved, that Lewis isn't hiding out, preparing to slip into a life of luxury in the jungle with Mutual Life's stockholders' hard-earned money. The representative actually seems to consider this the most realistic scenario; and though that undermines his earlier arguments, it leaves Helen with Lewis's death again being the only reasonable explanation. After the call she sets the phone down carefully, as if to deprive the action of any kind of finality.

Outside the snow has retreated to a few unmelted, dirty piles, hiding under the bushes. The grass is matted and brown. It smells like mold. Shane is in the living room, playing with toy soldiers that spit and fight and fall to mournful, tormented endings.

LILOKI—LA MAGIE—MAGIC

KOFI SEEMS TO KNOW where he is going, and he moves so fast and comfortably in the forest that Lewis nearly has to jog to keep up. Still, he is moving better than he first did. After a while they stop to drink from a creek. Hundreds of small white butterflies dance in the glint of sun that shines through the thick canopy onto the bank. Nearby a chorus of frogs competes with the hum of insects, a brittle, musical clicking that sounds like breaking glass. Lewis sits down and rests his head back against a gambeya tree, looking up its fantastic height the way a boy on a summer day anywhere might, breathless with vibrant life. It's ludicrous, but he feels as though he has done something completely and unexpectedly right. There is something in this moment, some ease in his heart, that he would not trade for any rescue.

Kofi sits with his legs crossed at the edge of the water, his hands in the fine sand, making a sort of castle.

"Where do we go now?" Lewis asks in English, just to have the verbal accompaniment to his signing.

Kofi looks at him, puzzled. Lewis points to the forest again, the path they have been more or less following, and tries again. *"Où?"*

Kofi points ahead and offers a long explanation in Lingala. Lewis nods with a smile, as if this is absolutely satisfactory to him, whatever the plan may be. He points to his own stomach. *"Faim?"*

Kofi gets up without a word, and he is gone in a moment. There is a sudden gust of wind high in the canopy. It sounds like a wave rushing up onto a pebbled beach. Then a misty rain falls from the highest leaves, cooling Lewis's face. He closes his eyes just to listen to the rain and wind ruffling the top of the canopy a hundred feet over his head.

Kofi returns with a handful of mushrooms. They're big, almost pure white and shiny, and smell of wet dirt and of the water Lewis just drank. His stomach welcomes them.

"Good!"

Kofi nods and finishes his. Then they stand up, brush the leaves from their knees and travel until dusk. Lewis rests against a silk-cotton tree that Kofi is using to make a shelter. The tree is at least twenty feet around at the base, and the roots reach down from the trunk in long, four-foot-high ridges that form the walls; Kofi lays broad leaves and branches across them to make the roof. The forest is noisier at night, and there is something oddly reassuring in it, in the rhythms he has become familiar with. A mile off, some chimpanzees are creating a racket making their beds, and there is some strange bird, which at first he took to be a monkey, that calls out at irregular intervals, its song more optimistic now than disturbing. By the time Kofi finishes the shelter, it is dark. Lewis watches him lie down in the mulch under the trees as if it is the most comfortable bed, and then Lewis closes his eyes and falls easily asleep.

His dreams come to him vividly, with a sense of clarity much greater than his memory can normally muster. The first is of Shane, three years old. He has his hands over his own eyes, as if he is playing peek-a-boo. Lewis waits anxiously for the small hands to come away from his face, from his eyes, and the simple action seems to take an eternity. Somehow Lewis has the idea that what is to be revealed will be new and perfect eyes, shimmering with light.

"See my magic?" Shane asks, still holding his hands tight over his eyes.

Lewis tries to speak, but he cannot even shake his head. He looks sadly at his boy's face, knowing that he means something he must only imagine as seeing. There is no way to explain to Shane that his father cannot share that part of his experience. Then he realizes that Shane is not covering his eyes for any effect it has for himself. He is showing his father what he needs to do.

Lewis covers his eyes with his hands. At first he sees what he expected. But when he is able to see beyond the darkness of his closed eyes, beyond the warm color of his eyelids, there is a brilliant, sparkling light.

Shane laughs.

Then the dream changes. He is looking at Helen's face, an ageless version that is more his awareness of her, more the part of him that she occupies, than a real image. She is looking away, and he realizes that this is the same image that has come to him so many times. She is kneeling and writing a letter. He touches her arm, and she lays the pen down.

He utters a stream of apologies that she does not hear. *I'm sorry. I'm sorry to have forgotten you.*

He takes her hand, and she stands up. It is barely light enough to see. She stands before him at the window. Behind her, behind the glass, the world is calm and distant. She eases into his arms.

"Shhh," she whispers.

WHEN THE RAIN STOPS in the middle of the night, the sudden quiet wakes him. He cannot get back to sleep. He lies on his back for a long time, looking up at the impenetrable canopy, searching for the first glimpse of light. Then he hears a faint rustling nearby and a subtle, low cough. Adrenaline races through his body. He sits up, and just when he is ready to convince himself that he imagined it, the cough comes again. It's not quite human; it's deeper and raspier. Is it an ape? Or something else?

Lewis touches Kofi's arm to wake him, and immediately, as if responding to the subtle movement of Lewis's hand, the animal takes another step in the leaves and growls. It must be less than a dozen yards away.

"Nkoi," says Kofi quietly. "Le léopard." They listen for a moment, for any clue, but if the cat is moving, they can't hear it.

When the leopard growls again, the sound is so low that it's almost a purr.

Kofi smiles. Now he seems more excited than worried. He calls out to the animal in Lingala the way he might call to a friend.

"Ozo kende wapi?" he asks. Where are you going?

The leopard answers. It seems a little farther off now.

Lewis relaxes. Kofi laughs out loud.

"Kande nayo. Kolya mutu te." Go away. Do not eat any people tonight.

There is no answer. When Kofi yells again at the beast, Lewis joins him. They shout and yell, saying ridiculous things that the other doesn't understand. Challenges to the beast. Offers to eat it instead. Insults and profanity in each language, and then quiet laughter. Lewis falls into a weary sleep.

THEY WALK FOR MOST of the next day without seeing any sign of the leopard. The forest seems unusually quiet when they stop for a rest. If Lewis's sense of direction is any good at all, they have been walking now for two days away from town. He had thought that they would merely skirt the roadblock, give it a wide berth and then head for town, but Kofi clearly has something else in mind. They cannot afford to run into the soldiers.

A twig snaps. Something is out there again.

"Kofi?"

Kofi is already scanning the bush. He touches Lewis's arm and points to a tree about thirty yards away. Lewis sees eyes camouflaged among the leaves like jewels shining in the greenery. An electric shock of fear weakens his heart and arms as he prepares for the leopard to charge. It seems to have the same effect on Kofi, who is now absolutely still. Then Lewis sees another set of eyes. He is puzzled until he sees hands, a bow and arrow, and realizes that the eyes are human.

"Mbote." Kofi greets the men with as light a tone as he can manage, but Lewis can tell he is afraid of them.

One of them steps out of the bush, and at first Lewis wonders if it is some trick of scale or distance in the forest that make the trees seem so unnaturally large; the man looks only four feet tall. Then two more small men step out with their bows drawn. Kofi raises his hands and stands up. Lewis stands, too.

"Toxique." Kofi whispers to warn him that the arrows are more dangerous than the toy sticks they appear to be. He begins talking to the Pygmies, who seem to know Lingala well. They are dressed like Kofi in T-shirts and cheap, worn pants, but with a few pieces of clothing made of bark and animal hide, and they are all barefoot. He shows them that he is not armed, and Lewis holds his hands out, too, and then suddenly the strangers break out in laughter, lowering their bows and slapping their sides with their hands and snapping their fingers to express their hilarity. It's infectious, and soon Kofi is also laughing. There is no doubt that they are laughing at Lewis, but he never learns why. Perhaps it is just the fact of him, a white giant seeking refuge in this forest.

The Pygmies wipe the tears from their faces and without a word turn and walk away, into the forest. And Kofi, who at ten is taller than any of them, follows. Despite his long legs, Lewis, the exotic foreigner, has trouble keeping up; the Pygmies move much faster than even Kofi, and no matter how careful he is, Lewis takes several hard falls. Though the forest is cooler than the direct sun, the humidity makes walking feel like swimming. After three hours of marching without a break, he is exhausted, bruised and dirty.

"Where are we going?" he asks between gasps for air, then gestures in an attempt to sign his question and ends up looking more like he has gone mad.

"*Ils auront de la nourriture. Est-ce que vous avez d'argent?*"

Lewis shakes his head, confused. Kofi rubs two fingers together to indicate money. "*Mbongo?*" he asks quietly so the Pygmies don't hear him.

"*Un peu.*"

The Pygmies have come to a halt where the forest thins out a little. They are smoking from a long pipe made of bamboo. Lewis notices for the first time that one of them has a kind of rucksack made of old canvas. At first it appears that the man is carrying an infant, except that protruding from the top, by its small head, is the tail and hand of a Mona monkey. It is clearly dead.

The Pygmy catches Lewis staring at the monkey. He says something to Kofi, pointing at Lewis and then rubbing his hands together.

"No. No. I just . . ." He shrugs as if he has none.

The Pygmy seems put out by Lewis's response, and the others stop talking. He says something angrily to Kofi, holding out his hand and gesturing aggressively. He expects money. Already the other Pygmies have put away their pipe and are getting ready to leave. The man with the monkey is shouting now at Lewis, waving at him and pointing to the way they've come.

"On doit leur donner l'argent, seulement," Kofi whispers.

Lewis looks at him.

"Mbongo," Kofi tries.

Lewis reaches into his pocket, and the men stop. He would like to be able to do this in a more private way. He realizes that they must not find out how little money he has. He needs to save as much of it as he can, yet give them some now, enough to pique their interest and not offend them. The problem is that he doesn't know the value of the unfamiliar currency, and he cannot simply take it all out and look at it. He needs to give it to them quickly.

He takes out a few coins and watches Kofi's eyes to see if it is too much or too little. Kofi hardly reacts; it must be okay. The Pygmy takes it with a broad smile, satisfied. The men put their bags back down and retrieve their pipe, which seems absurdly long given the size of its owners. It's hard for Lewis to imagine how they carry it without getting hung up on every low branch. They unwrap a small package of green leaves and use a tiny ember they've kept burning to relight the pipe. The blue smoke curls upward, strong and pungent. They pass it to Lewis. He takes a short obligatory drag, managing not to cough too much from the astringent smoke. Then they hand him the bag with the monkey as if it were the greatest of riches. This is Lewis's reward, to carry the dead creature. He slips the backpack over his shoulder as he begins jogging again to keep up. The monkey's small hand sticks out of the top and scratches at his neck like a child begging for attention.

———

To Helen the thought of institutionalizing her mother is defeating. It feels like giving up again, like another loss. But taking care of her has become simply more than she can do. If she falls again, Helen doubts she will be able to pick her up by herself. Any thought she might have had of keeping her mother at home is destroyed by the obvious fact that she has been crippled and is too old to recover. Her decline has been so precipitous that Helen feels like she must be falling, too.

Her mother sits quietly in a chair in the corner of her bedroom, pointing out the things she would like to take with her. The awareness that she is packing not for a trip but for an irrevocable departure gradually overwhelms Helen. Her mother seems more resigned or at least seems to have distanced herself from the reality of it. Helen holds up a dress that she knows her mother will never be able to make use of at the retirement home, but she does not want to exclude it automatically, as if a symbolic point would be made by that choice. There is a such a feeling of finality and significance to each of these decisions.

"You have to have this one, don't you think, Mom?"

"No, dear. I won't need that."

"But you look so pretty in it."

"It's too fancy. It won't get used."

Helen puts the dress back in the closet, hoping to keep herself from crying by getting on with the packing. She turns back, and her mother reaches a hand out to her.

"I'm sorry, Mom. I never . . ."

"It's my fault."

"No."

Her mother puts a hand on her cheek, and though it is too cool and shaky, it calms her. "Come on now, don't be silly. I just got old faster than we thought I would."

It's a struggle, but her mother sits up enough to get both her arms around Helen to give her a hug. And for Helen it feels like a mother's hug—just strong enough to release her. She sits down on the floor and takes her mother's cool hands into her own. Shane's play in the living room, crashing cars and battling spacemen, brings a smile to her mother's face.

"Listen," she whispers. "Who do you think is winning?"

There is an especially loud crash, followed by a wild, spitting laser effect. Helen smiles, too.

"How's he doing?" her mother asks softly.

"He asks about Lewis almost every night. He's been dreaming about him. He's convinced that he's just trapped somewhere in the jungle and he will come home soon."

"What do you tell him?"

"I tell him that he might not be able to come back. I try not to say too much—I don't know." Helen stands up. She gives her mother's hand a squeeze and then lets go to straighten her blouse. She sighs and forces a smile. "He's still just a boy. Never means no more to him than forever."

Her mother looks down at her own frail body. "Funny how your perspective on that changes."

• • •

HER MOTHER DOESN'T LOOK back at the house as Helen helps her from her wheelchair into the car. Shane scoots close to his grandmother as soon as she is settled. He tells her more about Africa as they drive to the retirement home, about the hawk, the monkey that stayed on the boat, about his friend Malik, the boat and the noise and smells of the jungle, the parrots that woke him in the mornings. Helen watches her mother smile in the rearview mirror.

Shane continues talking as they walk her down the hall of the retirement home to her room. It's new but not too sterile. Helen examines the small kitchenette and refrigerator; it won't take much to banish the hotel room feeling. She unpacks the clothes first. Shane carries the empty hangers back to the box as she sets about transforming the room.

"When are you going back to New York?"

"Pretty soon," Helen says, and pounds another nail in the wall, "but not right away. I can stay for a little while."

"No, you should go."

Helen gets off her stool and scoots it over a few paces. "Really, Mom, I'm not in any hurry to get there."

Her mother watches her unpacking for a moment, studying her. "Don't count on me to keep you busy. You'll have this room fixed up in no time."

It takes Helen maybe an hour more to empty the boxes. Her mother has fallen asleep in her chair. Helen helps her take off her shoes and pushes the recliner into a more comfortable position. Her mother opens her eyes without fully waking.

"I'll be here tomorrow morning, Mom. Do you want me to ask someone to help you get ready for bed?"

"No, please don't. I'll be fine."

"Okay." Helen kisses her lightly on the cheek. Shane takes her hand, examining it carefully for a moment before letting go.

ON THE WAY back they stop for gas, and Shane wants a hot dog. She starts to say no, but then she gives in. She pays the attendant with plastic, and he hands her the microwaved frank, which is so hot that she nearly drops it. Through the window she sees Shane waiting on the passenger seat, his hands resting on the smooth dashboard. This scene looks so familiar to her, so mundane, it seems so close to normal—if only it were simply a matter of turning the right corner on the way home to find her life restored. She opens the door and gives Shane the hot dog. The sweet smell of the unnaturally yellow mustard floods the car.

"I think we'll go soon, Shane."

Shane bites into the hot dog. "Hmmgh?"

"To New York." She would like to continue as if it were all just a great a vacation plan, but she can't. "Shane, we're going to have a memorial for your father."

"What's that?"

"That's when . . . Honey, Daddy is gone. You understand, right? He's not coming back. Not ever. That's why we're having the memorial—to remember him."

Shane wraps up the remainder of his hot dog. Then he is absolutely still for a few minutes. When he speaks, his voice is calm and simple.

"I remember him already."

ELILI—L'OBSCURITÉ—SHADOW

IN HALF A DAY'S march they reach a part of the forest that has never been logged. There is less brush to thrash through, but it is more somber under the denser canopy. At the edge of a swamp they catch up with the Pygmies, who have stopped to eat a lunch of dried meat. It's salted enough to look palatable, and Lewis is hungry enough to ignore the flies. The men hardly move as they sit and eat in silence.

Then one of them points across the water, which is choked with yellow flowers and a mat of green leaves. A broad manlike shadow is moving at the edge of the swamp. He is much bigger than any of the Pygmies, bigger even than Lewis. He edges through the brush to the water and wades chest deep to the middle. Lewis's heart skips a beat. It's a gorilla. When the silverback sees them he barks a warning and stands up to his full height, thrashing his mighty arms in the water as if he might be inviting them all to a water fight. The Pygmies fall over themselves laughing.

The animal rushes out of the water and back into the forest. Before he disappears from view, he turns and faces the men again as if puzzled, like a man hesitating at the edge of a clear lake, unsure of his reflection. Then the Pygmies fall suddenly quiet, too. One of them says something so softly that it is almost a whisper. He seems to be speaking to the gorilla. Lewis imagines he can see into the animal's eyes, and there is a startling connectedness, the feeling of a shared past, then the gorilla calls again abruptly, violently. He beats his chest, but there is nothing comical about the haunting sound reverberating in the forest. Lewis can see the yellow teeth in his mouth and the deep red of his tongue.

He looks over at Kofi. He has his fetish out. He handles it secretly, where the men will not see, rolling it over in his hand like a rosary. It's a finger cut off at the middle joint, except for its color, it could be a man's instead of a gorilla's. He slips it back into the satchel and pulls the red tie. Lewis is stunned at his own naiveté, the feeling he had begun to entertain that he had something to connect him to this mad wilderness. Kofi looks genuinely troubled, worried by the sighting of the gorilla, but the Pygmies seem to have already forgotten it.

They move on and eventually come to the Pygmies' camp by a small river. The children are the first to spot Lewis among the hunters. They run over from where they have been playing in the mud but stop a few yards away, giggling and whispering in their nervousness. He is too tired to smile back at them and collapses by one of the cook fires, rubbing his leg to keep the muscles from cramping. When he looks up again at the children, they laugh and run off in mock terror. The women by the fire give him an occasional sideways glance, but mostly they ignore him and go about their business, preparing a meal of bush meat as if it were hardly a strange thing at all to have this white man as a dinner guest.

———

Helen's instinct to run is nearly overpowering. Six girlfriends sit before her in postures of such concentrated empathy she feels like a trapped animal. She senses that they want her to cry, that they are worried by her apparent lack of emotion. She vacillates between guilt for the flashes of anger she feels and gratefulness for her friends' genuine sympathy. Margaret, who has arranged this support group, is pouring tea. The china clinks and rattles softly, and the quiet requests for honey and cream and skinny milk offer a welcome distraction.

Margaret pours a cup of tea for Helen and then sits next to her on the couch. Unconsciously the group hold their breath. She lays her hand on Helen's knee. If there ever was a time to cry, this is it. Helen could break down right now, burst into tears, and they would all join right in. Boxes of Kleenex would be sacrificed to the eventual relief of laughter that would follow. But she cannot. She looks up at them and inhales, taking in a little air, getting up the courage to defy the circumstances and tell them it is all off. No dumb memorial, as Shane put it. But that's impossible. She frees her breath, and they all exhale with her.

Then Margaret turns to the group. "We have work to do," she says, and squeezes Helen's hand. "I know Helen wants to keep this short and sweet. We can do most of it for her."

Helen hears very little of the rest. Plans are being set. Margaret is efficient. She already got Helen to commit to a date, even narrowed the choices of place. Helen chastises herself. Her friends seem sincerely pained and wholly prepared to help.

Perhaps it's that she is so used to eschewing the sympathy of strangers for her and her poor blind child that she has gotten into the hard habit of mistrusting the authenticity of people's intentions.

"Margaret," Helen says quietly, and the whole group falls silent. "I'm going to go peek in on Shane."

"Okay."

Helen gets up and smiles at them all.

It is a relief to be out of the room. She turns the doorknob and slowly opens the door. He's playing with Legos and has already built an elaborate spaceship.

"What's that, honey?"

"Escape pod." He holds up part of the construction in his hand. She walks over and sits next to him on the floor. "I don't want to stay here. I want to go home to our house."

She dreads going out to Westchester, to that empty house. "We'll go after dinner."

She gets up and looks around Margaret's office, a room that has been waiting for years to be a child's room. How much simpler her life once was, much more like this—when she had the freedom to chart her own course. Shane makes a sound effect for the spaceship lifting off, and then it breaks apart in the middle.

"Emergency!" he shouts. "Brrrrp! Brrrrp! Man the escape pod!"

"I've got to go back in there, Shane."

"Okay, Mom. Watch out for alien ships in the hallway!"

Helen laughs.

She shuts the door and walks toward the buzzing voices in the living room. She stops after a few steps. It isn't because she means to eavesdrop. It's more that she is afraid to go back into that room.

"In her heart you know she still believes he might be alive."

"How long has it been?"

"At least three or four weeks, a month, I think."

"My brother was in the Marines. He did jungle training in Panama. He said you wouldn't last more than a week."

"How do you live with the thought that his body is just out there somewhere?"

"I don't know."

It occurs to Helen that she cannot just walk into the room. They need to know that she is coming. She opens the door next to her. It's the bathroom, so she silently sneaks in and shuts the door, turns on the fan so she cannot hear them anymore. She catches her reflection in the mirror. She's horrified to think that this is what her friends see. Her eyes are harsh, her jaw set. Do they hold this against her, that she seems so unfeeling and hard? She wishes she could tell them, in a way that they would understand—she had no premonition of this ending.

She opens the door and flushes the toilet. She hopes this has warned them that she is coming back now. But the conversation is on to food, anyway. She does her best to be helpful and be helped. Their hugs are strong, and feel good, and there are moments when she can actually imagine accepting this inevitable conclusion.

Margaret whispers in her ear at the door after they have loaded the car. "Just take it slowly."

BY THE TIME HELEN and Shane get to the house, it's dark. As they pull into the driveway, Helen's heart takes a sudden leap. The lights are on and it looks like someone is home. Lewis's car is in the driveway. She exhales. He must have left it this way, taken a cab to the airport.

It takes her a moment to unlock the front door. Shane hurries in after her. The house smells bad, like something was left in the refrigerator. The TV is blaring. She turns it off and hears Shane thumping his way upstairs to his room. Otherwise it is silent, and the rooms have an acoustic ring to them, like a new house that needs pictures on the walls, curtains and furniture.

She sits down at the bottom of the stairs and starts to go through the mountain of mail that accumulated at the front door. Catalogues, bills. If she thought it was hard at her mother's house, this is much worse. It's intolerable. How can she live here now? His name is on everything.

NSOMO—LE PRÉSAGE—PORTENT

WITHOUT WARNING THE RAINS have stopped. The bed of the forest has begun to dry out. Daily, Kofi asks if they will be leaving, but the Pygmies are in no hurry. For a while Lewis expects Kofi to decide to leave on his own, but he realizes that there is no way they could hope to find their way out, and now the Pygmies want more money from Lewis. Small groups of men come over in turns, on the pretext of a visit, and bring up the question in an offhand way. Kofi has been trying to hold them off, but eventually they start threatening.

"*Mbongo*," says Kofi.

"How much?" Lewis raises his hands.

The Pygmies press around him now. Kofi doesn't seem worried, more put out, as though he's dealing with children who are not worth his time. His attitude offends them. One of the men shouts and shakes a fist at Lewis. He can see that these small men have no fear of him, his size or his whiteness. He decides that he has nothing to lose; he digs into his pockets and without letting them or Kofi know it, he gives them everything but a few tiny coins he figures are worthless. They don't seem impressed. But Kofi argues, showing them he is not afraid, either, and after some discussion they grudgingly decide to accept the money. There is a brief argument about who will take it, but once it is decided they all seem lighthearted again. Still, they are not offering to take their guests anywhere.

Most of the time Lewis sits by his hut, playing with the children or sleeping. His fevers return once again. In his delirium he's vaguely aware of a small woman who feeds him something from a gourd that makes his face instantly numb. Even after the fever eases, he sleeps so much during the day that he is awake most of the night. He feels he is on the verge of something, and though nothing is forthcoming, his anxiety only grows. It develops into a fear, like a kind of stage fright, a *Trema,* the anticipation of some inevitable cataclysm. He dreams of the edge of the world, a great, bottomless waterfall, where the water is so black it reflects no light, and though it has a surface, it allows no perception. When he pulls back from the edge, when he is able to, the world is empty, and he wakes up knowing for a few lucid moments that he is on the verge of a breakdown. But then that clarity fades, replaced by a transparency even more terrifying, and again Lewis loses himself.

In the middle of one of these endless nights, when his hips are sore from lying in the pile of leaves that are his bed, he gets up and walks down to the river. The moon is bright on the water, and he sits there for a while, listening to the rush of the current over the rocks, and gradually he realizes that he has also been hearing a human voice disguised in its babbling. He follows the sound up the river, away from the camp, pressing through the bush, which is wet with heavy dew. At the edge of the river, in a shallow eddy, one of the Pygmy men is dancing in the water, splashing it over his head into the moonlight, laughing and singing. Lewis quietly crawls away through the brush so that the man does not notice him, and then he sits down, and he cries.

Helen sits on the floor of the kitchen with the answering machine in her hands. She has been trying to change the outgoing message, but she hasn't been able to come up with a version that is usable. When she plays the message back she can hear the shakiness of her voice struggling to sound matter-of-fact. It seems to her like a silly thing to be stuck on, but this is never going to feel right, this omission of Lewis aloud. She realizes she shouldn't have picked this moment to do it, but she has been waiting for Shane to get ready for half an hour.

"Come on Shane, let's go!"

He yells back from the other room. "Where are we going, again?"

"To do some errands. Come on!"

While she waits for him, she studies the notice that she has a registered letter from the U.S. State Department. Her hands are shaking. She knows what it is. She will forward the letter to the insurance man, the state department's first, unofficial assertion that Lewis is presumed dead. She knows it represents nothing more than an official response to her own request for such a document, but it comes now as a kind of notice, a confirmation, as if it were the news, the final word.

When Shane comes down the hall, he is buttoned straight; even the colors of his outfit work well.

"You look handsome, little man."

Shane smiles.

Helen is in no hurry to get to the post office. She puts it off by shopping for groceries and going to the hardware store for a knob that came off the kitchen cabinet. By the time they get to the post office the line is long and slow. It's lunchtime, and Shane is getting hungry. He pulls on her arm, punches her leg, and then when she is able to get him to leave her alone, he pulls on the stanchions that hold up the cord, threatening to knock them over. He is unusually aggressive about it, and she isn't getting the kind of sympathy she normally would from the people near her in line. He is acting too much like a monster.

"Shane, calm down," she snaps, knowing it will have the opposite effect but hoping at least to register some credit with those around her for making the attempt.

He growls back at her and pretends to shoot fire.

By the time they make the head of the line she has nearly destroyed the notice with her sweaty hands. The woman gives her a disapproving look, both for her treatment of the notice and for Shane, who has started hopping on one foot. Helen looks at the line of faces for a grandmother, anyone who will empathize with her, but their hostility allows for no understanding of what she is going through.

The woman hands her a package.

"Is this right?" Helen asks.

The woman takes the package back and looks at the number and address on it. She taps the black ink scrawled there.

"This is you?"

"Yes, but I was expecting a letter, not a package."

"Well, you got a package, dear."

She takes the package. The woman leans past her and shouts for the next person. Helen takes a step out of the way. Shane is hanging on her leg and nearly trips her.

"Shane, please."

She opens it. There is a letter, and then wrapped in a plastic bag, like evidence at a trial, are Lewis's wallet and passport. She pulls them out and stares in utter disbelief. Shane nearly knocks her over with another push, but she doesn't respond.

"Excuse me, Ma'am," says the clerk, with scant politeness. "Can you move to open your mail. You're blocking the line."

Helen moves in the direction that the woman is pointing, awkwardly dragging Shane with her. She lays the wallet on the counter, takes a breath and opens it. There are Lewis's credit cards, but not his driver's license. Tattered and worn, there is the picture of her from the photo shop. She forgot that he still carried it. A chill spreads over her.

"What is it, Mom?"

"Your father's wallet and passport."

She looks at her own disapproving image. If there is to be a record of the first moment he saw her, why does it have to be this one, this snapshot now faded to cyan with time, and so cold? He asked for it back after they had been seeing each other a little while. It was still in the envelope with his phone number, lying on her desk. She was surprised that it hadn't already gone out with the trash.

"This isn't really me, you know."

"It's a moment of you."

She remembers his taking the picture out of the envelope and holding it up to the window to get more light.

"What do you see?" she asked.

"A woman who won't take no for an answer."

She sat down on the kitchen floor next to him, where they had the Sunday newspaper spread all over the tile.

"You have to admit, it's not a great picture."

He held it up to her for comparison. "You're prettier. Softer."

She rolled her eyes.

"No, really."

"Then let me throw it away. It's served its purpose."

"No. Not yet it hasn't."

"What are you going to do with it?"

"I'm going to carry it with me." Lewis put the picture in his wallet.

Helen closes her eyes. There was something in the confidence of his desire for her that she had never wanted to escape. She holds this photograph in her trembling hands. She looks at it again. She could have been an easier woman. If once she knew what she believed in, it has betrayed her now.

"Mom, can I have it?"

She hands Shane the wallet. It looks big and worn in his hands. She thinks of all the intervening time that has worked to destroy this artifact, and yet here it is, like a flare shot up from the wilderness where he disappeared. It is proof of nothing, no more reliable than the feeling she can't shake that the officials have rushed the conclusion that he is dead. Tears well up in her eyes and make reading the letter difficult.

Dear Ms. Burke,

This has been forwarded to us from Mr. Corbeil, in Africa. Apparently, it was given to him by a missionary who was leaving worsening conditions in the countryside. He says that he never met the man, presumably your husband, to whom it belonged. In fact, he got it from someone who worked for him, who offered no explanation of how he came by it. We therefore cannot say with any certainty what it might indicate: when it was taken from your husband or under what circumstances. In the absence of any other evidence to the contrary, we still must assume that Lewis Burke is deceased. Official notice will come after a reasonable waiting period. Nonetheless, please find attached the notarized letter you requested which explains the circumstances of his disappearance. We hope this is helpful. Please accept our most heartfelt regrets.

A hand lightly touches her shoulder. "Are you okay?"

She turns to the stranger, an elderly woman. "Yes, no, yes . . . I'm okay. I'm just . . ." She shrugs to indicate there is nothing to be done about it in any case.

"It's bad news? I'm sorry." The woman smiles and moves back into the line. Shane is suddenly quiet. Helen takes a deep breath, gathers her purse and the package and then looks around as if she has forgotten where the door is.

On the way home Shane holds the wallet. "Are we going back?"

"Where?"

"To Africa."

"No, Shane. No."

"But he's alive."

"No, honey."

"But the wallet . . ."

Helen slows the car and pulls over, afraid to continue driving. She stares ahead and breathes heavily. The cold, overcast day looms dully beyond the windshield. The well-insulated car muffles the sounds of traffic rushing by.

"I know Dad is still alive."

"Shane."

"You shouldn't have made us leave," he says.

Helen is stunned and doesn't answer him right away. "We can't find him, Shane. It's impossible. We tried that. We have to wait this time."

"What if he needs help, Mom?"

She leans awkwardly across the seat to hug him. At first he feels stiff and unwilling to accept the affection, but finally he gives in and hugs her back. She holds him for a long time before easing the car back into traffic.

Kofi is not among the hunters when they return from the bush. The men walk by Lewis's hut without offering any explanation. One of the women lays some food down in front of him and leaves, avoiding his eyes. He is impressed by the helplessness of his situation. He never could communicate that much with Kofi; still, he got some basic ideas across, mixing the few words he knows of French with sign language. Now he cannot even ask after Kofi. Even if he could, he might not be able to interpret the answer. If Kofi has gone off on his own, Lewis will have to hope that he will be tolerated as a guest here until the day the Pygmies decide to take him out of the forest or until they drive him into it.

He looks down at his body. He has lost a lot of weight to the sickness and rations that are only a fraction of what he is used to having. He wonders if, when it comes to it, he will be able to walk out.

After the evening meal, the women and children go to bed earlier than usual. The men seem to make a show of chasing them into their huts. Then they return to the fire and silently wait for something. Lewis looks across his own small fire and the gathering of shadows. Unreal as it once was, it has all become familiar to him. Then there is a sudden, frightening sound from the forest. It sounds like a leopard at first, but louder and somehow otherworldly, as if the forest itself is calling out. The Pygmy men sing, answering back, and then the animal calls again. The younger men in the camp get up to dance, leaping over the fire, daring it to burn them. The older men chant as if singing to that part of the forest that is joy and fear, and life and destruction.

He falls asleep aware of the light of the fire on his eylids, and sometime during the night Kofi comes back. He lays down on his mat of leaves without saying anything to Lewis, and falls into the dead sleep of a child. Lewis wakes and stares at him, wondering if this illusion of death is real or just another mis-interpretation of his trembling thoughts, the sense of dread that has gripped him since coming to this camp.

Another dancer leaps through the fire and lands like a leopard.

IT'S BEEN LIGHT FOR more than an hour. Kofi has been sitting patiently by the hut, waiting for Lewis, making him eat before they leave. The sweet fruit and nuts hurt his stomach, and Lewis has to fight to keep them down.

"*Venez*," Kofi says. He has a short spear in his hand, and he points with it toward the edge of the camp, where a group of men are gathering.

"I can't," says Lewis. "I'm too sick."

Kofi shakes his head. He gets up to walk away. Then he turns.

"*Allons-y!*" He seems anxious. This must be their chance to get out. The hunters are leaving. Lewis stands up with a great effort. Kofi gives him a long staff to help him walk.

The hunters move quietly through the forest with nets and bows. They travel so far that they have to camp overnight. They make beds of leaves without the shelter of a roof. Despite the hard march of the day, Lewis cannot sleep. Faint moonlight filters through the trees. They have made no fire, but he can see the sleeping men in the dim light, his eyes have grown so accustomed to this nocturnal wakefulness. Their faces are still and calm. He wishes that he could borrow their dreams.

At dawn they are walking again, and they walk all day. Lewis has not tried to keep track of their direction. He follows like a child who simply must keep up. They don't even stop for a midday meal. They cross a shallow river that runs clear over some rocks and barely pause for a drink. Lewis looks up at the blinding sun—he has gotten so unused to its full light. When they reenter the forest it is denser than before, and they travel more slowly. The day is almost gone when they come to a road, a muddy rip in the forest.

The Pygmies squat at the edge of the clearing, staring out at the wound. They stop the way an antelope would, waiting for the fear of the open space to subside, to make sure it is safe. As Lewis waits, though, his fear only grows; the forest at his back feels safer, a place to hide. With a low sound from one of them, barely a word, they walk out into the road.

KOZONGA—RETOURNANT—RETURN

THE WALLET SITS FOR almost a week on the countertop, begging for some explanation. It unbalances the house. Whenever Helen puts it away, within a few hours she has it out again. It does not prove that he is alive. It could have been taken from his dead body or while he was held hostage. Nonetheless, the doubts nag. What about this man who worked for the missionary; what if he actually saw Lewis alive? How far is the mission from where the plane landed? Did Lewis make it that far? Did he make it farther? She can't avoid the slim possibility that Lewis is alive, or even if he isn't, that she could find out what happened to him.

The wallet is heavy in her hand. She thinks of the many times she helped him find it when he was leaving in a hurry to catch the train to work. It was a relief to have him on his way, have the house to herself so she could finally get something done. Now the house is so empty that it seems to shout at her. What is there to do here in this place where she cannot find an acceptable moment of peace? Perhaps she is losing her grip, finally. The option of going back to Africa beckons to her as much as it compels her. At least, she thinks, she could escape there, no matter what else comes of it. She imagines Malik's surprise at their return, his willingness to help. His undaunted spirit that would be a welcome relief.

She hears the back door open and Shane's quiet progress through the house.

"Mom?"

"I'm here, Shane, at the table."

As he walks through the kitchen it strikes her that he makes his journey through life, like crossing this room, with much less to go on, but he does it with an uncanny confidence. Every step looks full of hope. She's sure he got this optimism from her. What has happened to that now? She feels so shaken that she is afraid to take her eyes off him, as though everything would be lost if that tenuous thread were to quietly snap. She reaches for a chair to turn it for him, and he adjusts his course to the sound of its scooting on the floor. He sits down next to her, reaching for her leg with his hand, for balance, but he finds the wallet instead. He inspects it silently for a moment, feeling how she holds it.

"If Dad is okay, he might need this," he says, with a maturity that startles her. He takes the wallet from her and opens it. Without Lewis's credit cards or his driver's license it looks empty, but its message is shouting at her. He could be alive. So much time has been allowed to pass. How could she have given up and come back? How could she have waited here this long?

The Pygmies come around a corner in the road and run smack into a small military patrol. It's night. The rebels shout, and one of the Pygmies shoots a poison arrow into the group of ten or more soldiers, not one of whom is older than fifteen. When the arrow sticks into one boy's arm, he yells and falls to his knees, crying as the poison burns like fire into his arm. The boys start shooting their rifles at the Pygmies, who are already running for the bush. Red tracers streak through the blackening forest, strike a tree or wing off into the night like mad fireflies.

Lewis runs. He gets to the edge of the road, but then he trips and falls into the deep grass, hurting his shoulder. Some of the Pygmies have circled behind the boy soldiers, and they have taken a rifle from the first, who is already dead. It is ridiculous, this fight in the dark, but the contest is more equal. The Pygmies can flank the rebels and sneak up to bow range, but with only the moon providing light, their aim is poor. Lewis lies with his head in the grass to protect it from the wildly scattered bullets. Kofi does the same a few feet away. Lewis can't understand why the Pygmies aren't just running back into the bush.

Then it is quiet. He can hear the soldiers talking, but he can't hear the Pygmy men at all, and he wonders if they have run off. The voices are approaching him, agitated, wondering, too, where the small men have gone, if they are preparing an ambush or if the they have retreated. Lewis hears the crisp sound of clips being reloaded and set in the rifles as the boys get closer. If the rebels continue coming as they are, they will walk right over them.

When the soldier shouts, he is standing less than three feet away. Lewis hears his boots settle in the grass. He closes his eyes in an attempt to concentrate on the choice before him. If he pulls the boy down, he has to get that rifle and be prepared to use it immediately. Odds are the boy has a round chambered and the weapon is ready to fire. Unless there is a safety to fumble with in the dark, Lewis will be all right. Still, the soldier will not give up his life casually, and he isn't going to go down quietly. But if Lewis does not take the chance, and the boy discovers him, he will have lost any advantage he might have had. Lewis tries to calm his breathing. He should have a plan, some goal—to pull the soldier down, take his rifle if he can . . . and then what? The soldiers are so keyed up with the game of hide-and-seek with the elusive forest men that if he is discovered, they will definitely shoot Kofi and him right where they lie.

The soldier takes another step, then inexplicably stops again. He may be waiting for the others to catch up. Lewis grabs the boy's leg and pulls him off his feet so easily that he, too, is caught off guard and doesn't move to the next step as quickly as he should. The boy yells. Lewis leaps up and jumps on top of him, hitting his face as hard as he can. It distracts the soldier long enough for Lewis to get his hands on the rifle. The soldier is still holding on to the weapon, but Lewis's size gives him the advantage. With a force that surprises both of them, he shoves the soldier back down and pulls the rifle from him. Then just as suddenly Lewis hits him in the head with the butt of the weapon. The jarring blow causes Lewis to lose his grip. The boy rolls away, yelling and holding his head. Lewis takes advantage of the moment to back away and get a proper hold. He turns and sees Kofi getting up, and beyond him he can just make out the soldiers rushing at him from about a hundred yards, raising their rifles. One of them has a flashlight, though he has not found Lewis yet.

Lewis has the rifle aimed at the soldier who is still thrashing on the ground. He holds it awkwardly. If he tried to fire this automatic weapon holding it this way, he would instantly lose control of it. Even so, at such close range he can see into the young soldier's eyes, see the fear, and he would undoubtedly manage to seriously hurt the boy. His finger rests on the trigger, a tiny squeeze away, but despite the gunfire now coming at him and the rage that came to him in the attack, he doesn't shoot. The boy gets up and runs away. He is nearly killed by his comrades instead. Lewis lifts the weapon up and fires randomly at the shadows of the rebels. He feels invincible, and they somehow perceive it, or perhaps they are merely surprised to see the shape of such a big man where they were expecting only the poorly armed Pygmies. They aren't prepared to be shot at, and they turn and run. Lewis lowers the weapon, burning his hand on the breech. Then he sits down. A cloud covers the moon, making it impossible to see anything.

"Lewis!" Kofi shouts.

"Here."

Kofi creeps over to Lewis, staying low. *"On ne peut pas rester ici. Tokende!"*

But Lewis does not move. Kofi takes the gun, which is now lying in the grass by Lewis's feet. He hefts it, appreciating its weight and its power.

"Venez." Kofi starts walking away beside the road, where he can duck into the bush quickly if it becomes necessary. The moon is out again, just enough to see the trees against the sky. Lewis finally gets up to follow. He walks in the grass on the edge, afraid for some reason of walking in the bare dirt. Then he stops. There is a dark shape in the grass at his feet, like a crouching leopard, but something is wrong with the animal. He kneels to see it better and realizes that it is one of the Pygmy men. He touches the warm body. His bow is still tight in his hand.

"Allons-y," Kofi hisses again. *"Les rebelles reviendront bientôt."*

Lewis suddenly feels sick. He backs away from the body and drops to his knees. When he looks up, trembling, the sight of Kofi standing a few feet away, holding the rifle in his hand,

262 • MARCUS STEVENS

gives him a start. He could so easily be one of the rebel soldiers who attacked them or the boy Lewis knocked down, the boy who once carried this rifle and who will want it back. Kofi motions for Lewis to follow, and they run down the road until Lewis has to stop to catch his breath. He looks behind him between gasps. He can just make out the road; no one is there, nothing to suggest that the rebels were ever anything more than phantoms.

———

The dull roar of the plane silences Helen's doubts. The smell of Africa, the damp swimming air, the mad noise that invades the cabin when they open the airplane doors, welcome her back. The line in customs is long, and this time no one spots her and Shane and calls them to the front. Already she feels a shift in the progress of time or her perception of its urgings. It's good to be closer to Lewis—whatever has happened to him—and a relief to be doing something again. At least it puts off the inevitable.

When she cancelled the memorial, Margaret seemed disappointed in her. "This will only make things worse."

"They cannot be worse."

"Just don't stay too long. There has to be a reasonable end to it."

Helen wonders now if that can be true—that there has to be a reasonable end to anything. She looks at the faces of the people around her in the line, people whose lives have been so different from her own, and she doubts that they would think so.

Malik meets them outside the airport. It's easy to find his smile amid the throng. For a moment she could forget what she has come for. They load her two bags into his old Toyota, and Shane scoots across the sun-scorched seat to the window. Helen fights a sudden pang of anticipation or dread that turns her stomach and concentrates instead on Malik's firm hand on the steering wheel. Palms race by dizzily in her peripheral vision, and Shane floats his hand out the window like a soaring bird.

Malik takes them to his store so Helen can get some food and basic supplies. He's found a place for her to rent, nothing special by American standards, he says, but it has a kitchen and it's a short walk to his store and the embassy. After Helen has a few groceries, mostly snacks for Shane and a little UHT milk for her coffee, they drive the few blocks to the apartment. He opens the door wide, clearly eager that she like it. The apartment is on the second floor, and the windows look out on a blossoming jacaranda tree full of birds. Shane hurries to the window as the birds light into song like a welcoming band. Malik grins, taking the credit.

"It feels like this will be home, Malik."

"The woman who lives downstairs will cook for you."

"Oh, that's not necessary, really. I enjoy cooking."

He looks disappointed. "Perhaps there are other things she can do."

Helen realizes her mistake. "Certainly."

"I have a present for you, Monsieur." He hands a bright yellow ball to Shane, who takes it and lifts it like a sun into the air over his head. Malik laughs.

"I'm not sure what I'm going to do first, Malik," Helen says casually.

"You will think of it, Madame," he says, still laughing. Helen has the impression that he has his own idea about what to do but is not saying.

"It's hard to know," she continues, hoping to draw it out of him.

He nods.

"Of course I will go to the embassy."

"Yes." He still seems to be stalling.

"Malik. What do you think I should do?"

"The authorities will not be much help, of course. But there are other ways, if you are willing."

Helen hesitates. There is something in the offer that makes her uneasy. He misunderstands her hesitation.

"Not too expensive."

"Malik, I'm sorry, I don't know what you are talking about."

"*Une féticheuse.*"

"A witch?"

"A healer."

Shane bounces the ball, and it gets away from him. Helen catches it awkwardly.

"We'll see, Malik. I don't know."

Malik takes the ball from her and holds it over Shane's head for a moment, and Shane reaches for it, stretching his arms; then Malik slowly lowers it to him. He leaves without saying anything more about the *féticheuse*. After the rattle of Malik's Toyota is lost in the general din of traffic, Shane sits with his ball on the couch.

"Can she do magic, Mom?"

"Who?"

"The *féticheuse*."

"How do you know about that?"

"Can she?"

"I don't know, Shane. Maybe it seems like magic."

Sometime after the cool fog of the morning has burned away, Lewis and Kofi come to where the road ends at a broad river. There are monkeys everywhere—in the trees, on the dilapidated landing at the water's edge, digging through piles of garbage, and climbing on the nearly collapsed frames of market stalls. They scream when they see the boy and white man, but they hold their ground, retreating a few yards only when Kofi waves the rifle at them. He sets it down by a tree, threatening the monkeys again with his fists, and begins searching for something along the banks of the swollen river.

Lewis sits next to the rifle, relieved to give his exhausted legs a rest. He squints at the searing sparks of light reflected off the river. The water doesn't look cool or inviting; it looks more like warm syrup. Along the bank a tangle of driftwood has washed up into the brush. When one of the logs moves, he realizes that they are actually crocodiles.

He looks back down the river; Kofi is out of sight. The monkeys have quieted enough that he can hear Kofi splashing in the water as he walks along the shallow edge. One of the monkeys has taken a particular interest in Lewis. It sits only a few feet away, watching him. It has the rind of some fruit, which it chews on as if in contemplation.

"What?" Lewis says to the animal.

The monkey spits some of the rind out and tilts its head.

"What are you looking at?"

The monkey makes a soft, clucking cough and scoots closer. Lewis picks up the rifle and the monkey stops. He lays it across his lap. The monkey has canines like a dog's but sharper. He wonders if it means to bite him. It is so close that he couldn't really use the rifle quickly enough to defend himself if the animal did decide to attack.

"I might eat you."

The monkey shrieks as though this has to be some kind of joke. Lewis must not look like the monkey-eating type. Or perhaps it is trying to say that it might just eat the white man it sees collapsed weakly under this ragged palm. As if to confirm

it, the monkey opens its toothy mouth wide in a yawn. Then
Lewis realizes what interests it so much. All this time he has
been unconsciously fiddling with his few leftover coins, rubbing
them together nervously in his hands.

Suddenly the monkey makes a dash at him and grabs the
coins. It happens faster than Lewis can react, and he recoils at
the sharp scratch of the animal's fingernails as it digs into his
hand for the coins. It runs away screaming and shrieking in
triumph.

"You can have them!" Lewis yells after it. "They're worthless."

Now the other monkeys join the thief in taunting Lewis. They
shriek and run up and down the trees, shaking the branches, then
jumping to the ground and spinning in a chaotic sort of dance.
He grabs several rocks and throws them, scattering the monkeys.

"I don't care," he shouts. "Do you hear that, you goddamn
monkeys? I don't give a shit."

He closes his eyes. When he opens them again, he will be in
New York or back on the airplane, or waiting at Orly or calling
Helen to apologize, if he can, for years of turning away at precisely the moment he should have stayed. He wishes he had her
picture and Shane's. They're the only things he had in his wallet that now seem worth anything. Then he feels hands on his
face, like Shane's hands looking at him. It nearly makes him
jump and open his eyes, but he forces them to stay closed. The
hands are cool and small, just like Shane's. He has the sense
that if he can keep his eyes closed, resist the temptation to use
his sight, this really will be Shane. The thought makes his heart
ache.

When the hands lift away, he continues to hold his eyes shut
until he hears Kofi splashing back toward him down the bank.

He's wading in the shallow water, pulling a pirogue. It's in terrible shape, holding water, rotten at one end, but Kofi seems delighted. He waves triumphantly to Lewis.

The pirogue floats, just barely. Lewis is particularly big for it, and though Kofi has taken the rotten end, where Lewis rides it still sinks partway into the river. The water washes around his legs, and it would be something of a relief out here where there is no shade, if it were not for his fear of the crocodiles that occasionally float past. Lewis points them out. Kofi laughs and mimics their great biting jaws. He guides the pirogue with a broken pole that he also managed to find somewhere along the bank. Water drips from the pole as he lifts it, sending small drops dancing across the surface. Otherwise it is almost silent on the river.

Though the water appears placid, Lewis can now feel the strong current, and as the afternoon wears on, its pull seems to intensify. He remembers the *ndoki,* her warning about *la rivière,* and touches the talisman at his neck, wondering if it is a blessing or a curse. The river pulls on the banks, creating eddies behind fallen trees that swirl into whirlpools. Kofi uses the pole to keep them straight or to push them to the protection of one of the banks when they think they hear human sounds coming from the shore. It is an uncomfortable place to travel. The branches hang low, and they have to duck and push them away to get through. As soon as it feels safe again, they pole out into the open current.

———

Helen wakes slowly, not yet adjusted to the regular rhythm of the equatorial sun, which rises and sets exactly every twelve hours like a warm heartbeat. She sits up, letting the sheets fall back onto the bed, and turns her face to the sun.

There is something here that makes her feel more comfortable than she has since Lewis has been missing. Perhaps it is merely something in the first impression of the sun, that side of Africa, which seems to offer life so easily and generously. Perhaps it is the search itself, transformed from an urgent rescue to deliberate waiting.

She listens for a while to Shane in the other room. She hears him get off the old couch where they made his bed and find his way to the small refrigerator, which labors with a loud hum and rattle in the kitchenette. He is still learning the room, and she hears him bump into things, then step back and find a new way. It's hard on her to hear his small shins bang into a chair or his elbow strike an unexpected table.

They rise this way every day, without an assigned purpose. They wander late into the street to Malik's store to buy a few things, then on various errands. They have gone to the bank to set up a system for wiring money and then back again several times to try to get the system to actually work. In her barely adequate French she has asked local people—the woman who cooks downstairs and people at the market—what they have heard, listening for news that may have reached here from the countryside. She has not called the embassy. She's savvy enough now to know that she must find another way around impossible obstacles like the government officials and roadblocks.

Helen gets up, pulling her clothes on before the jacaranda tree. She finishes her breakfast with Shane, who eagerly chats about their plans for the day. He is a man of action, excited to meet the *féticheuse*.

"A real sorceress!"

Helen widens her eyes in mock fear, forgetting herself, then puts her hand on his shoulder, imparting a different and unintended tone to her response. "Aren't you afraid?"

"What will she be like?"

"She will be pretty much like anyone else, Shane. Don't be disappointed."

Malik knocks on the door and comes in. He, too, seems excited. He stands anxiously by the door as Helen gets a few things together so they can leave. Shane holds his hand as they walk the main street and then turn into a series of side streets, dirt alleys with gigantic potholes. Soon Helen is completely lost.

The sign says in French: "Madame Courouis, Féticheuse. Miracles. Will cure every kind of sickness and blindness, also love and financial problems. Look for evil in the hearts of men, not in God."

The air in the tiny house is hot and claustrophobic, overheated by a bare tin roof. The pale blue room is hung with religious pictures, and a crucifix hangs over the door. The *féticheuse* sits on a low, carved stool. She looks first not at Malik or Helen, but at Shane. She reaches out a hand for him, and before Helen can stop her she has pulled him away from Malik, clasping his small hand in her two hands. There is something odd in the way she regards Shane, as if she cannot yet see what most can spot from across a room: that he is blind.

"*Il n'est pas malade.*" She laughs. He is not ill.

"*Non,*" is all Malik says, so Helen offers her own voice.

"That's not why we've come," she blurts out, and then offers her explanation. As she listens to Malik translate her words into something that sounds much more like a plea than she intended, she wonders to herself why she has come. Still, she smiles through it all, endorsing the unknown message. The old woman looks directly at Helen for the first time. She looks normal. Her eyes seem glazed with cataracts, and her hair is nearly white. She looks more like the family's forgotten relic than a powerful healer.

"*Asseyez-vous.*" The *féticheuse* coughs hoarsely as she invites them to sit down.

There are no chairs, so they sit on the floor on a bright orange and green rug that seems to be there for that purpose. Helen pulls Shane away from the *féticheuse* and holds him protectively in her lap. Along one wall a roughly hewn table is suspended from the ceiling like a cot meant for a patient to lie on. Next to that is a low shelf with gourds and small vials. The room smells strongly of spice, more like a kitchen than Helen's idea of a healer's chambers.

"She wants money. A thousand francs," says Malik.

"What? You're kidding. She hasn't done anything yet." She glances at the woman, who doesn't seem to know any English; still, Helen lowers her voice to a whisper. "Suppose she is a fake."

"Fake? I don't know this word."

"A fraud. She needs to demonstrate that she is worth the money. A thousand francs is a lot."

"She is no fraud," says Malik, offended. "Everyone knows who she is."

Helen looks at the woman, who can tell from Malik's tone the nature of the conversation. Helen addresses her directly.

"I am not looking for a miracle." She stops. It occurs to her that even in the most Cartesian view of the world, she is looking for precisely that—for some colliding of accidents or chance connections that will find its way to the truth. The old woman smiles, and she seems so generous that Helen regrets her tone.

Malik's voice, translating, is calm. "She asks you, what is a miracle? Is it a mother's touch that calms a child's nightmare?

If she tells you about the future, is it merely chance when it is fulfilled? Who can tell? She says you must believe what you wish, Madame. But how can you say, for sure, that your own dreams are only fantasy?"

The *féticheuse* lays a hand on Helen's, and it is cold and trembles slightly. As she speaks in her raspy French, and as Helen waits for Malik to translate, the old woman studies her eyes.

"You will have to wait to know what has happened to your man. I cannot see or hear the answer. When I listen, I hear only a deafening roar. Maybe I am too old. You must listen, too." The *féticheuse* lets go of Helen's hand. "Perhaps a dream."

She begins gathering odd pieces of stone and bones and shells and twisted roots into a small bag. The way she handles them, their presentation, alters them from the ordinary things they are. Helen reaches out for them, but the woman pulls the bag away and pushes it into Shane's hands.

"These are for the boy, who can already see without eyes," she tells Malik. "These will help him hear his father when he is near. They will help him know what to listen for. The song of a bird, or the cry of a monkey that is of significance."

Then she turns to Helen again. Her tone is very matter of fact. "Everyone will be looking for him now. Does that help?"

For this she wants another five hundred francs. Malik explains that her stocks of medicine are low: this would be a kind of donation. Helen grudgingly pays the additional money. And they leave without further fanfare; no crystal ball, just the pragmatic solution Helen would have asked for, that the word get out so people know to be looking for Lewis—and a souvenir for Shane to keep. Helen turns back as they walk out. The old woman is counting her money.

Boeta—Les Cataractes—Cataracts

Sitting in the old dugout, half wet for three days now, Lewis's face is burned and chafed, and his waterlogged legs feel like they may actually rot. At first it seemed like the best way to travel: to be carried, pulled by the river to its end, but it has become a stunning kind of torture.

Lewis motions to Kofi. "I must get to the shade."

Kofi looks up at the searing white ball overhead. Lewis points again and shades his face with his hand like a man expecting a blow. Around the sun the sky is white. Kofi dips his broken pole in the water and slowly pushes the pirogue toward the shore. They will need to travel in the evening and at night from now on. Lewis closes his eyes tightly and does not open them again until they reach the shade and he feels the pirogue sink into the silt of the shallows.

"*On doit se reposer.*"

The spot where they have landed is hardly inviting. They

struggle to get just a few feet away from the water and muck. The bush is low and cramped and swarming with bees and flies. Lewis is exhausted, so any respite from the river is miraculous enough. He lies down like a winded dog, curling up to keep his feet out of the water. The shade is cool, though even here it must be ninety. A layer of motionless air hovers over the ground and seeps out of the impenetrable vegetation that has acquiesced this spit of mud.

"*Lala,*" Kofi whispers, closing his eyes and resting his head against the twisted trunk of a small tree.

Lewis's lungs struggle weakly with the humid air. He hears a voice. Shane's. All he has to do now to be in his son's world is to close his eyes. He listens for the whisper, as insects crawl over his body, some biting, some merely crawling as if waiting for rot to begin its intimate softening of the skin.

He thinks of his empty coffin and the eulogy that attempts, and even momentarily succeeds, in conjuring a sense of momentousness. It lends a certain weight to the now irrelevant fact of his existence. More convincing is the inevitable ending—the moment the river rises with the floods of the rainy season and soaks into his body, what remains of it, pulls the last vestiges of him into the muck. Helen walks outs of the church with more of him in her heart than Shane has, who will one day struggle to remember him. She has all that's left—the memory of his smell, the sound of his voice, his most foolish secrets, and his brief successes. With an impassive equity these are in her hands now. It is Helen's warm hand, and her lips, the soft curve of her arm, the confidence of her eyes that matter. What were these laurels he expected from living, for something that will pass faster than wood can rot in the rainforest?

Lewis opens his eyes. Kofi is shaking his arms, trying to get him awake enough to move.

"Réveillez-vous, Lewis. Réveillez-vous!"

He lifts himself somnambulently into the pirogue, vaguely aware that the afternoon is gone and the sun is easier on his eyes. He sits down again in the tepid water, swamping the hull of the unsound boat, coughs deeply and nods to Kofi that he is ready.

Kofi pushes them into the current, leans hard on the pole once or twice to straighten the pirogue, then lays it into his lap and lets the current take them. At first the river draws them with the same monotonous, inexorable pull that they have come to feel like a quiet dread, and then it seems to quicken, accelerating steadily with each mile. Dusk gives way to a night of brilliant stars and half a moon. Then Lewis first hears the dull roar of the cataracts.

"What is it?"

"Les cataractes."

"Cataract? A waterfall?"

Kofi shrugs, but he is not pulling the boat out of the current. The pirogue dips and rocks in the small waves of the rapids that lead to the real cataracts.

"We should not do this at night," Lewis whispers.

Kofi doesn't understand. Lewis raises his voice.

"Not at night. . . . *Nuit . . . non.*"

"Pourquoi pas?"

Lewis sits up abruptly, shaken out of his stupor now. The cataracts are rising to a deafening roar.

"We should walk around." Lewis signals with his hand.

Kofi looks blankly at him, waiting patiently for him to catch up with the reality of their circumstances. They cannot walk around. They cannot carry the pirogue. Waiting for day will not change anything, only delay the inevitable; the cataracts will be the same. It won't make any difference to plunge in without the dubious benefit of being able to see before them what they simply must risk.

Amid the slick blackness of the river, the white foam of breaking waves glows faintly in the moonlight, teasing the limits of Lewis's vision. Soon the whole river seems to be churning, and the roar of the cataracts is deafening. Kofi does his best to keep the pirogue out of the main current and keep them straight. They have almost made it halfway when a standing wave pushes them hard from the side, into the thick of the current. For a few exhilarating minutes they manage to stay upright. Then for a long, extended few seconds they are with the pirogue even though it has been completely submerged.

Suddenly it is completely quiet, and the darkness is absolute. To his eyes there is only the faint whiteness of the turbulent water. He does not breathe what is now more water than air. And the river pulls him down with a force so unappeasable that he does not attempt to resist it. He spins and twists and falls and is lifted up, thrown and embraced in rapid succession. As water floods into his body, his orientation fails him, and he begins to feel ethereal, as if he is nothing more than a suspended thought spreading through the river. It feels good, this escape from gravity. But there *is* some voice that is shouting at him, *Swim, swim!* The burning in his lungs makes him try it, but he is so disoriented that he accomplishes little in the attempt. His body strikes heavily against a rock, sending pain through his right arm, and jars him into struggling to survive. He claws at the water with his good arm and kicks like an animal. Then, although there is no light and he can see nothing, there is air, and he sucks a great gasp of it into his lungs before going under again.

Then the river takes his body, and his consciousness washes away into dreams. Miraculously he has left the river and the forest. He walks into his house, already bracing for it to be empty. The door swings open with barely a click. He reaches to turn on the lights, but they don't work. He stops; the power is out. There is no hum from the refrigerator, no mechanical sound at all to greet him, and he can sense the lack of it, the electricity that should be trembling inside the walls, warmly wrapping his body in its magnetic field.

His muddy shoes on the parquet oak floors feel like a violation, like some breach of manners, as if he's walking on someone's dining room table. He kicks his shoes off and walks carefully to the stairway with the idea of calling up to see if the house is really empty, but he is afraid to disturb the formal silence. He wanders through the house into windowless rooms he doesn't remember, afraid to touch anything, aware of the muddy, wet trail he is leaving behind, wishing there were a way to clean it up. The mess becomes worse with every step. Great, improbable globs of sludge fall from his hands, slick pools of water already choked with algae, wet gravel and stones, pieces of bone, black ragged feathers, and then matted hunks of hair that at first seem to come from some animal but then he realizes that they are coming from him. He pulls at the *ndoki*'s bundle. It reeks. He tears it from his neck and drops it amid the debris on the floor.

The dustless, antiseptic smell of the house is overwhelmed now by the smell of wet, unwashed animals, urine, sharp with the scent of hormones, and excrement. He steps in it and tracks it across the white carpet of the bedroom. When he touches the aluminum-framed window by the bed, it rusts and begins to fall apart. The fumes of cleaning agents coming from the bathroom are burning his eyes, and suddenly he begins coughing uncontrollably as if his lungs are filled with toxic liquids. He falls to his knees; blood and bile mix with the sulfurous water that pours from his mouth, and the whole strong mixture is swimming with parasites that swarm and spread across the carpeting. Lewis yells in terror and runs from the house.

The light outside is stunning, as if the sun has been fantastically amplified. He covers his eyes, afraid of being blinded, and stumbles a few steps across the perfectly trimmed lawn, which cuts into his bare feet. He tries to yell again, and he does, but he cannot compete with the blinding light that seems to drown out the sound. He runs out into the black asphalt of the street. The pavement is so hot that it blisters his feet. He is trying to find another person, but no one is outside. He runs down the block. The houses are all white. Their windows are like dead eyes. Still no people. No dogs or cats or children. The cars are as empty as the streets.

He opens the doors to one of the houses and takes a few steps in, but he is afraid to go much farther than the threshold. He screams dryly into the entryway and gets no answer.

At last Lewis finds a tree that has some size to it, not one of the hopeless seedlings dying in the shrill manicured lawns, but a tree with shade, an old tree that must be left over from a time before the houses were built. It has been scarred by lightning, and there are huge rips where great limbs were torn off by the wind. Nonetheless there is still a good canopy to it. He sits in its cool relief and closes his eyes.

Boyebisi—Le Messagère—Messenger

THE MESSAGE COMES IN the afternoon, when the rain is beating
down on the red dirt as if it might be angry. Shane is sitting by
the window, eating soggy Weetbix and playing with a small
Braille typewriter Helen brought with them. He hears the footsteps long before the messenger arrives. He hears them through
the storm and the traffic and the noise of the children playing
downstairs. He walks his fingers on the same two keys, back
and forth in rhythm with the sound. Helen is about to ask him
to stop when a sharp knock at the door startles her. She gets up
and opens it to a young African girl, maybe fifteen, leaning on
one hip, one foot resting on the calf of the other leg.

"*Venez, Madame. Le blanc était vu sur la rivière.*"

When Helen doesn't seem to understand, the girl repeats her
message. This time Helen can make out "white man" and "the
river."

"Is he alive?" Helen desperately searches her mind for the right word in French. *"Vivant?"*

The girl shakes her head, but she doesn't seem to be saying no.

Helen tries to tell her to wait. She leans against the doorjamb with such relaxed patience it makes Helen feel self-conscious about her sudden hurry. She points to the couch and tries again. This time the girl understands the intention, and she sits with her hands on her knees, her legs crossed.

"Where are we going, Mom? Is he okay?"

"I don't know, Shane. She said *'la rivière,'* the river. Malik will have to help us."

Helen hurries into the bedroom to pack. Her mind races, as she tries to remind herself that this could be nothing, a rumor or, worse, the bad news she has been dreading.

Shane sits down next to the girl, who studies him curiously. "I don't speak African."

She smiles and picks up his yellow ball, turning it in her hands. Shane hears the movement, and he guesses what she is up to. He lifts his hands, and she tosses the ball the short distance to him.

"Zua," she says softly. Catch.

Her voice helps him time it. The ball lands in his hands, and he manages to pull it to his chest before it bounces away. The girl laughs, and he tosses it back to her without giving her enough warning. His aim is off. She reaches for it, but the ball bounces off of her fingers and across the room.

"Sorry."

The girl doesn't say anything. She gets the ball and hands it to him. He sits there for a moment, as if he's unsure of where she is. Then she begins to sing to him, a simple song in Lingala that rhythmically repeats the words *bandeke,* birds, and *bazo pumba*, fly. He listens for a moment and then realizes that she is singing to help him with his aim, and this time when he throws the ball she catches it.

THEY FIND MALIK AT his home. It's in an area of Kinshasa that suffered from the looting by the army before the war. There are a few ruined houses along the way, but his is well kept and bustling with children. His Toyota sits prominently in front, as if in a reserved spot, and the kids give it plenty of room as they rush to greet the visitors with peals of delight. Shane tightens his grip on Helen's hand a little as they gather around. Before they get to the door with their entourage, Malik comes out to greet them. He seems happy that they have come to his home.

"Welcome, *Madame et Monsieur.*"

He repeats his questions to the girl several times, as though there is some part of her story that does not make sense to him.

"What is she saying, Malik?"

"A white man was seen going into the cataracts of a river, a tributary of the Congo, in the north."

"How does she know about it?"

"I don't know. Her answer is not so clear. She says she is just passing on the message. I don't know how the news got all the way down here; perhaps someone from the ferry. Or you never know, perhaps the visit to the *féticheuse* was not so foolish."

Helen smiles. "How far is it?"

"Days by car. In fact, I don't think it is possible to drive there anymore. I am going to telephone a friend about this. Can you wait?"

They sit in the main room of the small house, which isn't as big as the apartment that they've rented. There isn't much light. Heavy drapes hang on the small windows, and the walls are a dark blue, which only makes it darker. But it is cool. They hear his wife in the kitchen with an older child, and in a few minutes the two come out with a plate of food, yams with slightly charred skins.

Malik's wife looks much younger than he, in her twenties, probably. She's wearing a neatly kept dress of colorful West African fabric, and she smiles as she offers the yams to Helen.

"*Merci*," Helen says, and takes a piece for Shane, too. Malik's wife laughs. Maybe it's Helen's accent or nervousness. She offers some to the girl, who takes a whole yam, not bothering to hide her obvious hunger. Helen feels awkward to sit in silence, and she is aware of Shane's noisy eating. She lays a hand on his leg to try to quiet him. When Malik finally returns, he looks ready to leave.

"You must take a bush plane. It's the only way to get in there. I can fly in with you to set things up."

"You can't stay?"

"Someone has to make sure the airplane goes back when it's time. Otherwise they just forget about you. Something more important comes up."

"How long?"

"I don't know, Madame, that is up to you."

"Four days?"

"It will be enough, I think."

"When do we go?"

"When you are ready, Madame. We can take this girl home on the way."

"Malik, is this a waste of time?"

He smiles quietly, remembering this concern of hers with "wasting time." Then he shrugs. "Who else could this man be? It's a desperate thing to take a pirogue into the cataracts. But if it is your husband, he went a long way from the jet."

"Is it possible?"

Malik doesn't respond immediately. He's thinking about it. "A man can walk a long way if he has to, farther than he might think."

"Why would he take the river, not take the road?"

"There is no road up there, Madame."

"No road?"

"There are a few footpaths, if you know the way, a few fishing villages. There is not much at all."

"Could he be alive?"

"Those cataracts are very bad, I think, Madame."

"If he was alive, he would have been found by someone, don't you think?"

"Yes, I think so. A white man does not walk out of this river every day."

Helen feels a shock settle in her heart. She leans back into her chair, trusting it to catch her.

"Do you think there is even one chance in a million, Malik?"

"I think there is what happens to a man. Not much else."

Helen turns to Malik's wife. Her face is quiet and empathetic. *"Bonne chance, Madame,"* she says.

THEY DROP OFF THE girl on the way to the airport, on what seems an indiscriminate stretch of road. There are no buildings to be seen, just footpaths cutting into the thick brush that crowds the road. The girl takes some money from Malik with very few words and turns away without waving. She disappears into the forest like a breath of wind that will be forgotten as soon as the leaves on the bushes cease to tremble.

The bush plane looks all right, not what she expected, not like the rundown cabs in town. The well-educated Congolese pilot seems to have spent most of his life in Belgium; his French is natural to him. His manner with Malik is tense, possibly a bit racist, as though he prefers the white miners and loggers who are his usual fares. While he preflights the plane, Malik helps Helen load her bags. Shane sits by the plane and waits while his mother rechecks her packing to make sure she has everything they have to have—particularly money and malaria pills. Finally she looks up, satisfied that everything is there.

"Okay, I'm ready."

Most of the way, the plane flies over the Congo river. The forest hides any villages and roads that might be down there, and there are only few barges now and then. Otherwise it is a vast basin of bush and forest, flat and infinite. At this low altitude, it does not feel like they could ever escape this green universe. The river lies spoiled and rotten like a worm in its verdant bed, fat and pregnant with silt. Helen tries to describe the landscape below to Shane, wondering what his imagination makes of the information, abstractions like *green* and *wild,* and what his idea of *forest* must be.

A flock of pink flamingoes rises out of one of the many channels that braid though the islands. She describes it to him as a pink cloud, and then reconsiders. "It looks like the sound of rain when there isn't a wind—just a mist that feels good on your skin."

The plane drones on for hours, and Shane falls asleep. They leave the big river and follow a tributary away from it. At first there is a road below them, and then it peters out. Finally the river narrows, and the landscape begins to have some contour to it, not just a wide, flat, undifferentiated carpet of green. The pilot dips a wing and begins a wide circle over the river, descending dramatically. Under the wingtip the color of the river has changed from a deep brown to almost white, and she realizes she is looking at the lower end of the cataracts. As they get closer a chill spreads over her. No one could survive that.

The approach to the dirt runway is difficult. They bounce in a crosswind only a few feet over the trees and then drop in hard on the narrow strip. The small plane rattles and shakes when the pilot slams on the brakes. Shane bangs his head on the window as he sits up and the plane makes a last hard brake at the end of the strip. Helen puts her arm around him to comfort him.

The pilot doesn't plan to wait very long for Malik. He begins refueling almost before they can get their bags off. Half the town has come out to see who has flown in. Among them a schoolteacher. He presents himself to Malik and Helen as Manou, a sort of spokesman for the village. He speaks some English; it seems that it will be enough. Malik negotiates with him for a while and then comes to an agreement, just as the pilot gets the airplane started up again. Malik looks irritated at being rushed.

"I have told them you will pay two thousand francs a day for the boatman, the boat and his fuel, and eight hundred francs for a house and food. You can give this man, Manou, something, but don't pay them any more. They will just keep raising the price."

"Don't worry Malik, it's okay. We'll do all right." She means it to sound confident, like a statement, but it comes across a little shaky.

"I think you will have success, Madame."

Helen takes his hand. Then, though she senses that it might not be the kind of thing a woman is supposed to do in public, she gives him a hug. When she takes a step back, he keeps hold of her hand and warmly smiles.

"*Bolamu!* Good luck!"

Malik climbs into the plane and after a moment gets the door shut. The pilot reaches across him to open the window for air, and it flops up and down in the prop wash. They have to back-taxi the runway to get a heading into the wind. When they take off the plane is close overhead; Helen can see Malik waving, his bright and optimistic smile. The plane banks and then drones slowly away beyond the trees.

When Helen turns back, her bags have already been picked up by various boys and are on their way to the village.

"To the river?" Manou suggests, indicating the foot trail that winds down a low hill. Though the cataracts must be at least a mile or two off, the dull roar is unmistakable—and unsettling.

HELEN LIFTS HER HAND from the river. The water feels too warm, muggy like the air that rests upon it. There is nothing to see, nothing to be fathomed in these opaque depths of brown. Shane is asleep on a narrow bench in the small, dirty boat, and the sweet smell of gasoline mixes in the humid air and wafts over them. The boatman's lean brown arms have a slick sheen of moisture. He is staring at the opposite bank, looking for anything floating there that might be a body, washed up on a bank or caught in the crook of a logjam. The whites of his eyes are reddened from the work, and his hand on the outboard looks tired. She suspects that he has viewed this project as hopeless from the outset.

They have covered at least two miles on each side of the river. They even found a body within the first few hours. But it was not Lewis, and it seemed to have been there for a long time, lolling among the sleeping logs, stubbornly refusing to slip back into the oblivion of the great river. She guessed that no one ever called out a search party for this man, that his disappearance was taken for granted, natural and not that unusual. The river

is so vast and deep in its currents that the odds of actually finding Lewis are almost nil. This has become an exercise in something else, in proof, perhaps, dullness of proof—something that
she will have to beat into her soul.

Shane wakes up hungry. He scoots along the side of the boat
and lays his head against his mother's shoulder. This has been
hard on him.

"The smoke makes my tummy feel sick, Mom."

"Mine, too."

She waves at the boatman to get his attention. "Can we go
back?" she says softly. *"Revenir?"* She realizes that these half-
communications she can manage in French have a certain blunt
rudeness to them. *"S'il vous plaît?"* she adds softly.

The boatman slowly turns the boat in a wide arc toward the
bank, and the wake folds over itself, brown and green. Then
even as he speeds up to head back, Helen spots something. She
has seen many things like this floating in the water, and all have
turned out to be nothing, bits of garbage or things rotting. But
the possibility of leaving something to doubt is intolerable. She
cannot help herself. She points, and the boatman slows the motor. The wake, catching up, gently lifts the stern as if to give him
a better view. Then he turns to her, and he shakes his head and
guides the boat to the shore.

Manou waits for them on the bank of the river with a wide
smile. He seems happy with his role as interpreter. An elder of
the village sits next to him with a posture that does not anticipate anything, his feet tucked under his legs the way a child
kneels. He barely looks up as the schoolteacher helps Shane and
Helen from the boat.

"This man has information about the white man."

"Oh, good, Manou. Good."

The bang of the outboard against the tin side of the boat

startles her. It reminds her that she must pay the boatman. She hands him a few worn bills, and he takes them almost delicately in his rough hands. Helen turns to Manou and the elder, who have been watching her closely. She has the impression that they are assessing just how much cash she might be carrying. Manou smiles. He isn't going to rob her.

"Are we looking in the right place, Manou?"

"Oh yes, certainly the right place."

Helen watches the elder, waiting for him to say something, but he remains silent. Manou will be his spokesman; his tone is earnest now. "There was a boy with him. This man saw them both. He was hunting above *les cataractes*."

"A boy?"

She looks at the elder. His skin is like the bark of a poisonous tree. "But there is bad news. They went into *les cataractes* at night, Madame." He shakes his head, overdoing the sympathy a little.

"So we're looking for two bodies, then?" she says numbly, trying to imagine how this information can be of any use. "Does this man know who the boy was?"

"No."

"Okay, Manou. *Merci*."

She starts to leave, but Manou just stands there smiling. She looks at the elder, whose fingers are rocking subtly on his walking stick.

"Madame," begins Manou, the advocate, "this man is a very important elder in this village. That is why he asks me to speak for him."

"Yes?"

Manou smiles, confident that she will understand, without his actually having to come out with it, that a tip is expected for this information. It's an expectation created by generations of

Europeans before her. She looks at Manou and the elder—though it seems to be their system, it is really hers. She digs through her purse for a bill. She hands it directly to the old man, who catches her eye for just a moment. There is something unapproachable in his gaze, as if she has just reached across an ocean to touch his hand.

"Thank you," she says quietly. "*Merci.*"

Manou takes them to a cinderblock building at the outskirts of the village, one of the few constructions in town that he seems to think is appropriate for a white woman and her child to stay in. Besides two hammocks to sleep in, there is nothing else in the small room. Two of the walls are lime green. The others are deep magenta. The combination makes the room seem to spin or vibrate. A young woman has been waiting for them with some simple food in a basket. Helen pays her, and they take their food outside to eat it on a small cement pad that forms the threshold of the building. Before they can finish, an army of ants finds them, so Helen tosses the leftovers into the bush, hoping to draw them off. She and Shane sit quietly, listening to the day end. Birds and insects trade shifts, but evening brings no relief to the gummy heat; if anything, the air is only more suffocating.

After a while she finds a candle for some light and helps Shane get situated in his hammock. She rocks him gently to sleep, then goes back out to sit on the stoop. At the edge of her skin, she senses a world that is completely alien.

KOLAMUKA—ÉVEILLANT—AWAKEN

FOR THREE MORE DAYS she goes to the boat. Shane stays behind with Manou and listens to his stories about gorillas and forest elephants. They build villages of sticks and gather piles of stone. Helen sits in the bow, watching the water occasionally gather a riffle from a puff of wind, feeling the boatman subtly shift his weight from one foot to the other. She is no longer fooled by every floating piece of plastic or twisted bit of driftwood. She sees as well as the boatman now—she sees things for what they are. The surface of the water reflects the vivid blue sky, and she is caught holding her breath between the two.

Every morning Manou has come to her with more people who wish to trade dubious information for her dwindling supply of cash. There are two categories of stories: those that offer the possibility that the white man was seen alive below the falls and those that claim that a pale body has been seen drifting by on its way to the ocean. The latter are easy to discount;

she knows now how easily a floating piece of garbage can be mistaken for a person. The stories of survival seem calculated to be worth more money, on the speculation that she will pay extra for hope. She plays the game, and Manou politely takes his percentage. Eventually she pays less or nothing for the survival stories until they stop offering live sightings, and all she hears about are the bodies of white men afloat in the crocodile-sick water.

"Manou, I will not pay for any more information. It's enough. You must tell them all."

"Will you go out in the boat again tomorrow?"

She looks at him. He is smiling, as always. He must tell the boatman so he will know to get gas. The man walks half the night to the closest supply, carrying it back in the dark on his head. He needs to know. Though she is now convinced that they will never find Lewis's body, there is a fatefulness to this search, like a kind of surrender or faith, that draws her to the river.

"One more day, Manou."

After he has left them at their concrete home and they have eaten inside because the ants have anticipated them and are already swarming the step, Shane says he wants to walk into the village. A low drumming is coming down the river. Even though it is late, they might find some of the small, sweet bananas that he has come to love, and he wants to hear the drums better.

They pass a couple of houses with radios on in candlelit rooms, but most of the homes are empty. The drumming is interrupted every few minutes, and each time it returns it seems to grow louder. Eventually they find the crowd, which is gathered beneath a great broad-leafed tree. At the center of the group is a storyteller. He stands with a bamboo staff in his hand, performing a tale. Often he is interrupted—someone from the audience shouts back at him or steps in to take over or even change the story—and then the drums overwhelm them both and everyone joins the singing, even the youngest children, who lie on their bare stomachs in the dirt where the light falls away.

Though she cannot understand the words, Helen is caught up in the moments of drama and suspense or the humor of a comical twist. Then she steps back a half step. A young couple in front of her are holding hands, and Helen can see that the boy is gently caressing the girl's palm with his thumb, making small circles. Though their attention seems to be on the story, it is not; it is there at that small point of contact, at that quiet meeting of experience. That touch.

Helen takes another step back. She feels her breath tightening in her chest. She looks at the strangers who surround her, arms and legs, wild laughter and smiles, people of another world who will forget this foreigner and what has happened to her the moment she leaves. They have already forgotten. She lays a hand on Shane's shoulder to get him to leave, and at the same moment Shane moves closer to the crowd, pulling at her hand.

"I want to hear the drums, Mom," he says, drawn to the music that does not have to be seen, that is not in another language.

Reluctantly she allows him to hold her there at a kind of border. Then she notices someone far outside the circle, just at the farthest reach of the light. He is looking at her; his gaze must have caught her attention. As her eyes adjust slowly to the darkness, she can just make him out sitting against a tree, a boy of about ten with his legs held in his arms. He lifts a hand and waves subtly, as though he wants her to come over but doesn't want to be noticed by anyone else.

Helen pulls on Shane's arm, but he resists.

"I don't want to go, Mom," he says too loudly, drawing the attention of a few people around them.

"Just for a moment, Shane."

"No, Mom, I want to stay." He is even louder now; his voice carries through a quieter moment in the story. Manou notices them from across the group.

"Shane, I'm not asking you again. We'll come right back." Shane follows reluctantly, making her tow him along. Of course, she knows that this boy is up to the same thing everyone has been up to. He will tell her that he saw the white man's body three miles upriver or six miles downriver and will ask for money. She is irritated by the time she gets to him.

"What do you want? *Que voulez-vous?*"

"*L'homme blanc—*"

She interrupts him. "I am not paying for information. *Je ne paye pas pour l'information.*"

Manou steps past her. She is a little surprised; she didn't hear him come over.

"*Kende nayo,*" he says in Lingala. Go away, boy. He waves a dismissive hand at him.

The boy catches Helen's eye. He addresses Manou.

"*Je veux simplement lui dire—*"

"*Kende nayo!*" Three men from the circle have joined Manou. The boy stands up, ready to run off. His clothes are filthy, and he looks like the worst kind of street urchin. They shout at him, and he takes a few steps away from the tree.

"*Va-t-en!*"

"It's okay, let him talk." Helen says, too softly for the men to hear. Manou picks up a stick.

"Don't worry, Madame, we will chase him off. This kind of boy is up to no good. *Dangereux.*"

The boy is hurrying away, and the men wave their arms at him and threaten him, hazing him like an animal. A couple of times he pauses to say something, but their shouting pushes him on, and Helen can't hear what he says.

She shakes her head. She hates to be the cause of this. She calls after them.

"Manou, it's okay. Just . . ."

The men chase him to the edge of the forest. There's no place else for him to go. Though he is only a hundred feet away, in the dark Helen can hardly see him. The men have stopped, confident that he will keep going on his own. The boy turns and shouts something, looking past the tormentors and directly at her. He is instantly drowned out by their shouts, but a few of the words make it through.

It sounds like "*mon ami.*" And then her blood turns cold. Did he say "Lewis?" Did he say the name, or was it something else?

"No, wait!" She tries to stop them, but it's too late. One of the men throws a rock and nearly hits him. "Wait!"

He ducks into the bush, and he's gone. Helen is shouting now.

"No, Manou, wait. Wait, catch him. Wait!" She is immobilized by Shane's grip. She cannot let go of him to follow, and the men shout and throw rocks into the bush until he is long gone.

Shane tugs on her hand. "What did he say, Mom?"

"I don't know, honey. I'm not sure."

She stares at the abrupt wall the forest. How could he know the name? It's impossible. Did she imagine it? If she heard it at all, it was so faint. The only thing left, the only evidence now, is her awareness of thinking that she heard it. She cannot recreate the sound of his voice saying the name, and it could so easily be some word in French distorted by the distance and the shouting men. She sits down with Shane and pulls him tightly into her arms. She tries to force herself to stop shaking. She knows it is scaring Shane.

"This is it, Shane. This is all I can do."

Shane kisses her cheek.

"Tomorrow we are going home."

Manou comes back, looking satisfied with himself. The boy has been run off.

"Who was that boy?"

"He is not from here."

"Couldn't he be *the* boy?"

"What boy?" Manou has forgotten the elder's tale, along with most of the others, true and not true, that he translated for her.

"The boy who was seen with the white man."

It takes him a second. "No."

"Are you sure?" She looks into his eyes, but across this cultural distance there is no way to test for truth. She knows they were all lies, anyway, all those stories, perhaps even the original report.

"There are so many boys like this now. *C'est à cause de la guerre.*"

His usual smile fades to an expression that is oddly cold. He can read her mind. She hates this place, or worse, she despises it. It is contemptible. She has always had her fairy tale home to return to, no matter how long she stayed here. Now she is leaving. There will be no more money, and there will be no more pretense that she was ever welcome or that she ever wished to be. Manou turns away from her without saying a word, and he walks back to the circle of the drums. Any Western stiffness he has affected slips away as he relaxes his joints and begins to dance with the villagers, his hands high over his head.

Helen stands up and takes Shane's hand, and they start back

to their concrete hut at the edge of the darkness. They walk carefully, more used to sidewalks than dirt trails in the night. Helen's back is straight and her shoulders are so taut they hurt her. *Get me out of here,* she thinks. *Just get me out of here.*

She lifts Shane into his hammock. He kisses her and lays a gentle hand to her face before he turns onto his side and falls quietly asleep. She lies back in her hammock. As uncomfortable as it is, she's glad to be off the floor, away from whatever crawls there. Her eyes adjust slowly to the unlit room as she listens to the dull throb of the drums in the distance. It keeps her awake, this rhythm so utterly syncopated to the beat of her own heart.

So this is defeat. She has found the limits of what she can do, and it isn't much. If she ever was a strong woman, even if she was merely reckless, this is the end. Perhaps it was mere vanity, the thought that she could do anything, be strong enough for all of them. To some degree it *did* shut Lewis out. She saw it in his face in every fight, every time she silently condemned his cowardice, every time he turned his back to walk away. She lifts her hands into the darkness above her, and they look transparent and weak.

What did Malik once say? He was explaining the tribal scars on a stranger's face. He said that the man's mother must have lost her first child as an infant, so when her next child was born she marked him with two fine scars on his cheeks. The idea was that some souls are unwilling to stay in this hard life—they keep quitting the world. If the second child died, too, she might recognize him by the markings the next time he was born.

He said, "In Africa a woman builds her house, she paints it and the rains tear it down, and she puts it back up again. When her child dies she weeps, but she does not blame him for leaving."

Helen dreams of not being able to sleep. She dreams of her hands gripping the hammock so tightly that they begin to cramp. She dreams that she can hear the boy's voice just outside the glassless window.

"Lewis. Lewis," he whispers. "Lewis."

She listens, afraid to hear it. She tells herself that she is imagining it. She dreams that she is dreaming it. But the voice will not go away.

"*Il est mon ami.* Lewis."

She gets up and walks quietly to the window and looks out into the forest. Though it is night, she sees as well as day. She looks for a moon, but there are only the shadows of tree branches and beyond that an unnaturally bright sky of stars. The boy stands by the trunk of a great tree, about fifty yards away. He has a light in his hand, beckoning her.

She goes out without putting her shoes on. It's something she ordinarily would never do. The damp, spongy detritus of the forest is cool under her feet. Before she can get to the boy he turns away and disappears back into the rainforest. She turns once to look back to where Shane is sleeping. He'll be okay, she dreams. I won't go too far. He will sleep.

She follows the boy through the forest, never quite able to keep up, but somehow always sure of where he is, even in the thick brush. There are animals everywhere, monkeys sleeping in the crooks of the trees and snakes coiled in the vines or slithering out of her way as she passes. The trail at her feet is swarming with bright green ants. They crawl so mechanically that she can almost hear the metallic whisper of their movement. A leopard slips silently through the brush ahead of her and then is gone before she is sure she saw it. She runs to catch up. Then she sees it again, just for a second. She imagines that the boy is riding on its back, but then she corrects the image: it is just the boy standing there, finally waiting for her. A candle lights his face. She turns to where he is looking.

There is Lewis. He is propped up among the tangled roots of a tree. He looks pale and unconscious. His skin is wet and puffy as though he was in the water a long time, like the body she saw.

"Lewis?"

Helen kneels next to him and lays her hand on his shoulder. It's cold. She turns to the boy, but he shakes his head. She puts an ear to Lewis's chest. It is silent. He's gone. She is alone. She yells and hits his chest, and her fists fall flat on the waterlogged corpse. The dull thud is like the drums, which she hears still beating in the distance.

She wakes with a great sob, gasping for air. Her heart leaps from her chest as she jumps out of her hammock.

Shane is gone. His hammock is empty. She races her hands over it wildly as if there were any way he could be hidden there.

"Oh, God."

She runs to the door. On the way she steps on something very sharp. It cuts her deeply, then scurries away, but it doesn't even slow her down. She throws the door open wide. The night is utterly black.

"Shane!" She screams at the darkness. "Shane!"

And he is there, sitting on a small stool only a few yards away. Next to him is the boy. Helen runs at him with the intention of driving him away.

"Get the hell out of here! Leave my son alone!"

The boy stands, but Shane is holding onto his hand. "No, Mom."

Shane's face is so completely calm that it stops her.

Then the boy speaks, quietly inviting her to come with him. *"Je peux vous amener chez Lewis. Est-ce que vous pouvez aller maintenant?"*

Lewis. That's all she understands of it—Lewis. He wants to take her to Lewis.

"Who are you? *Qui êtes-vous?"*

"Je suis Kofi."

"Kofi?"

"Oui. Lewis est mon ami."

She stares at him as she struggles to decide what to do.

"Come here, Shane."

She leads him inside. She is absolutely sure that she should not go back out there. She should chase the boy off. But he knows Lewis's name.

"Put your shoes on, Shane." She hands them to him and then slips her own on.

"No matter what happens, don't let go of my hand. Do you hear?"

"Yes." He squeezes it tightly.

"Okay," she says to Kofi. She gives him a flashlight that the villagers loaned to her. His hand brushes hers as he takes it, and it feels warm and relaxed.

They turn to the forest, and Kofi finds the path that leads in. The night is black among the trees, like something that is physically hard. The beam of the flashlight dances ahead on the trail, feeble, like a dying firefly. They see no animals. Once, something scrambles away into the trees, or there is a flash in the light, and two red-green eyes stare back at them before retreating. Her foot is numb from the injury.

Then the light goes out. Helen stops. It is too dark to see the trail anymore.

"Why did we stop, Mom?"

"The flashlight went out. I can't see."

"It's okay, Mom. Follow Kofi, he knows where to go."

"*Venez*," says Kofi confidently, and she finds him from the sound of his voice. She can just make him out as a deeper shadow in the darkness. She follows as much by the sound as by his image, which is so tenuous that she must maintain it by faith.

She dreads the end of this journey. She worries that she will be unable to keep her sanity when they find the body. She should not be doing this. Not with Shane. His small hand in hers is like a challenge. It says *You must control yourself. You must survive. No matter what.*

Kofi stops abruptly.

"What is it?"

He doesn't answer. She thinks he must be lost. But then there is the bright flash when Kofi lights a candle. The light dims to something warm and reassuring. It does not penetrate the darkness much beyond the three of them. But Helen is thankful for it. She exhales.

"That smells funny," says Shane.

"It's a candle . . . a light."

Kofi moves it back and forth in front of him, looking for something. The flame dims with the movement and threatens to extinguish. But when he stops, the flame finds more oxygen and the light glows, reaching a little farther into the forest.

There is Lewis. Leaning against a tree. Helen's heart leaps. He looks different from her dream, not as pale, and he is sitting more upright.

"Lewis?"

Helen moves closer to him.

"Lewis?"

His face is bearded and scarred. His hair is matted with dirt, and his clothes are torn and filthy. He smells foul. Up close he looks dead. Helen takes in a deep breath, preparing herself for the shock, afraid to touch him. Shane lets go of her hand and finds his father's face.

"Is he sleeping, Mom?"

"Yes, I think so." Helen reaches for Lewis's hand, expecting it to be cold, but it is only cool.

"Listen," says Shane.

"I can't hear anything Shane."

Shane lays a hand on his father's chest. Kofi is sitting close to them, holding the candle up. He looks calm and unworried. She lays her head on Lewis's chest. And after a moment she can hear, just faintly, his beating heart.

If this were a dream, he would stand up and they could walk or dance right out of this forest, or they could fly over its moonlit canopy—they could do impossible things. They could crawl backward together through the mud until everything was undone, the whole story. But when she looks at his inert body, it seems irrevocably changed and unfamiliar. He smells like this world, like the roots and the broken leaves, the worms breeding in the sand and muck. She grips his shoulders tightly. She took a chance, once a long time ago; she let her heart settle here, like a breathless bird. The trees loom over them, these usurpers of the sky, like conspirators, as if they might steal him away. She lays her arms over his body to protect him. And then she closes her eyes and imagines his waking. It's the only thing she can do now—create a miracle as a feat of imagination.

She sees him coming back to her, walking slowly down a long, red dirt road. At first he is just an indistinct shape, fading in and out. He looks as though he has come a long distance and found in walking an ease for his soul. His stride is certain and his shoulders are relaxed, held with an easy strength. When he sees Helen where she sits under the tree, he doesn't speed up, but he veers casually off the path, and then when he gets close enough for her to see his face, he looks into her eyes and grins.

"What do you think of this Africa?" The sound of his voice brings him closer. And then he is standing under the same tree, an arm's reach away.

"It's beautiful, lover."

LEWIS'S RECOVERY AT THE small colonial hospital by the river does not happen in the world of ordered time. After moments of awareness, he slips back. Helen and Shane seem to come and go with each breath. Most of the time he cannot distinguish his emotions from the reports of his senses, and he has no perception of time passing. He can feel air in his lungs. He has the sense of being lifted, moved. Sometimes the scent of flowers is indistinguishable from the sound of Shane's laughter. There are long spaces of silence. Smells of medicine. The sound of something dripping slowly into his blood. A bird fluttering against the glass of the window. Footsteps in a distant hallway, the grit of dry dirt on the soles. And through it all there is this warm touch, which never leaves him.

Though in some ways his senses seem heightened, it's as though a leaden blanket lies over his body, weakening him. He has lucid moments when he knows he must sit up, breathe, open his eyes and stop hiding in this false blindness. But then a powerful sense of timelessness traps him, until finally something happens that gives him the sensation of sequence, an order to events. It begins with the air, as it shifts from a dead, stifled presence to something suddenly alive. He feels hands lifting his shoulders. Something cool against his back, a sense of motion. He hears the sound of tropical birds, a breeze and then water, like a river below him. He remembers what happened.

The pirogue tipped. He fell in. Kofi. The waves pulled him under, and he thought he must have drowned.

All I have to do now is open my eyes.

At first he is afraid to do it—terrified to discover that he has drowned, perhaps to see his own body floating face down in the water. But the sound of the river is getting closer, and finally he has to open his eyes.

In front of him is the balcony of his hospital room, the shifting tops of a grove of palms and beyond them a river. He can hear the laughter of people bathing there. Then, at a corner of the building, just a few feet away, he sees Shane and next to him Kofi leaning on the railing. Kofi looks just the way he always did in the forest, relaxed but ready, waiting for Lewis to revive so they can continue their journey. Both boys are turned away from him. No one has noticed that he has opened his eyes, but he can feel Helen's hand resting lightly on his shoulder and the slightest stir of her touch that awakened him.